K

SILVER MOON

SAM KEATON *Legends of Laramie*

Books by
Sigmund Brouwer

SILVER MOON

Sigmund Brouwer

BETHANYHOUSE

MINNEAPOLIS, MINNESOTA

Silver Moon
Copyright © 1994, 2000
Sigmund Brouwer

Silver Moon is a revision of *Moon Basket*, published in 1994 by Victor
Books/SP Publications.

Cover illustration by Chris Cocozza
Cover design by Ann Gjeldum

Published by Bethany House Publishers
A Ministry of Bethany Fellowship International
11400 Hampshire Avenue South
Minneapolis, Minnesota 55438
www.bethanyhouse.com

Printed in the United States of America by
Bethany Press International, Minneapolis, Minnesota 55438

Library of Congress Cataloging-in-Publication Data

Brouwer, Sigmund, 1959–
    Silver moon / by Sigmund Brouwer.
      p. cm. — (Sam Keaton legends of Laramie)
    ISBN 0–7642–2365–8
1. Laramie (Wyo.)—Fiction. 2. Sheriffs—Fiction. I. Title.
PS3552.R6825 S55 2000
813'.54—dc21
                                          00–009973

SIGMUND BROUWER is the award-winning author of numerous books including *The Carpenter's Cloth*. In addition, his coolreading.com reaches out to instill good reading and writing habits in the next generation. Sigmund and his wife, recording artist Cindy Morgan, divide their time between Tennessee and Alberta, Canada.

To L.D.

I've always loved the glories of the old Wild West, and I would like to express my gratitude to the historians whose dedication has preserved that era, allowing the rest of us to cherish its spirit of freedom.

To them, and to you who may be reading this as more than a mystery, I would like to apologize for any of my research mistakes which I may have passed on during my attempts to make the fiction as historically accurate as possible.

CHAPTER 1

HALFWAY THROUGH HIS SERMON, Brother Lewis lifted from beside his Bible an old hog-leg cap-and-ball pistol fully eighteen inches long and, with a single shot, killed two of the three hounds whose fight had spilled out from below the bench closest to his pulpit.

It wasn't his shooting the dogs that caused me the most concern.

If circuit preachers don't know how to handle distractions, they find other work. I've seen one excuse himself from the pulpit, take a troublemaking drunk outside from the back pew, thrash the drunk into submission, and return minutes later to finish the sermon. Dog-fights, too, are common enough. Some Sundays you'll find a dozen or so hounds have followed their owners inside, and a preacher learns to raise his voice above the growling and barking that often ends in a dogfight as glorious as the threats of hell from the pulpit.

No, it was how this revivalist shot the dogs that got my attention.

After all, these were not the perfect circumstances for a shooting. Brother Lewis had raised folks to a frenzy of holy ecstasy. The darkness in the tent shifted with the flickering of oil lamps, and as the dim yellow light moved, it revealed faces that glowed with agonized joy and rows of arms raised in waving fervor. The sawdust-and-dirt floor had dampened with the sweat of their heated bodies trapped beneath the low tent roof, and that smell of wet wood mingled with the ripe odor of flushed and long unwashed skin. Some of the women had already begun to babble in low moans. Others wept. Men raised shouts of hallelujah or cried out for forgiveness.

And above it all, Brother Lewis preached and worked them like a gasping trout at the end of a light line.

"Have you been saved, brothers? Have you been saved? When the angel of vengeance appears, can you look him straight in the eyes and declare that his sword of fire is meant for another? Can you? Can you now? Can you? Are you saaaa-ved?"

I doubted a person could ever face a more important question. We either have souls. Or not. If not, everything in life truly is dust. But too much in my past pointed me toward believing we do have souls. Why leads to the frightening questions. Why? Where will our souls go after death? And yes, have we made peace with God?

But my innards tightened in anger listening to this man. I doubted if he cared about any souls in this audience.

His voice rose as he lifted his hands to point at the crowd, so his final words were barely short of a hoarse yell.

"Amen! Amen to that, Brother Lewis!"

"Bring me salvation, Brother Lewis!"

"Oh, Brother Lewis! I feel it! I feel it now! The Spirit is upon me!"

Brother Lewis dropped his voice. And his chin. The lamp beside him cast his entire face into shadow, and his next words were a whisper from the mouth of the avenging angel himself.

"Have you cast aside the sins of your youth?"

Brother Lewis pushed aside the flaps of his long black jacket. He rested his hands on his hips and bored his black eyes into the crowd. Two women in the front row fell to their knees, adoring eyes cast upward at the tall lean figure at the makeshift pulpit.

"Yes! Yes!" Brother Lewis continued that penetrating whisper. "I have learned from the sins of my past, sins of the flesh so terrible I can only shudder"—he shuddered on cue—"to recall. Sins that would cause you to weep in sorrow. Sin upon sin with Satan at my side and lust in my soul. Time and again, until the day I approached the Cross and bared my heart."

His white shirt beneath that black jacket was divided by a black string tie. I saw hair slicked back on a narrow skull, a long, strong nose—almost a hook—clean-shaven, furrowed skin. His frown promised hell as he shouted and smiled like the devil as he whispered.

And when the hush fell, he paused, then roared as he raised his arms. "I ask again! Are . . . you . . . saved? Will you approach the Cross and bare your soul?"

The wails of torment and rapture that answered him almost drowned the snarling of the dogs as they chose that moment to boil into action between the two kneeling women.

It was then, cool as the midnight air outside the meeting tent, not even pausing as his words rolled thunder, that Brother Lewis lifted the pistol, held it steady—it had to weigh a good ten pounds—and sighted briefly down the barrel to pull the trigger.

I sat among chairs at the front of the tent and saw clearly, even in the dim light, the mushroom of blood that exploded from the shoulder of the largest hound stopped mid-howl, and its dance of death joined with the hound below it. That casual accuracy in the midst of his passionate plea and the poor light was my first indication of what to expect from any confrontation with Brother Lewis.

Worse for me—his voice still rising in a wave that pulled the crowd with him—Brother Lewis smoothly loaded the pistol and set it down beside the Bible on his makeshift pulpit. These were the slick, efficient movements of a man accustomed to more worldly ways. One accustomed to challenges.

Add to it the reaction of the crowd to the shooting of the dogs. Rather, lack of reaction. The people were so bound by his words and so bound for glory that they were deaf to his gunshot. They continued their frenzy as if the shot had been just another hallelujah and the drift of gun smoke a whiff of the brimstone they were so determined to escape in their cries against the devil. Not even the owners of the dogs had risen in rage, a bad sign when hounds were sometimes more loved than a wife and generally considered easier on upkeep.

Bad enough I'd arrived here to confront the man. It now appeared I'd find no friends in the mob.

I could only take comfort that his action had dismissed any doubts about the reason for my presence here. Were this truly a holy man wrapped in bliss, I would have been troubled at my need to be here. There *is* more to a man's life than what he can see or touch—something I'd recently begun to understand—and I would have been glad to learn more in this tent. How could a man ever hope to fully understand the God of this universe? And to ponder the life and works of Jesus and the grace extended through Him? I'd fill a year's worth of nights in this tent if I thought I could get those kinds of questions answered with any degree of truth. But spiritual help wouldn't come from this man. His cold, calculated shot to kill the dogs only proved to me how much of this was an act and that I should feel no shame for sitting as I did, waiting for when I would no longer be able to wait.

"Brothers and sisters," he shouted. "Is it enough to say you've been forgiven? Is it enough to walk away without proving the Spirit of the Lord rests upon you? Or will you approach the Cross tonight?"

As he spoke, his eyes flicked down to the dead hounds and to the surviving dog beside them as it lapped up the blood that soaked into the sand.

His eyes flicked to me.

No surprise.

I could not fake involvement in what was happening around me. To be sitting without moaning, or shouting praise, or clutching the nearest person was to make me as obvious as a cactus in a bed. Even if Brother Lewis did not know I was the law here in Laramie—and I'd bet he'd have made quiet inquiries upon arrival—even the most unobservant fool would have known I wasn't part of the crowd. Thus, by judging his method of pulling folks in to set them loose and pull them in again, this definitely was not an unobservant fool.

Instead, I'd guess Brother Lewis had marked every single person in the crowd and, were he to step down from the pulpit, could continue to wave his arms and point his accusing finger, all the while informing me how much each would leave at the basket for collection, and who would be the first to accept his call for the test of faith.

What he could not expect was that I would be the first to answer that call.

Or maybe he did. Maybe his shooting of the dogs had been just another part of his calculations, a deliberately bloody way to tell me whatever the reason for my presence, he would not be deterred from the fattened money baskets that would be collected at the height of the crowd's frenzy.

Brother Lewis lifted both his hands high and tilted his head back, way back, as if watching the heavens open to pour down glory.

The hush of response was instant.

"Lord, Lord, Lord, do they have it?" He spoke softly with his head still tilted back.

Several moans from the center of the crowd.

Brother Lewis brought his head down, staring into the people with his arms still high and widespread.

"Do you have it?" His voice remained soft, and he stared until the moaning rose.

"Do you have it?" He roared now. "Do you have it in you to show the Lord your love?"

"Amen, brother!" came a shout.

"We do!" came several more.

"Weep with joy!" Brother Lewis exhorted. He dropped his hands and shook fists of victory at the crowd. "Weep with joy at the redemption that is within your reach!"

I knew redemption was within the reach of any man, but I doubted this was the way.

Brother Lewis stepped away from the pulpit, paused to tuck the hog-leg pistol in the belt of his pants, and, with the briefest glance in my direction to see if I understood the significance of that action, walked to a wooden crate.

The hush fell again.

I knew why the slats of that crate had no gaps. I knew what was inside, as did every person in the tent.

Snakes. Rattlers. Caught that day from the dry hills outside of Laramie.

Brother Lewis rested a hand on the outside edge of the crate and began to speak. "Living witness, brothers and sisters. Tonight we give living witness to the power of the Spirit."

I wanted to look away. Recently, I'd seen a man die because of rattlesnakes as thick as clubs that had struck with enough force to drive the man backward in his chair. Snakes with jaws open so wide it appeared they were clamped onto the skin of his neck and arm. I had to search my mind no further than that image to find a waking nightmare.

But it wasn't that memory that accounted for the anger and revulsion I felt to observe Brother Lewis as he shouted.

Nor was that memory the reason for my presence here.

"The Lord says if you believe, you may take up snakes and cast them aside!" he shouted again.

Brother Lewis smiled. Stepped away from the crate. They all knew he would reach inside. Why not play them longer?

He launched into a tirade against the devil and sin. Spittle flew from his mouth and his voice grew hoarse.

Moans and screams of joy rose accordingly from the faint-hearted.

It bothered me greatly that Brother Lewis—so powerful in acting, so skillful in oration, and so charismatic in presence—would abuse his gifts to twist these people.

There *was* something beyond this life. Events of previous months had shown me that, and I was determined to continue my search for understanding. But was this show the way to find God?

Unfortunately, my badge did not give me the right to act upon my anger. While indeed Brother Lewis preyed upon people so hurt in spirit each begged to be swept along in a rush of emotion, in the end, a man can blame none other than himself for the spiritual choices he makes, and, as well, he had a right to those choices. For me to interfere simply because I did not believe in the cult of the snakes would be stooping to the preacher's level, the only difference that my show of power would consist of a drawn Colt .44–40.

No, I was here on business, not personal anger.

Brother Lewis had moved back to the side of the crate. His eyes burned as he pumped himself on the emotion of the crowd. His voice rose and fell and he cried to the people.

"We shall show that the Spirit is among us!"

He rolled back his sleeves and, with several loud hallelujahs, plunged his forearms deep inside the crate. When he pulled them free, he held, clenched in each hand, a coiling, writhing snake—rattles shaking in fury, jaws spread wide in rage.

Brother Lewis held the snakes high—careful, I noted, to keep his grips just below the triangle heads of the massive snakes—where he would be safe from a strike. "I have reached into the lair of the devil and stand unharmed! Proof, brothers and sisters! Proof that the Spirit of the Lord has descended into this tent!"

This brought renewed wailing and moaning.

"Brothers and sisters," he shouted and shook the rattlesnakes, "who shall give further glory to the Word? Who shall make testimony? Who shall come forward to cast snakes aside and give living witness to their faith?"

I took a deep breath. Already a trembling woman, her petticoats dragging in the dirt and sawdust, was moving up the aisle from the back of the tent. I could no longer wait.

I judged, for the twentieth or thirtieth time, the space between my guns and Brother Lewis. I confirmed yet again that if I were forced to draw and fire from my position, any shots that missed Brother Lewis would hit none of his flock.

And I started to rise.

Before I could complete the movement, cool air reached me and I looked to the rear, as did a few others, to see the tent flap now swinging back into place. A tall, stooped man carried a torch as he marched forward to Brother Lewis. His manner was direct, the anger in his face so obvious, that each row he passed fell into expectant silence, and when he reached the front to stand within five paces of Brother Lewis, no person in the tent was able to ignore his low words.

"She died, preacher man. A half hour ago she died. Five children left behind."

I knew the man. Cornelius Harper. Doctor Cornelius Harper. In the same dull brown suit he wore in his office, at funerals, as he set out in his horse and buggy—a dull brown suit well short of his wrists and his ankles, which gave him the appearance of an awkward schoolboy. Except Cornelius Harper was at least forty years beyond school age—obvious from the thatched hair almost white, eyes deeply sunk in a worn face, and in his crooked carriage, as if bone rubbed against bone with each of his slow movements.

"You, sir, have interrupted a man of God," Brother Lewis intoned. "I request that you depart and leave this host of believers in peace."

"Did you hear me, you miserable excuse of a cur? She died." There were traces of accent in Doc Harper's voice. New England, I'd heard. A successful practice abandoned some time back.

"A woman in your care dies. What concern is that of mine? Unless you are here to ask me to pray for her soul. Or perhaps to ask forgiveness for your mistake in doctoring." Brother Lewis continued to hold the snakes high. Their tails wrapped and unwrapped around his forearms. He spoke, indeed kept his arms aloft effortlessly, as if the snakes did not exist. "Perhaps God in His infinite mercy shall—"

"The concern is that she died because of you." Doctor Harper spit out the words. "She accepted your call last night. And reached into hell."

"Ah, the young lady of little faith."

The young lady of little faith was my reason, too, for enduring the revivalist. Dorothy Kilpatrick. A downtrodden woman married to a shiftless stable hand. Mother of five. Barely twenty years old. Looking for any hope at all in her bleak world. Before they dragged her out of the tent last night, her arms had swollen to the size of melons, her face and neck as if she had been pumped with water. Someone had counted ten sets of puncture wounds on her arms.

"Dismiss these people," Doc Harper said between clenched teeth. "No one else shall die."

"Brother, brother, brother," the revivalist said in soothing tones. His eyes glittered. The snakes in his grasp appeared to be staring at the doctor as well. "Your arrival, instead, dictates I must ask all to remain."

Brother Lewis spoke past Cornelius. "Last night sadly proved that the young lady did not believe in the protection of God. She was of little faith and did not have the Spirit upon her. Brothers and sisters, we must bow our heads and pray that her lack of faith will not lead to punishment in the afterlife."

The rolling cadence had begun to return to the revivalist's voice, and a few amens greeted his words.

"No." Doc Harper raised his torch in threat. "You'll bundle this tent and leave town."

"I think not," Brother Lewis said.

I admired Doc Harper. He showed plenty sand in his craw to refuse to back down from a man easily two decades younger, sixty pounds heavier, armed with the gun so obvious beneath his belt, and, more importantly, armed with the righteous support of a crowd in full passion.

Doc Harper took a step toward Brother Lewis.

I stood. Only the blind would not know this was a showdown. The expectant silence of the crowd became a pressing blanket.

Doc Harper took another step.

What he intended to do, I could not guess. Nor did I have a chance to find out. Brother Lewis had intentions of his own, intentions signaled by the slight movement of his arms as he pulled them back.

Without thinking—because when it happens like this, the luxury of thinking will paralyze a man—I reached for my Colt as Brother Lewis began to fling his arms forward to cast the raging snakes at Doc Harper's upper body.

Six shots, a Colt will hold. Five because I carried mine with the hammer down on an empty cylinder. My right hand was full of iron as I pulled loose from my holster, while my left hand, fingers spread, was raking across my body to fan the top of the hammer with my thumb.

That shot clicked dry and advanced the next bullet into position.

The snakes were already in the air as the meat of my index finger hit the hammer. Done right, a man can fan three shots in one pass. Thumb and two fingers—so fast the shots sound like one.

I didn't have the time to worry myself into a panic, and the next two shots fell into place like rapid blinks of the eye. Which shot got the first snake, I don't know. Firing from the hip demands that you point the index finger of your gun hand at your target and trust in instinct and luck and prayer and whatever else you believe it will take.

One of the shots ripped the head off the first snake so that it landed like a chunk of heavy rope across Doc Harper's chest. Another shot caught the second snake somewhere near its tail, enough to slam it off course, and it landed in a frenzy and turned on itself to slash at the source of its pain.

Impossible shooting? If a man were using bullets. But when I carried in town, I'd taken to the habit of loading with cartridges that sprayed chunks of lead no bigger than unground pepper, a trick that guaranteed accuracy at close range and, as the lead lost all power more than a stone's throw away, cut down on the number of innocent bystanders who might take a stray bullet. Here, all I'd needed was fast shooting and to place those shoots within a foot of the snakes.

No one else knew that, though, and in the shocked silence that followed those blasts, I earned my own share of hallelujahs from the crowd behind me.

Brother Lewis spent no time in praise. He swung a hand downward to his belt.

"Nope," I said as I spun to level my Colt at his chest. "I've got two shots left. You're a bigger target than those snakes. Slower, too. Unless you're anxious to shake hands with Saint Peter, I'd advise against anything stupid."

Less than twenty minutes later, Brother Lewis was in Laramie's one-cell jail, the back portion of the marshal's office.

Early the next morning, when I returned to make coffee and check on my latest prisoner, I immediately began to feel sorry for myself and the problem I'd put upon my shoulders. Not only was I subject to Brother Lewis's considerable talents of verbal abuse, I was still searching for an appropriate charge to lay.

Has any man ever faced a judge for throwing snakes?

Unfortunately, those problems became minor in a big hurry.

Before my coffee had finished brewing, Laramie's newly elected mayor busted through the doors of my office to inform me that two men had been found dead in the vault of Laramie's most prosperous bank.

His bank.

CHAPTER 2

"DIDN'T YOU HEAR ME RIGHT?" Mayor Crawford sputtered. "I told you clearly that I opened the vault this morning to find two men dead inside. And money gone!"

I nodded but didn't let that stop me from finishing what I'd begun before he'd taken five minutes to repeat the same message a dozen different ways. I rubbed the inside of my coffee mug with a clean rag, inspected it, and blew it free of imaginary dust.

"Then do something! There's money gone!"

Mayor Charles William George Benedict Crawford—a short man in a wide frock coat and a top hat, and fat enough to carry a couple of *more* names—was almost childish in his frustration at my apparent lack of concern. His was the fat that covers more softness beneath, and he wobbled as he shook, his thick lips pouty, fists clenched at his sides. It wouldn't have surprised me if he soon stamped the floor in anger.

Brother Lewis had moved to the cell bars

and listened with sullen interest. Outside of that cell, my office was hardly big enough for a man to pace twice before turning. Brother Lewis had no choice but to hear. It didn't bother me. His silence was a relief after all of his unkindly oration.

I stepped over to the potbellied stove in the center of the office, and with the rag to protect my fingers from getting singed, I lifted the coffeepot lid to check the contents.

"Either of those dead men named Lazarus?" I asked.

Mayor Crawford glared at me. Not effectively. His cheeks, blotched with growing red, puffed outward and gave him an appearance that matched the face of a hissing goose.

I said nothing to deflate those cheeks. He could not know that during our first meeting a week earlier I'd decided any man who insists on letting you immediately know all four of his given names is a man in love with himself, petty power, and the sound of his voice. He hadn't proved otherwise in our meetings since, and a man like that needs straightening, or every encounter down the road gets more difficult.

I set the lid back into place and repeated myself. "Either of those men named Lazarus?"

"Calhoun and Nichols," he huffed. "Why would you ask if—"

"Because short of putting them to bed with a pick and shovel, there's not much to do before my coffee's finished brewing."

"What about the money? Do something! You're the marshal!"

"One who ain't even tasted his first coffee of the day. Five minutes won't make much difference to the whereabouts of the money." I faced Mayor Crawford squarely. "Go on back to the bank. Ask those dead boys if they mind that I take another few minutes to get there. Unless they answer yes, I'll be along when I'm ready."

He removed his top hat and shook it at me with one hand

and pointed at the jail cell with the other. "You're mighty big for your britches considering that only a few months back this town had you behind those bars on murder charges."

"Town Council," I said calmly, "wrote me a letter of commendation for ridding this town of the marshal before me. That letter's in the same drawer as the letter of pardon from the territory governor."

"Some folks wonder about you, Keaton—"

"They'll have a good excuse when I kick your butt out of this office."

"I'm the newly elected mayor. You can't talk that way to me."

"Not when you're out of earshot." I sighed at his lack of movement. "And that was advice."

Mayor Crawford slammed his hat on his head and tugged on the brim with both hands to make sure it was secure. He turned on his heel to prepare for a grand departure.

"Mayor?" Brother Lewis called. "Mayor?" He lowered his voice. "You'd be just the one to correct this grave injustice. Order my release and your reward awaits you in higher places."

Mayor Crawford slammed the door so hard behind him that it popped open again.

I set my mug down on my desk, moved to the door, and shut it so that I could reach for my hat and holster where both hung on a long nail. Hat in place, holster cinched, I returned to the potbellied stove and lifted the coffeepot.

"Take coffee?" I asked Brother Lewis.

Brother Lewis mumbled he did.

I found another mug and handed it to the man. In daylight, the skin of his face seemed gray and dead.

"Anytime you want more," I said as I poured, "just ask."

He raised his eyebrows in surprise at my courtesy. What he didn't know was that I figured getting coffee into his mouth appeared the fastest way to shut him up.

I poured my own coffee, then set the pot back. Cup in hand, I moved to the door. I wasn't looking forward to my visit to the bank.

Aside from establishing the tone of our working relationship, I had another reason for insisting to Mayor Crawford that I wait for my coffee.

I wanted a comforting distraction when I first viewed those dead men. I'd seen my share over the years. Violence and sudden death were no strangers to Laramie or the rest of the territories, but long ago I'd held my brother as he'd coughed blood and died in my arms after a gunfight. Since then I'd known—with my soul, which is a knowledge much deeper than any knowledge of the mind—the damage and pain a bullet brings. In short, the sight of a man's blood hits me hard. Puts my dying brother back in my arms. Brings the churning horror and disbelief back to my stomach.

So that's how I stood in the doorway of the steel vault. Hat low over my eyes. Coffee mug at my mouth. And doing my utmost to keep my hand from trembling as I slowly tilted coffee into my throat. Any excuse not to react.

The vault was deep enough that it needed two oil lamps to light the interior, even with the morning sunlight now streaming through the front windows of the bank. I guessed it to be roughly the same size as my office. That's where any similarities ended.

Unlike my office, no worn desk sat to one side beneath a cracked window. Instead, there was a wall of deposit boxes. On the other side, no racks stood to hold rifles. Instead, here, metal shelving held various bundles of bank notes and small closed boxes of various sizes.

In the center there was no potbellied stove, but a man, dead.

The man was on his back, arms sprawled at awkward angles, revolver clutched in his right hand. His hat was off and crushed beneath his head, showing the white of his forehead against short-cropped dark hair. He was dressed as a cowboy: boots with spurs, dusty jeans, leather vest, checked flannel shirt. His gray-and-black beard was matted with blood, blood that had pooled from a hole torn into his throat and formed a black puddle on the wood floor.

At my feet, as if he'd been facing the cowboy to be knocked backward into the vault door, then fallen face first toward the cowboy, was the second man. Not a cowboy, he wore dark blue pinstripe pants. His shirt back was starched white, except for a jagged circle of dried blood, and in the center of that stain was the star-shaped exit wound of a bullet that had already ripped through ribs and lung before smashing past the spine and out through the cloth. A revolver lay on the floor beside him. And like the cowboy, blood pooled beneath him, sticky with the print of a bootheel.

I didn't know the man on his back and had little urge to turn the other over to see his face. I drank more coffee, glad for how it burned my throat.

When I felt my stomach settle, I tried my voice.

"Crawford, you mentioned their names."

"That's *Mayor* Crawford."

His hot breath washed my ear. He had moved up to stand behind me, on his tiptoes, craning to look past my shoulder. I was glad for any reason to turn away from the dead men. Glad to replace weakness with anger. I drained my coffee and faced the mayor.

"Crawford," I said as quietly as a man can speak. I lifted his top hat and dropped it on the floor. His slicked hair glistened. My chin almost touched the pastiness of his sweating forehead. "One's dressed to work here. The other's dressed to be in debt here. Sort them out for me. Quick."

He flinched. Stepped away. Spoke in rapid bursts.

"Bob Nichols. Owns . . . owned a ranch west of here. The

Rocking N spread. We held a big mortgage on it. And Lorne Calhoun. Vice president of the bank."

"Calhoun always carry a gun?"

Crawford shook his head. "He must have grabbed it from where we had one hid in a safety deposit box. In case someone did try something like this."

I studied Crawford without really looking at him. My thoughts were on the dead men.

This was an unusual situation for a marshal. We're called on to settle drunks, shoot stray dogs, settle disputes, and occasionally try to stop robberies in progress or begin pursuit when we're late. Most of the action required within the realm of our duties, while sometimes difficult, is clear-cut. A man dies; someone is holding a gun with a hot barrel nearby. Or there's a dozen witnesses to point out which direction the murderer left. In short, marshaling has no resemblance to what Pinkerton men do for a living, which is to ferret out secrets and piece them together for a semblance of truth. For a marshal, the truth is usually there in what is happening before his eyes.

These bank vault deaths, however, put me in a difficult position. Laramie had no Pinkerton man. And no one else in the public domain for this duty to fall upon. As marshal, I had no choice but to begin unraveling what had led the two men to their deaths. It was nothing I had experience with, and I hoped it was as simple as it appeared: that the men had shot each other.

Unfortunately, not too long back, someone had tried to arrange *my* death to appear the same way. From the git-go, I wouldn't be able to ignore that possibility here. And there was the fact that money had disappeared. Which would indicate a third party was involved, whether he arranged the murder or ran from it—unless one of these two had hidden money earlier and come back to finish the job, only to be interrupted by death.

I felt like a dog circling for its own tail.

Where to start?

Mayor Crawford was babbling something at me.

I stared through him again. "Crawford, you should understand a couple of things," I said. "For this race, I am the town's horse. I wear a badge and take a salary. But I'm the kind of horse that runs harder without the whip."

He shut his mouth.

"We're going to close the bank down," I said.

"But customer deposits—"

"We're going to close the bank down. I'm going to sit you at a desk, and you're going to answer every question I have."

"For how long?"

"Until I can't think of any more questions to ask. And then we'll start over."

CHAPTER 3

THE BANK INTERIOR WAS BUILT with a small open area in front of the two tellers' wickets that were set side by side. Behind those wickets were two other desks, stacked with papers. Past that, in the corner, with an outside window to overlook Main Street and another window to the inside that let him watch employees and customers, was Crawford's office.

He had a huge oak desk that filled most of his office and a comfortable padded leather chair. Opposite his desk was a coatrack and three narrow chairs.

I moved to sit behind Crawford's desk. Made him take the uncomfortable straight-backed chair on the other side where folks sat when they had to beg him for a loan.

He cringed as I reached for a writing instrument set neatly beside a short pile of documents.

"That's a fountain pen," he said quickly. "Latest thing out of New York. Very expensive. It takes special care not to—"

I splotched dark blue on the polish of his desk. "High-strung, all right. Where's paper?"

I admit I was pushing him hard. Taking his chair. Messing his desk. I wanted Crawford on edge. If he had anything to hide, he'd find it more difficult flustered. While I didn't know he had anything to hide, it was his bank, he had found the men, and new as I was to this process, I didn't figure it would hurt to be as thorough as possible. Which was also why I'd decided to make notes of anything pertinent to the deaths of these men.

"Paper?" I repeated and began to shuffle through the documents stacked so neatly on his desk.

Crawford wheezed as he struggled to get his body out from the confines of that narrow chair. After securing me some lined paper, he grunted his way back into it.

"Bob Nichols," I said slowly as I wrote the name on the pad. "He owe money here? He behind in payments? How much land did he own free title?"

Crawford sputtered. "That's confidential to bank matters!"

I set the pen down and leaned forward. "Let's put our guns on the table, Crawford. Money missing, and yes, I'll get around to asking how much. Two men murdered. And a cold trail. I'll be throwing this badge around mighty hard to find out where that trail leads. And the less you answer, the more it'll look like you're at the end of that trail."

His eyes widened, a considerable feat, lost as they were in the fat of his face. "You're not suggesting I had anything to do with this!"

Probably not. It took guts to kill. But it wouldn't hurt to continue to pressure him. "I'm suggesting you're the first person anyone would investigate."

Crawford sagged, another considerable feat given that his body always seemed as low to the earth as possible.

"Nichols had a year left to prove up his homestead,"

Crawford said in a quiet voice. "We loaned him some money against that. He also held notes on a thousand head of cattle, but he expected to ship this week. He was behind a couple months but promised to make good with his cattle profit."

"Did you believe him?"

Crawford shrugged. "Didn't matter. We had all of the notes secured, on cattle or on the land he filed for homestead claim. One way or the other, we'd get it back."

I took satisfaction in blotching another ink puddle plainly within Crawford's view. It wasn't much punishment for the banker's coldheartedness, but it was immediate, and you take justice where you can, no matter how small.

I studied Crawford's twitching face. While it made no sense to steal money from himself, Crawford might have had any number of hidden reasons for arranging these deaths. One reason came to mind easily.

"The Nichols crew any good?" I asked.

"What?"

"Will the Rocking N run without him? Will his payments still be made?"

Crawford shrugged again. A man could learn to hate that shrug, especially if a man owed this bank money.

"Crawford, what I'm asking is if it would be worth killing Nichols to be able to foreclose."

His face grew puce. "How dare you—"

"It's a question folks will be asking among themselves. Clear it now. If you can." My hard accusation was like a slap across his face. He lost all bluff.

"I . . . I'm not sure if he had a good crew. I hadn't given any thought to what any of this means . . . and now you're saying folks might believe I killed my own employee. . . ."

Loud rapping sounded on the glass of the door that led into the bank.

"Sign's up, isn't it?" I said. "Posted that the bank is closed till further notice?"

Crawford nodded. Without the energy to speak, he was sunk in misery, and against my will, I had my first stirrings of sympathy for the man.

The rapping grew louder.

"Find a place to get comfortable," I suggested. "I'll tend to the door."

The shadow outside the opaque glass showed the impatient visitor to be tall. Even with that warning, Doc Harper in his brown suit was the last person I expected to see when I pulled the door open. We hadn't met before; he was known for keeping to himself. Yet if he was here to thank me for saving his life, I needed to put effort into being polite.

"Doc Harper, what brings you this way?" I asked pleasantly.

He brushed past me and scanned the interior of the bank.

"You fool," he said after a moment. "I hope you didn't already move the bodies. Lorne Calhoun was a good man."

It'd been a long time since I'd been called a fool. Often I'd deserved it, but my size was enough that folks either decided against saying it or said it where I couldn't hear. From Doc Harper, it didn't come out as an insult but abruptly honest, as if moving the bodies might indeed be the act of a fool. I was surprised to be aware of quick gladness that Doc Harper did not have that reason to call me a fool.

"The bodies are in the vault. And good morning to you, too, Doc." He gave me a sharp look at that reply.

"Two men dead. Murdered. One a friend. It is not a good morning."

Now I did feel the fool. Away from the sight of their blood, I had begun to think of the deaths as a problem to be solved. Doc's blunt words reminded me that two men had stopped living. Two small pieces of lead had robbed them of any future joys, sorrows, hopes, or dreams. The two men had left behind folks who would not coldly view their murders as the beginning of a tangled chase, but instead would grieve the loss deeply.

"You heard already?" I finally said. "Word gets around quick."

"Sharp for a lawman, aren't you? Take long to realize that earthshaking revelation about a town as small as Laramie?"

He started to walk ahead in that slow, painful way he had of grating his bones into motion.

"Doc."

He heard my anger. Stopped. Slowly turned to me.

"I'll agree it is not a good morning," I said. "You have my apology for that. And if the bodies had been cleared, you might have cause to call me fool. But lay off spitting nails in my direction. I ain't the cause of whatever is stuck in your craw."

"What if I decide not to lay off?"

"You'll only shame yourself, throwing stones at someone who ain't gonna throw back. I'm particular about who I choose for an enemy."

He thought that through. Snorted. Looked, for the first time, directly at me. "Samuel Keaton, that's the name?"

I nodded. I'd been marshal here a few weeks, and he would know my name. I took the question as a grudging hello.

"Maybe you're more than a gunslinger." No smile. "You'll excuse me."

He moved to the vault.

That left me nothing to do but return to Crawford in his office. He was standing beside his desk, wringing his hands as he stared at the wall.

"Lorne Calhoun began work for the bank in '70, right when it opened," Crawford said without being prompted. "Started as a boy who swept the floors. Worked his way up."

I sat at the desk, picked up the fountain pen. Splotched

again, this time by accident. "Was it unusual for him to be here at night?"

"No. Not at all. More like unusual for him *not* to be here. All he did was work. He had the keys, of course."

"Combination to the vault?" I asked.

"Combination to the vault. He probably knew the workings of this bank better than I did."

Without the pomp that he kept around himself, Crawford seemed like the sad little boy he must have once been. I wondered—and knew I was mean for doing it—how long it would take for him to puff himself up again.

"How much money missing?"

"Twenty-four thousand, three hundred and fifty dollars in bank notes. Twelve thousand, six hundred and twenty in gold."

When a cowpoke made thirty dollars a month, that was some kind of money. I didn't hold that thought long.

"Sit, Crawford."

"What?"

I sighed. "Sit."

He did.

"Lift your feet."

"What?"

I wanted to slap him.

"Lift your feet."

He did.

I squatted for a closer look. His left bootheel had tiny splashes of dull black-red on the side.

"Crawford, you stepped over the bodies to count."

He nodded—without the grace to blush.

That, at least, explained the heel print in the blood beneath Calhoun. I found myself happy to be able to dislike Crawford again.

"What time was that, Crawford?"

"I get here at seven-thirty. I walked in, saw the vault door partly open, and—"

"And took a half hour to reach me with the news."

He flapped his arms to express helplessness. "There's the money."

As if that said it all. He'd worked with Calhoun almost since Laramie had become a town.

"Why so much on hand?" I asked. "Seems risky."

"Payroll," Crawford said. "We handle payroll for the Union Pacific rolling mills."

Did I imagine extra nervousness? Why was he loosening his tie?

"What else do you know, Crawford?"

He swung his head sharply, as if trying to decide whether my voice had been accusing.

"I know I didn't murder anyone."

Before I could ask anything else, the outside door banged shut.

No one had entered the bank, so I assumed Doc Harper, not a model of Southern gentility, had left without calling a good-bye.

"You'll put a reward out for the return of that money?" I asked Crawford.

"Fifty dollars for every thousand recovered. Be close to two thousand dollars to whoever turns all of it in."

He'd given that thought, too, stepping over the body of the man who had served this bank for so long.

I hid my disgust and asked the most obvious question I had left. "Who else besides you and Calhoun could get into the vault outside of banking hours?"

There it was again. The little twitch. A tug at the tie. Unless I was looking too hard, grasping at anything.

"No one," he said.

Too loudly?

"But what if you died when Calhoun was out of town? Or the other way around?"

"Then the bank would be closed until he or I returned."

A defiant tone? Nor did it make sense he'd want the bank closed. Not from a man who had wanted the bank open to customers while his vice president lay dead in the vault.

I rubbed my eyes. I searched my mind for anything else to ask.

Crawford wheezed each breath as he waited.

Trouble was, I couldn't think of anything else to ask.

I swung out of Crawford's chair and motioned for him to occupy it. When he was seated, I handed him the fountain pen and gave him the remaining blank paper.

"Write down everything you knew about Calhoun. Everything about Nichols. When you're finished, and only then, call for the undertaker."

"I've got a bank to run. A town to oversee and—"

"I can't do everything myself, which is the only choice I have," I said, "being as when Town Council considered hiring me a deputy, you worked so hard to swing the vote against it."

I left him there. Maybe something would show up on his list that would point me toward a third person. Or at the very least, toward someone else who might point me in the right direction. More importantly, I wanted Crawford occupied while I went back to the vault.

I wondered what would possess Doc Harper to make an appearance when he knew the men were beyond his help.

The bodies had been shifted.

Lorne Calhoun was now on his back. Doc Harper had placed his brown suit jacket over the man's head and upper body. I realized, almost with a shock, how tall Calhoun was. Death in my mind had shrunk him, but Doc Harper's jacket showed me wrong.

It took more willpower than I knew I had to lift the jacket.

There was the blood to discourage me from that action. And the disrespect of uncovering a man covered by a friend.

Calhoun's eyes were open wide in what looked like surprise, if a person wanted to put emotion on his face. His shirt had been opened to show where the bullet had entered the center of his chest. The bullet hole, wiped of blood, now appeared clean and black against marble skin. What kept my eyes open so wide was that I was trying to see Calhoun, instead of my brother in his dying moments. Even on closer inspection, I could not find anything unusual about the bullet hole, and I straightened.

Bob Nichols had been moved, too. He was on his side, moved a foot away from the blood that had emptied from the front of his throat. The exit hole of the bullet was lost in the matted hair at the back of his skull.

Death filled my nostrils, and the coffee now rising inside me as bile was a good indication that I should leave.

My search, however, was not complete.

I swallowed hard and stepped around each man to take the revolvers. A tentative sniff told me that each gun had been fired recently, and a quick check of each cylinder showed an empty brass shell where the pin had last struck.

Lastly, I took one of the oil lamps from its stand. I knew too well that flesh and blood offer little resistance to the smashing velocity of a chunk of half-inch lead, so I held the oil lamp close to the back wall and slowly raised and lowered it until I saw a shiny dent, shoulder height.

I looked at the floor and saw bits and pieces of the slug that had caused the shiny dent.

I should have felt more at peace to discover the proof that a shot had indeed been fired in here. And even more relieved to find another slug mark slick on the inside of the vault door, chest high, almost centered in a blood smear—proof that Calhoun had been shot from where Nichols had stood.

I told myself maybe that's how it did happen. Nichols

finds a way into the vault and is surprised by Calhoun. Or maybe they're in on it together and have a falling-out. Or maybe Nichols forced Calhoun in here at gunpoint late last night and didn't expect a banker to have a gun hidden nearby in a safe deposit box.

However it happened, everything in the vault did add up to a point-blank shoot-out.

Except, of course, for two things. Doc had told me it was murder.

And, of course, the missing money.

CHAPTER 4

I'D BRIEFLY SPENT TIME in Laramie when it was little more than Fort John Buford. That was '68, when Union Pacific laid tracks across the Wyoming Territories in barely more than a year's time. I'd been earning wages then by shooting buffalo to feed the Union Pacific work crews, and after the push from Cheyenne to get the tracks and construction crew through both the winter and the Laramie Mountains, it was a relief that spring to get down here into the plains between the Laramie and Medicine Bow ranges, especially with the tent town and fort that awaited us to offer some form of civilization.

We didn't stay long in the new town of Laramie—at two miles of track each day, we never did in any of the end-of-track towns—but my memories of it had always been favorable.

I suspect much of that good impression simply had to do with the weather. Misery inflicted by the fierceness of winter had ended, and we had yet to hit the blistering dryness of summer that would make for such arid, windswept torment through the basin flats into Rawlins and Rock Springs.

When we left, the army left with us, moving west with the tracklayers to protect them from Indians, and Laramie was abandoned to the ruthless and lawless, who managed in our departure to run off what was left of city government. It left the town without law and order for five months, until in October of that year a vigilante committee formed among the citizens. In one bloody night, five outlaws were killed, fifteen wounded, and four others hung from telegraph posts.

I saw none of that action, of course, as we were near to Green River by then, but news traveled fast up and down the tracks, and I heard soon after. So did many of the gamblers, army deserters, and assorted outlaws, who suddenly decided that prospects for better health lay west of the Laramie Plains and searched for it accordingly. Things turned so peaceable, I'm told by old-timers here, that by the summer of '69, Laramie had one school and four churches.

———

Now—barely six years since I'd seen it as a town of dirty white tents clustered around a fort—Laramie had secured its future. Other end-of-track towns—Bryon, Benton, and Bear River City—were dying, but Laramie had its rolling mills to make rails for the mighty Union Pacific. It also had a three-story territorial prison made of limestone bricks on the west bank of the Big Laramie River and cattle ranches spread up and down the plains of the wide valley between the mountains west and east of town. There was money enough in this town.

I could walk down Main Street in the midmorning sunshine—as I was doing now—and see that prosperity alive in the steady movement of men on horses or driving buggies, and of women in cotton dresses as they picked their way along the wooden sidewalks or between horse apples while crossing the dirt street.

Aside from Crawford's bank, the First National with its obvious wealth marked by brick construction, there were three others, false-front wooden exteriors high and wide and freshly painted in vain efforts to match their hallowed competitor.

At the far end of Main, the Union Pacific rose against the backdrop of the far mountains. Set almost within the shadows of this forty-room hotel were the station depot and telegraph office.

Between the hotel and where I stood, a quick scan of the board signs that hung from the Main Street buildings showed more of the encroaching comforts of civilization. HILLMAN'S EATERY. THE BROADWAY SUITATORIUM—PRESSING—BOOTS & SHOES CLEANED AND SHINED. KELLER'S PHOTO PORTRAITS. MALCOLM'S QUALITY MILL & CABINET WORKS. THE *LARAMIE SENTINEL*—CUSTOM STATIONERY. OVERBAY'S DRESSMAKING & FITTING. GUTHRIE DRY GOODS & CLOTHING. ELVIN & NELSON ATTORNEYS AT LAW. And, sprinkled among those signs, others that gave cause for much of the reason for my existence in Laramie—the saloons. COMIQUE THEATRE AND DANCE HALL. RED ROSE SALOON—ICED BEER. LARAMIE SALOON AND SPORTING HALL.

A half-dozen side streets intersected Main, and those quieter streets were the places to find smaller hotels, blacksmiths, harness makers, and liveries.

That was why, instead of enjoying my usual breakfast at the Chinaman's café, I now walked along the wooden sidewalk, nodding at men, tilting my hat at ladies. I needed to visit each of those liveries, for the simple reason that Nichols had been a rancher.

He would not travel without a horse, saddled or buggied. The very presence of his dead body showed that Nichols indeed had ridden into Laramie to enter a bank vault late at night.

I'd found no horse tied outside of the First National. Perhaps that in itself was not a surprise. The last thing he would want is to have a passerby remember a horse with the Rocking N brand outside the bank he was robbing.

Yet the horse had to be somewhere.

If it was in one of the liveries, or if a hand who had stabled the horse for Nichols on his previous visits now recognized it somewhere tied to a rail on one of the streets, I might discover on that horse something—anything—to shed more light on the confusing issues that blanketed me.

On the other hand, if a thorough search showed that the horse was not in town, I'd be able to make one of two conclusions. Either some third party had been stupid enough to take the horse, a good sign that Nichols and Calhoun had not been alone in the shoot-out in the vault. Or some stranger had stolen the horse from where it was tied, awaiting the return that Nichols would never make.

Of the two possibilities, the second was unlikely. In these parts, getting caught on another man's horse almost always ended in a necktie party, no matter how good the excuse for riding a strange brand. If no trees could be found nearby, rope would be slung around a saddle horn, and the offender would hang as he was dragged behind the horse he'd stolen. In short, if you found a wandering horse, you stayed on yours and headed with the stray horse in a direct line to the ranch it came from or the nearest livery. That way, you were believed when you said the horse was on its return.

It was not much to go on, and I knew it, but at least it was immediate action of some sort, this search for Nichols' horse.

Later, when I'd breathed plenty of outside air, walked hard all over town, and cleared my body of the cling of death, I might be able to enjoy a late breakfast. After, I'd take more—and likely futile—action by riding to the Rocking N to ask further questions.

And given more time, maybe I'd be able to figure out something more useful to do about the double deaths.

But I wasn't hopeful about that possibility, either.

CHAPTER 5

THE PITCHFORK RECENTLY THROWN at my feet still quivered in the ground, inches from the toes of my boots.

"Men at the last three liveries say you run a good stable, that you're an honest man," I said to One-Arm Wilson as he hopped down from the wagon in front of me. "Hadn't heard about your distinctive manner of greeting visitors."

Wilson chuckled. "Seen you coming. Knew who you were. Wanted to be able to tell my grandchildren I'd made a marshal jump."

He looked down to where he had stuck the pitchfork with a throw from the wagon. "It grieves me that I didn't. What would it take, Marshal Keaton, to make you jump? A nicked toe?"

I shook my head. "Quicker reactions on my part. And call me Sam."

I stuck out my left hand to shake a greeting. He returned it with the callused grip of his own left hand. "Jake Wilson."

He chuckled again. "You needing quicker reactions? Not what I heard. Shooting two snakes clean out of the air, that ain't the mark of a slow man."

"It's the mark of a stupid one," I said. "Until a judge rides through, I'm stuck with a phony preacher that don't keep his mouth shut."

He nodded in sympathy. A broad-chested man of medium height with straw-filled blond hair and a blocky face, there was nothing remarkable about him. Except for his arms. I guessed it was for extra coolness during his work here in the warm, dark interior of the livery. He had torn the sleeves from the old shirt he wore. His left arm was massive, with sweat rivulets flowing down the tightened muscles. From the open doors at the front of the livery, I'd seen him atop the wagon just ahead between the stalls. He'd been pitching straw one-handed with the speed of two normal men. To do that, he had a sling nailed to the top of the pitchfork. It let him grasp the handle lower down with his left hand, and with the sling around his upper forearm, he was able to leverage the tines with considerable power.

His right arm, however, was barely more than flesh over bone, as if all the muscle had been stripped away. The arm hung slack at his side. Marbled scars, like ugly red worms, covered the skin on the upper half of that arm.

Wilson caught my glance.

"Stupidity, too," he said. No bitterness. "A stallion I'd kept for three years. I knew he was mean. Just didn't know he could be so patient. One careless moment. I was leading him to a mare and stood too close to his head with too much slack on the rope halter. . . ."

Wilson shrugged.

I could imagine the rest. Folks fear a horse's kick. With good reason. Stoved-in head or ribs are not uncommon. But it's the teeth that cause real horror. When stallions fight, that's how they damage each other. With lightning slashes, they tear from each other chunks of muscle that leave gaping holes in the haunch or the neck.

During Wilson's one careless moment, that stallion must have clamped its teeth on his bicep and ripped it from the bone in one swift motion. Most men would have fallen right there, leaving themselves helpless to be stomped to death, for stallions gone mean carry a bloodlust hatred for the two-legged creatures that prison them. That Wilson, in agony, had the presence of mind to escape was as impressive as his obvious determination not to let the handicap stop him now.

"Glad to make acquaintance," I said. "I'm hoping you might be able to help."

"The Rocking N horse." It was a statement.

"Someone get here ahead of me?" I'd offered a ten-dollar reward for the whereabouts of the horse at each of the previous liveries. In the absence of the help of a deputy or two, I expected that method to be as good as any to have the streets searched for the horse. Naturally, if a stable hand found it in one of the other liveries before I got there, he'd have a good claim on the ten dollars and have earned himself a couple weeks' wages.

"No. I hadn't heard." Wilson's voice was quieter, more serious. "When I saw the horse, I feared it might involve the law."

He turned away from me and walked along the edge of the wagon, wading through the straw that had spilled from it onto the dirt.

I stepped around the pitchfork and followed.

The front of the livery had doors open wide enough for a drawn wagon to pass through, but away from that opening, the livery grew darker each successive step inside. I saw dimly the tops of the backs of the horses that filled each stall—Wilson was good enough and, more importantly, known to be good enough that he had few stalls empty. I took in the clean smells of horse and the sweetness of hay dust and, a step later, discovered why there was so little stink. Two wheelbarrows were full with horse muck scraped from the ground. He'd cleaned the stalls first thing, and by the way he'd been pitching straw, he was also generous with bedding. I told myself to stable my horses here as soon as I could.

Wilson stopped at the last stall on the right-hand side. He opened the small door in the back wall of the livery. Light poured in to show the horse he led by rope halter from that stall: a large dun, rubbed down and blanketed. A saddle lay balanced on the top fence board of that stall, and I assumed Wilson had stripped it from the dun. Straddled behind the saddle on that same fence board, saddlebags draped the sides of the stall.

The sunlight also gave me a chance to note the brand on the haunch of the dun as it cleared the stall: a large "N," sitting atop a "C" turned sideways into a bowl. The Rocking N.

"Not a horse you'd forget," Wilson said with the same quietness as before. "Bob Nichols stabled it here more than once when he stayed overnight in town."

"He left it here last night?"

Wilson shook his head. "Some cowpoke brought it in about an hour ago."

"Why'd you assume I might come looking?"

"Cowpoke claimed he found it wandering just outside of town. Nichols is a careful man. He wouldn't let something like that happen. As soon as I saw the horse, I figured him to be in trouble."

I thought that over and knew it to be true. A horse without a man usually means just that. But Wilson had said . . .

"Trouble doesn't necessarily mean the law," I said. "Nichols could have been hurt somewhere. Why'd you expect me instead of family or a doctor?"

Wilson smiled sadly. "I'd heard already that Nichols and Calhoun had been found dead at the bank."

I snorted. Had Crawford stopped to place an ad in the

Sentinel before busting into my office?

I looked Wilson square in the face. "You know something about that horse I should know?"

"That cowpoke brought in this dun still saddled," Wilson said. He rubbed the horse's neck with his left hand as he spoke. "And I'm guessing if he'd known what this horse carried, he might have taken it for a long ride instead."

"The saddlebags," I guessed. "He'd minded his own business and not looked inside."

"Saddlebags were empty. Bare flapping empty. But not the blanket roll tied behind the saddle."

Wilson guided the horse back into its stall. When he stepped out moments later, he had a blanket in his left hand. He carried it by the four corners bunched in his fingers, and the bottom sagged like a sack, as if the blanket held something heavy.

It did. Something I'd tell Crawford about as soon as I could.

Twelve thousand, six hundred and twenty dollars in gold coin.

CHAPTER 6

I FOUND CRAWFORD OUTSIDE the Red Rose Saloon in a shouting match with one of Laramie's most well-known drunks.

"You flea-bitten souse, you'll return those notes to the bank!" Crawford's volume was impressive.

I stepped through the crowd to see Old Charlie beaming with joy as he leaned against the window of the saloon. Given that the whiskey bottle he held high in his right hand was only a quarter full, I could understand how he managed to sustain his joy despite Mayor Crawford's blustering rage.

"Marshal Keaton," Old Charlie slurred happily. On the occasions I'd had to escort Old Charlie to jail quarters, his thin coyote face had always shown that satisfied glow. "Care for a snort in toast to a fortunate turn of events?"

He pointed at Mayor Crawford, a movement that cost Old Charlie some balance, and he had to splay his feet to remain standing.

"Crawford here won't share the bottle,"

Old Charlie said. His pants were little more than worn canvas. His shirt had lost most of its buttons and hung wide open to reveal the faded, full-length red long johns he wore underneath. "In fact, Marshal, the mayor's a mite prickly this fine morning. I told him he had plenty money in his bank. No need to haul me into daylight and take what little I—"

"Keaton, arrest this man," Crawford sputtered.

I leaned close to Crawford. "That's *Marshal* Keaton."

Mayor Crawford contained himself with effort that made his jowls quiver. "*Marshal* Keaton, this man has been spending First National bank notes. I insist he return the money."

"Charlie?" I asked.

Old Charlie threw his head back and laughed. That put him into a coughing fit that only ended when he bent double and spewed a string of spittle onto the sidewalk between his battered boots.

He straightened and wiped threads of that phlegm from the gray bristles of his chin. "Marshal, who's got claim to money blowing in the breeze?"

"What's that, Charlie?" a male voice called from the crowd.

Old Charlie tilted the bottle and took a long gulp before answering. "In the breeze, boys. I found bank notes in God's wide open breeze!"

There were more stirrings of interest from the people gathering around.

"Shut him up," Crawford hissed between clenched teeth.

"Nobody'd be listening if you'd have left him inside."

"He smells," Crawford explained. Not softly. "Outside is the only place I can stand to be near him."

As if asked to uphold Crawford's complaint, Old Charlie passed wind with obvious thunder. "Rotten stomach, Marshal," he apologized. "Doc Harper says I gotta eat more greens."

"Hey, Charlie! Where in the breeze?" came another voice.

Old Charlie raised his bottle in salute. "Right outside my shack, boys. Like picking cotton!" He cackled and leered at Crawford. "Must be I'm living right."

Crawford stamped his foot. "Stop him. I insist."

"Appears like the damage is done."

By the expression on Crawford's face, he knew I was speaking the truth.

The crowd around us was already beginning to thin. Some men were in full run. A couple of women weren't far behind, held back not by spirit, but by the layers of skirt they had hitched at their knees.

Old Charlie lived past the edge of town. We'd be clear of our audience for a long while.

I turned back to Old Charlie. "Money in the breeze? How much blew your way?"

"Couple hundred, Marshal. Buy you a drink?"

I declined. Regretfully. Lack of greens or not, Old Charlie made better company than Mayor Crawford.

"Marshal Keaton," Crawford began. "It is unacceptable that you do not take immediate action. Those bank notes belong to First National."

"Crawford," I said, "you have no way of proving these notes are part of the missing money."

I watched the progress of the crowd as it strung itself out. The street now looked like a picnic footrace. One saloon dancer had knocked down a few of the slower men.

"Charlie," I said, "what say you give me that money for safekeeping?"

Old Charlie regarded Mayor Crawford with open distrust. "Marshal, I—"

"Charlie, the money will stay in my office until all this is sorted out."

With his right hand, Old Charlie nervously rubbed the white chest hairs poking between the buttons of his faded long johns.

I didn't let him hesitate long. "Otherwise," I continued, "Mayor Crawford will be gnawing on you every day until you manage to spend it."

Old Charlie frowned as he contemplated that complication to his otherwise simple life. It didn't take him long to reach into his pocket.

I accepted the crumpled notes and carefully counted. "Two hundred and twenty, Charlie. You want an official receipt?"

"Not from you, Marshal."

I nodded. "When you finish that bottle, you'll be hungry. I'll be dropping off some of these notes at the Chinaman's, and he'll keep it as credit for you. After all—"

"You can't do that! It's bank property!" Crawford blurted.

Old Charlie was still sober enough to give me a sympathetic nod.

"After all," I continued, "there's two good reasons you'd better take a good meal over another bottle."

"What's that, Marshal?"

"I'd hate to see this money wasted on fines," I said. I scowled as I thought of the next reason, a bothersome rattlesnake-throwing preacher. "And trust me, Charlie, you couldn't get drunk enough to endure the man you'd share the cell with."

Old Charlie grinned and saluted me with his free hand.

I tipped my hat in return and led Crawford away by his elbow.

"Crawford," I began as we walked back to First National, "how'd you know Old Charlie had bank notes?"

"You *will* return those notes immediately."

I sighed. "Crawford, how'd you know Old Charlie had bank notes?"

"I got word from a cowboy," Crawford said stiffly. "He hails from the Bar X Bar ranch. Said he'd found a horse grazing near Old Charlie's shack. And where else would the old drunk be but at the Red Rose?"

"You oughta be a marshal," I agreed. "What'd the cowboy tell you about that horse that put you onto Old Charlie?"

"He'd found it with the saddlebag open, and bank notes were blowing out from it."

"You believed him?"

"This cowboy plunked a bunch of them right on my desk and said it was all that was left in the saddlebags." Mayor Crawford smiled maliciously. "Let those fools run to Old Charlie's shack for whatever else blew free. My clerks have been combing the brush out there for the last hour."

"You're not worried about the clerks keeping some for themselves?"

The smile disappeared.

"By the way," I finished, "Jake Wilson found the missing gold. Figure on him showing up sometime this afternoon to claim his reward."

CHAPTER 7

BY THE TIME I SPOKE to Crawford again early that evening, I'd searched as many back-tracks as I could think to find and was forced to believe most of the pieces were in place.

I explained as much to him in his office.

"Nichols paid a visit on Calhoun last night," I told Crawford where he sat behind his desk with his paunch filling his lap. "Real late. They left the boardinghouse together."

"Calhoun! That snake was in on it with Nichols!"

I shrugged. "All I know is what the board-inghouse woman told me. She heard someone knock on Calhoun's door, and it woke her into peeking out her bedroom to look down the hallway. She saw it was Nichols, and as her rules only disallow women visitors, she turned back in and let them be."

"That proves it then," Crawford said. "Calhoun set this up. You got an eyewitness."

Darkness hit early now in the fall, and Crawford's office was already dim. I dug a match from my shirt pocket and snapped it into flame with the edge of my thumbnail. I continued to speak as I lit a nearby oil lamp.

"Why are you in such a hurry to crucify Calhoun?"

Crawford's eyes seemed to shrink in the light. "It . . . it . . . just seems logical. . . ."

"That after years of service, the vice president of your bank might be so unhappy he would conspire to rob you?"

Crawford began to puff with indignation at my choice of words.

"Yes, it's a possibility," I said. "Maybe Calhoun did let Nichols into the vault to set up a robbery, only to have a .45 caliber disagreement with his partner. But I doubt it."

I dropped the spent match on the edge of Crawford's polished desk. "Because on the other hand," I said, "for all you know, Nichols pulled a gun on Calhoun right there at the boardinghouse. Forced him at gunpoint to the bank. And of the two, that's where I'd place my bet."

Crawford stared at the burnt matchstick that littered his desk. He reached for it, but his belly brought him up short.

"Think it through, Crawford. If you were Calhoun, set on helping someone into a vault that would be empty by daybreak, and if you were about the only person in town with the combination to that vault, would you take a chance on doing anything late at night that might be remembered by anyone?"

Crawford grunted agreement. To keep his mind on our conversation, I picked the burnt matchstick from his desk and handed it to him.

"I did more trailwork," I said. "The wandering horse story fits, too. As much of it as you want to believe."

"As much as I want to believe?"

"Your cowboy from the Bar X Bar, he dropped how much of the missing bank notes on your desk?"

"Fourteen thousand, two hundred. When I get those notes you confiscated from Old Charlie, that'll make—"

I drew my finger across my throat and found it encouraging that Crawford shut his mouth so quickly.

"Add to it the gold that Jake Wilson returned, and you're still some ten thousand short."

Crawford nodded in painful agreement.

"A cowboy makes four hundred in a year of busting horses, cattle, and his own bones," I said. "Seems to me that ten thousand is considerable incentive to lie. Or kill."

Crawford may have frowned in thought. But in the dim light, and with the layers of fat on his face, any wrinkles that might have risen from that frown could also have been my imagination.

"Kill?" Crawford asked.

"Kill," I repeated. "Ask yourself how you'd best keep nearly half the money you stole and manage at the same time to appear innocent."

The flesh on his face began to work in thought.

I'd already done my share of thinking this day.

I was not a Pinkerton man. I did not have learning or experience in their kind of law enforcement. And I knew it. So upon seeing the two dead bodies less than ten hours earlier, I had decided against wasting any time in an attempt to think as a Pinkerton detective. Instead, I had spent all day coming at the problem from the opposite direction—standing in the killer's boots and trying to puzzle through how I'd have tried to hide a double murder, if indeed this was not as simple as two men shooting each other.

The first person I'd wondered about as a killer had been Crawford. While it made no sense to steal money from himself, Crawford might have had any number of hidden reasons for arranging these deaths. One reason came to mind easily. Nichols' ranch. Chances were Crawford could foreclose on something nearly three-quarters paid for, a sweet deal for any banker.

Crawford didn't know, and only would if his wife told

him, but my first stop after the Red Rose Saloon had been to his home, a two-story wood-frame building on a quiet street well away from the dust of the main thoroughfare. She'd told me his snoring kept her awake all night and made it a point to say his snoring was the only thing that ever kept her awake.

Following on the heels of that alibi came that conversation with the boardinghouse woman. When I'd asked if it could have been Crawford knocking on Calhoun's door, she'd made it clear that she'd have to be a total idiot to not recognize Crawford's backside—even in poor light, half-asleep, and squinting to the end of the hallway. I'd had to agree, and with two witnesses reluctantly speaking for Crawford, it seemed certain he was not the killer.

That left me next to wonder about the cowboy, a redhead by the name of Clayton Barnes from the Bar X Bar ranch. He claimed he'd found the horse as he headed back to the ranch from Laramie.

Yet the Bar X Bar, I'd discovered, was close enough to the Rocking N that he could have had dealings with Nichols, close enough that I could think of a way for the redhead to throw suspicion away from himself.

Were I in his boots, and not totally greedy, I'd pretend not to know about the gold in the blanket roll and turn it along with the horse to Jake Wilson, known far and wide for his honesty. Then I'd give half the bank notes right back to the bank, knowing it would appear, just as it did, that Nichols had secured most of the stolen money on his horse, then returned to the vault to meet his unexpected death, and afterward the horse had wandered away to lose most of the money.

I told all of this to Crawford to interrupt his wheezing thoughts.

"But I made a round of the saloons today," I continued, "and found a few of the boys from Bar X Bar. Learned two things. They'd spent most of the night carousing with this Clayton Barnes. And when they left, he stayed behind in a poker game that went through the night."

I took my Colt out of my holster.

Crawford's nostrils flared as he took a startled breath. I ignored his sudden and unjustified fear as I spun open the chamber and continued to speak.

"That means Clayton Barnes couldn't have been in the vault," I said. "So you have to decide whether that Bar X Bar cowboy found the horse with the saddlebag open or closed."

I held the revolver upside down and emptied the five bullets into my hand. Three I dropped into my shirt pocket. The other two I palmed.

"See, Crawford, was I him on my way home from an all-night poker game and I found a full saddlebag of First National money, I'd be real tempted to throw enough into the breeze to make it look like it did blow away and give you back enough to keep you happy."

Crawford did not look happy.

I found my pocketknife and flicked open the blade. "Of course," I said as I began to pry at one of the brass cartridges, "if I were you, I wouldn't speculate much on that possibility."

Crawford was staring at my actions with puzzlement. "Why not?" he asked.

"Even if you found him with a pile of money, unless you got a way to prove those notes belong to you, it'd be a real fight to get them back."

"No cowboy earns that kind of money!"

I pried more with my knife, working slow to keep gunpowder from spilling loose, until I finally popped the pepper lead free.

"He could find a lot of different ways to claim how the money came in. Or, if he was real smart and didn't want a whisper of trouble, he could wait a year, clear out, and spend it out of the territories."

Crawford's glum silence confirmed my suppositions.

He wheezed a few more minutes, and finally, as I nearly

finished working the second bullet, he asked me what it was I intended to do next.

I didn't answer.

Instead, I pulled a piece of paper from his wastebasket, tore corners away from the paper, and wadded the corners into small chunks that I pushed into each of the open cartridges. When I was satisfied with my handiwork, I loaded the two cartridges into my Colt, reached over his desk, and handed the revolver butt-first to Crawford.

"Take this into the vault. Close the door partway. Fire both shots at the floor. Don't worry about bullets. You'll be firing blanks."

He didn't try to rise. Just stared confusion at me.

"I'll be outside the bank," I explained. "If I don't hear those shots, it'll explain why I could find nobody that heard shooting last night."

Out on the street, it was near dark.

I stood and waited.

Barely a minute later, I heard the report of two muted shots. Had I not been listening, I might easily have decided a door had been slammed in a building nearby.

Crawford met me at the entrance to the bank. I accepted my revolver and decided it was not worth the effort to comment on the fact that he had not extended it to me with the barrel pointing in my direction.

"That seems about it," I said. "Best as I can tell, it happened the way it appears. Nichols more than likely forced Calhoun to the vault. Nichols maybe steps outside to pack the money on his horse, and that gives Calhoun a chance to dig a gun out of a safety deposit box. Nichols goes back inside for more money, and they have a shoot-out, which leaves the horse free to wander until it's found."

Crawford seemed satisfied with that. "Good work, Marshal. I'll pass on my favorable impression of your diligence to Town Council."

He looked at me as if he expected my tail to wag. It did not. I had nothing else to say, so I left him there in the doorway of his bank.

Down the street, I stopped.

The air had a bite to it, and I turned to feel the freedom of the wind in my face. The stars had brightened against the deepened purple of the sky, and a harvest moon hung low and yellow and clear to show the outlines of the building rooftops.

I did not need the moon as a reminder of the Sioux medicine bundle carefully stowed in the bedroom of my small rented house. It was the only physical proof I had of love from the woman now far from me and living among the Sioux north in the territory. I knew her as Rebecca Montcalm; the Sioux called her Evening Star in honor of how her mother had died. She'd given me her most precious possession, this medicine bundle, on our last afternoon together, telling me the Sioux legend about the first medicine bundle and a boy and girl parted, then reunited. The way we'd promised each other we would be.

Tonight when the moon was high and white would be a good night to ride, to leave the confines of my house, and go out across the plains to listen to the quiet. I knew exactly how it would feel, to be lost in the openness and to see in the night light the dark land as it stretched into the blackness of the far mountains. It would be a good night not to hide from the ache, to smile in mournful agreement with the lonely howls of coyotes, and to wonder in that cleansing infinity of solitude about Evening Star, where she might be, and if I were in her thoughts. Since I could not hold her, I would embrace the sadness that stole into my heart with the thoughts of her and accept that sadness as her presence. It was very little to have, but much, much more of her than I had once dreamed I could possess, and that made it bearable.

After I get through tonight, I thought, *there would be to-morrow, and tomorrow night, and the following day.* I knew that and, as always, steeled myself to think only of the moment I was in, not the time that remained until we met again, or what she might become by then.

As I stepped down from the wooden sidewalk onto the street and resumed my solitary walk, I told myself it was a small consolation that holding the truth from the mayor might help me find a way to pass some of that next stretch of time.

CHAPTER 8

CORNELIUS HARPER'S OFFICE did not appear to belong to a doctor.

Most offices I'd seen on the frontier held a collection of the doctors' handiwork—organs and amputated body parts supposedly removed from once-ailing human beings and then preserved in alcohol to impress prospective patients. If the doctor could afford the luxury of a waiting room—otherwise the next patient stood outside in the hallway or on the street—its shelves would be lined with those bottled leftover bits and pieces of former patients, pills and chemicals, jars of leeches, and displays of surgical instruments. The more curious and astonishing the contents of the shelves, it was felt, the more credible the physician.

By the plainness of his office, however, Doc Harper did not feel a need to impress his patients.

His waiting room barely fit the three cane-backed chairs set against a wall. It contained a potbellied stove and nothing else.

I knocked on the door to his inner office and received no answer. The door was unlocked, and I looked inside to see if I could find anything that would allow me to leave him a note.

It was an office as plainly decorated as the waiting room. On the left was a long low table. On the far side of the room stood two bookshelves, tidy but crammed with volumes and volumes of books—great luxury here in the territories. Alongside those bookshelves, a shorter shelf held splints of assorted sizes, bandages, and a few bottles of pills. Atop that shorter shelf was a small instrument I had not seen anywhere before, which appeared to be a narrow brass urn, its base screwmounted into the bottleneck of a tripod.

And on the right side of his office was his desk, a roll top of exquisitely polished walnut, set so that Doc Harper faced toward the window when he was sitting in the chair behind it.

Except for one sheet of paper and a pen and ink bottle beside it, the surface of that desk was totally without papers or anything else to indicate it might have ever received use.

I moved closer. The piece of paper was a note explaining, in neat script, that Doctor Harper had left before dawn to remove a gallbladder at the Thompsons' homestead. It also suggested that anyone who could read that note and needed Doc Harper's assistance should leave word for him with the pen and ink provided.

One person had already visited his office. *Betty got bad throte and cant hardly breeth nun. Abe.*

I jotted a message of my own beneath the scrawled words. *Please stop by marshal's office when best for you. Sam Keaton.*

Then I sat in the waiting room on the chance that Doc Harper might return in the next half hour. I had already taken a good breakfast, had nothing urgent of my own to do, and was in no hurry to return to the unwelcome guest preacher who was making my own office a prison for me.

I could also think clearly in this welcome solitude.

While I knew why I had chosen to mislead Mayor Crawford in delivering my opinion on how Nichols and Calhoun had shot each other, I did not know why I could not believe in the conclusion I had offered for Crawford's benefit.

Keeping my true thoughts from Crawford made sense simply because I felt he was involved in some way. Crawford seemed less than sharp for someone in his position of power. Or was it that he was so smart, he did a good job of playing stupid? And if that was the case, did he have a reason for playing stupid?

Furthermore, ten thousand dollars of his was missing. Why—especially in light of the fuss he had made trying to recover a few hundred from Old Charlie—wasn't Crawford visibly upset over how much still remained unfound? And why hadn't Crawford been the one—not me—to immediately point out how easily Clayton Barnes could have kept a portion of the bank notes?

Unfortunately, it appeared Crawford had a good alibi for his whereabouts during the night, and I didn't know if, despite my gut feelings, I could find anything to tie him into the murders.

As to my reluctance to accept the double deaths as the simple shoot-out I had described to Crawford, it bothered me that I could find no reason for the doubts that tugged at my mind every time I recalled the dead bodies. Unless something turned up soon—I felt I had done most of the important backtrailing yesterday—my public conclusion would have to stand.

Leaving the conclusion there, of course, would make it easier for me to continue quietly searching for the tracks of a third person in that vault—tracks that I was convinced existed, even with no good reason to back that conviction.

I poked at the same thoughts again and again as I waited for Doc Harper to return, telling myself that he had good reason for calling it murder, telling myself he had something that could start me looking in the right direction.

When I began to feel a headache from all my useless speculation, I borrowed a book from Doc Harper's inner office. After a half hour of reading, he still hadn't returned. I returned the book to its place and forced myself to return to my own office farther down the street.

"Lawman, that Injun squaw—did she look as good as folks say?"

I was glad that I stood at my office window watching the street for the Chinaman with lunch or Doc Harper with answers. Had I been facing Brother Lewis as he taunted me with that question, he surely would have caught the reaction that sent a tremor through me.

"Lawman," he said. "You heard me. Tell me about that squaw of your'n."

I took a deep breath and found the strength to turn toward the jail cell at the back of my office. If I continued to ignore him, Brother Lewis would know he'd managed to pull a scab loose from a painful wound—how badly I missed my Evening Star, Rebecca.

He leered at me as I gave him a level gaze. "Small town, lawman. First thing I heard about you was your Injun-loving ways. How you helped save a couple of Sioux necks before moving here. How one of those necks was real pretty."

"I ain't allowed you visitors, so you must have done your asking early," I said. My voice came out even and slow, remarkable considering how much I raged inside. "Most preachers have little cause to inquire as such. Where'd you find the need to acquire that habit? You on the run from the law?"

That shut him up but only for a moment. When he resumed, he exaggerated the backwoods rhythms in his words, as if it were easier to grind me down away from the loftiness of the educated tones he had used in the revival tent.

"Some folks wonder, lawman. More and more noise is reaching us about Injuns on the warpath. Whose side you on, I heard them ask. Like you're soft on Injuns. And on China-men, too, the way you spend your time in his eatery. You don't like regular folk? Or they don't like you?"

I sat in my chair, leaned back, and set my feet on my desk, easy and relaxed as if I were about to enjoy a nap. What I wanted to do was borrow a patch of Old Charlie's smelly long johns so I could roll it into a ball and stuff it in Brother Lewis's mouth.

I pulled my Colt loose from my holster.

"Aiming to shoot me, lawman? Figure that'll shut me up? Let me loose, boy, send me on my way out of town, and I won't be able to cause you more grief."

I took a small bottle of gun oil from the left-hand drawer of my desk. I found a piece of cloth from the other drawer. Without hurrying, I opened the cylinder and began to clean the revolver.

Where was the Chinaman with the lunch I'd ordered for the prisoner?

"Anyway, lawman, you can't rightly jail a man for drop-ping rattlesnakes. That's what it was, you know. I feared what that crazed pillroller might do, and I plum dropped those snakes in my panic. Judge'll see it that way, too, and he'll set me loose."

Once I got Brother Lewis his lunch, I could in good con-science lock the office behind me again and leave him alone for the afternoon. I would not worry about him making an escape. A few months earlier, my own time behind those same bars had shown me the futility of that attempt. The only way he'd get out was if he had help and dynamite, and the dyna-mite it would take to bust him loose would kill him in the process.

Another marshal might have set him loose already, but the more this man riled me, the more I was determined to make him stand trial. It bothered me, too, thinking about him setting up tent in another town and preying on folks so hurt in spirit they'd reach into a basket of snakes for a momentary illusion of glory.

"She going to come visit Laramie, lawman? The Injun squaw. Or you ashamed of her? She's fine and warm out of sight of respectable folks, but just an old blanket when you get back to civilization. That's it, isn't it?"

I smiled lazily from the chair. But my stomach muscles were clenched with rage, and it seemed my vision was clouded over with blood.

Fortunately for the preacher, the door banged open.

Unfortunately for me, it was not the Chinaman.

"Suzanne," I said. Suzanne from the Red Rose, a singer and dancer.

"Marshal Keaton." Her voice was breathless. Not the husky breathlessness she used on cowboys in the Red Rose Saloon when sweet-talking them into buying a whiskey. But the breathlessness of someone who had just finished running.

I stood.

"Here's a white woman you should show some interest in, lawman," Brother Lewis called. "She know about your squaw?"

During my stay in the jail cell a few months earlier, Suzanne and I had established something more than an acquaintance, with little said and much understood. The result had been friendship, not what Brother Lewis insinuated in his voice.

"Suzanne, got a moment to spare?" I asked. She nodded from where she waited in the doorway. Although she was a slim woman, the skirt hoops of her satiny blue dress made it appear as if the doorway blocked further entrance. Sunlight behind her bounced off her piled blond hair and put her face into shadow.

"Thank you kindly," I told her.

I loaded six bullets into the Colt, slid the cylinder shut, and held it chest high as I walked the few paces back to the jail cell.

"Put a hand through the bars," I told Brother Lewis.

He did not.

I pointed the barrel at his belly. He understood my face correctly and placed his hand on my side of the cell before I took the next step of cocking the hammer.

"Good," I said. I took his pinky finger and smiled mildly as I began to twist. "You can say all you want to me, but while I'm marshal in this town, I expect you to show manners around womenfolk."

He was on his tiptoes now.

"Understand?"

I took his grunt of pain as an answer and let go. Before I had reached the door to grab my hat, I already felt stupid for my childishness. He had just won a small battle by getting to me—and probably knew it.

"Suzanne?" I said.

"Come to the saloon, quick."

"Trouble?"

"Old Charlie."

"He hurt?" I could not imagine Charlie being the source of someone else's trouble, unless they were particularly sensitive to his need for greens.

"Probably soon," she said. "He called out four men in the Red Rose. Tie-down men. Then lit for his shack to fetch a shotgun. And Charlie's so whiskeyed up, they'll gun him down before he figures which end of the shotgun first gets into the saloon."

CHAPTER 9

TIE-DOWN MEN.

Before stepping into the Red Rose, I paused to look over the saddle-wing doors and saw the four gunslingers seated at the saloon bar with their backs to me.

It was a small saloon—five running steps could take me to them—and even in the dim, smoky interior, I saw enough. Three of the four wore old Confederate gray uniforms. Those three carried their guns in holsters tied against their right leg. The other had his tied against the left. I made a mental note of that, even though I didn't expect the knowledge to help much if it came down to a fight. For this was no front cover of a Ned Buntline dime novel. I'd never win a shoot-out against four men.

Because this was no dime novel, I could also hope the shoot-out might not occur. I've been led to understand eastern folks believe that in the territories, gunfighters fall in every direction, every day.

It doesn't even happen like that in Dodge City. While guns do speak louder than words, and most men carry guns, most men also prefer not to die, so guns tend to stay in holsters when men are sober. When whiskey blinds them to the prospects of easy death, their accuracy tends to diminish as well.

Still, I wasn't about to hope too strongly that their guns would not be drawn in the next few minutes. Unfortunately, because so few men will risk a gunfight, the rare ones who make it a profession are that much more dangerous. And they stop at nothing to ensure they'll be standing when the gun smoke drifts away.

Men like Jim Hickok, who's taken to introducing himself as Wild Bill ever since Abilene in '71, where as marshal he shot a troublesome drunk in the back and accidentally killed one of his own deputies, and is as nasty a piece of work as you'll find.

Tie-down men will do anything to get a jump and rarely hesitate at shooting a man from the side, behind, or from a darkened doorway—using rigged holsters, sleeve derringers, or boot guns when more is needed than a straightforward Colt.

Those habits, however, aren't the real reason to fear a tie-down man. Any gun-carrying cowpuncher could learn to fight in the same manner. What really sets a tie-down man apart is the unlearnable—how to kill another man without hesitation or remorse.

John Wesley Hardin comes to mind. I'd crossed his trail a couple times during my Texas wanderings, and he's caused more than his share of gossip in the saloons, jail offices, bunkhouses, and hideouts where cowboys and other gunfighters tend to congregate. At age eleven, it was rumored, Hardin stabbed another boy in the chest and back during a fistfight; he only got worse when he got his guns. At age fifteen he killed a former slave, then shot to death from ambush all three soldiers sent to bring him in for the slave's murder. That was '68.

The deaths didn't stop there, not for a man who once shot and killed a man for snoring in a hotel room next door.

Hardin was eighteen, already with a dozen notches on his gun handle in September of '71, when he approached two lawmen in Smiley who had been searching that town for him. The way I heard it, Hardin walked up to them as they were eating crackers and cheese in a general store. He asked the unsuspecting pair if they knew Hardin. When they replied that they had never seen him but certainly intended to arrest him, Hardin drew his gun, declared they were seeing him now, then emptied his gun in their faces.

The only defense against a professional gunman like Hardin is to avoid him or be prepared to meet him beyond the line of decency, where he waits, and hope if you survive, you're still the same man inside.

I took a breath and pushed through the saloon doors.

Tie-down men.

They remained sitting as I walked inside.

I did not like that.

In something like this, give me for an opponent someone goosey, someone so nervous that he'll jump and turn at the slightest noise, even though all he needs to do is lift his head and look into the mirror to see the entire saloon from his barstool.

These men looked into the mirror.

Suzanne had not entered with me. I'd left her on the sidewalk in front of my office, holding the front door key for the arrival of the Chinaman and the preacher's lunch.

I kept my right hand well clear of my holster as I walked to the saloon bar. I had no intention of forcing them into something I'd regret more than they would.

Inside here wasn't much different from any other saloon. Behind the bar was that large mirror and rows and rows of bottles. The other walls held life-size paintings, mainly of women dressed to catch a chill no matter how warm the evening and posed even less respectably than they were dressed. Unlit kerosene lamps hung from the ceiling. Sawdust covered the floor to soak up spilled beer or tobacco juice that didn't hit the spittoons. Draw in a breath, and you had your choice of the reek of smoke, liquor, horse liniment, tobacco juice, or sweat.

A few bleary-eyed men guarded a few poker chips on a table to my right. Early afternoon is not the usual time for a high-stakes game; later more chips would be in play, and the men would have been hunched forward in tension instead of watching me with still heads.

The piano playing did not start till after sundown, and most of the dance girls would be taking a nap, so there was very little noise to break the sound of my boots slapping against the wood floor on my approach.

None of the four men moved as I walked past their stools. Each had a shot glass of whiskey in front of him.

I did nothing except lean on the corner of the saloon bar.

"Afternoon, Samuel." The bartender—medium-sized, potbellied, and sporting muttonchop whiskers—had a nervous edge in his voice, and he wiped his hands against his apron repeatedly. I appreciated the fact that he had not called me Marshal. It meant he'd chosen not to let my presence be a straightforward challenge to the four men beside me.

"Got some coffee on?" I asked.

He nodded and stepped away to get me a cup.

"Gentlemen," I said to the four men just down the bar. They didn't seem too worked up at the sight of my badge, and I decided there was no sense in making this a long waltz. "I hear Old Charlie's got a burr under his saddle."

"The gray-haired drunk?" the closest one said. He appeared to be rangy, but that was only a guess because he was sitting. A couple days' dark growth smudged his square face.

"Promised he'd return with a shotgun. Seems he ain't heard The War Between the States is long over."

"It's caused him more than a few rough nights," I said. With Charlie, it was predictable. A happy glow, then later, in the jail cell as he began to sober, he'd come down some and let the memories work him over. "Lost his wife and both his boys in Kansas to Reb soldiers."

"He so informed us," the next one down said. His face held the same squareness as the first one's. "Town of Lawrence. Once we heard that, he didn't need to tell us more."

Nor me, the first time Old Charlie had broken down and sobbed in the jail cell. During the Civil War, a band of rebel guerrillas known as Quantrill's Raiders, numbering four hundred and fifty, had burned the town to the ground, slaughtering a hundred and fifty men, women, and children to do it. Old Charlie, who had been out on a hunting expedition, hadn't forgiven himself for not being there to die with his family. Knowing all this had made it easier for me to forgive the sleep I'd lost because of Old Charlie's habits with the bottle.

"You understand then," I said.

"He threw more than one insult our way, and we didn't shoot him." That from the third man down, who didn't turn his head to speak to me. "I reckon that's understanding enough."

"Safe to assume, then, you didn't ride for Quantrill?"

"Marshal, push on that accusation and you're in dangerous territory," the second one said. "What William Clark and his boys done was shameful. What we done for the South was duty, plain and simple, fighting other soldiers."

"That does set my mind at ease," I told him.

The barstool farthest down scraped as the fourth stood. He stepped away from the stool to face me. His jacket, the only one not Confederate gray, was tucked back to give him a clear path to his holster. His hand was poised above his revolver.

"Iffen that didn't ease your mind, Marshal," he challenged, "you figured on playing hero?"

Hero came out like *heee-ro*. All of them had Southern accents.

I pushed myself away from the bar. Slow and easy.

"Josh, git yourself down," the man closest me growled. "This marshal didn't come looking for trouble."

Josh, barely twenty, ignored the older man. I could see in the boy's eyes a light of courage that whiskey will bring.

"Is that it, Marshal?" Josh repeated. "You thinking of moving us on?"

I shook my head. "Old Charlie's a good man, sober or drunk. Sets my mind at ease to know I won't be doing him wrong when I take away his shotgun."

"We don't need your help," Josh said.

I snorted. "Four of you? And sober? Against one old man in his cups? I'd say you don't need help. And I'm guessing you're all men enough not to have to prove it."

Josh wavered as he pondered that. Especially since none of his older companions disagreed with me but remained sitting, faces straight ahead, expressions lost in the shadows of the brims of their hats.

"Fact is," I continued, "Old Charlie's the one that needs help if he makes it this far with a shotgun."

The man closest to Josh reached back without looking and pulled Josh back onto his stool.

That took a little strain off my ribs, holding my breath as I was.

I spoke to the bartender. "George, get these boys another round. Leave a whiskey for me, too. It'll give me an excuse to return after I speak to Charlie."

I only made it halfway to the saloon doors before Old

Charlie stumbled inside, his shapeless hat flopping at the brim.

Suzanne had been wrong. He *was* able to get the working end of the shotgun in first.

I stopped, remaining between him and the men at the saloon bar.

He lurched forward, shotgun leveled waist high. Both his hands were clenched hard. One to the stock. One to the barrel. That alone would have got him killed. His fingers were too far away from the trigger, his hands too tight to move quickly.

"Lay the gun aside, Charlie," I said in a voice I'd use on a spooked horse.

I watched his hands and prayed he would not reach for the trigger.

"They're Rebs, Marshal. It's plain to see." Anger had sobered him somewhat. "I hate Rebs. Alice died hard. So'd the boys."

"It wasn't them, Charlie. Lay the gun aside."

He jerked the shotgun up and down in threat. "Marshal, I'll go through you if I have to."

"Who'd sing along with you those nights you spend in jail?"

He shook his head. "I'll be dead anyway. But I'm taking as many of them with me as I can. Alice was burned to death, Marshal. Look at their gray uniforms."

"I told you, Charlie, it wasn't them."

He shook his head again and took another step forward. "They's lying dogs."

"No, Charlie. Quantrill's boys would've been shooting long before. Let this one rest."

I became conscious that a crowd had gathered on the street outside of the saloon. A few of the braver people stood on the sidewalk, peering in through the windows. Obviously

Old Charlie had made his intentions clear as he marched to his shack and back to here.

My focus returned to Old Charlie as he raised the shotgun to his shoulder. His forward hand started sliding back toward the trigger.

I heard the stools move as the men stood behind me.

"This is between me and Charlie," I said loudly without taking my eyes off Old Charlie. I was not being noble or protective. These men could take care of themselves. I'm not even sure I was worried about Old Charlie. What I did know was that I had no urge to be caught in a crossfire—shotgun on one side, four revolvers on the other. "You boys relax."

"Marshal, you best stand aside," Old Charlie said. "They's waitin'. And I'm ready."

I stared at Old Charlie. "Can't move aside. These men deserve protection of the law, same as everyone else in Laramie."

I didn't add that I was rapidly becoming more certain of the stupidity of having accepted a marshal's badge. And even more certain of the stupidity of pride that kept me from walking away from the job at times like this.

Old Charlie slid his hand another inch closer to the trigger.

"Aw, Charlie, don't make it tough on us both."

"Both my boys gone, Marshal. They'd be your age now."

It did not seem appropriate to mention that yet another wrong wouldn't make anything right.

I had maybe five seconds to decide if Old Charlie in his cold drunkenness was bluffing me. And if I decided it wasn't a bluff, then I'd need to choose whether I'd shoot Old Charlie to save my life, knowing that even if I tried to only wing him, the scatter effect of my peppershot cartridges at this close range would shred his flesh into rags.

The saloon doors creaked open. Old Charlie heard it, too, and his trigger hand hesitated. I dared flick a glance past Old

Charlie's shoulder, and I saw a slender silhouette. A woman had stepped through the crowd into the Red Rose.

I shifted my eyes back to Old Charlie and his fingers so close to the shotgun's trigger guard.

"Ma'am," I said without looking at the woman who had just walked in, "perhaps you'll return later."

The woman ignored me and advanced toward us. Out of the corner of my eye, I caught that her hair was blond and thick. But that was all the attention I was willing to give her, not with Old Charlie's trigger finger only inches from my death.

"Ma'am," I said with little patience, "you may notice we're at a delicate point in our discussion."

She stepped between me and Old Charlie, keeping her back to me. Over her shoulder, I saw Old Charlie's jaw drop in amazement.

"You don't appear to be a man so low you actually mean it," she told Charlie as she reached for the barrel of the shotgun, which was pointed directly at her face. "Marching down the street waving that gun and swearing to kill four strangers."

She slowly pushed the barrel sideways. Old Charlie didn't even hesitate. He extended the shotgun to her without a word, almost as if it were an offering.

"Ma'am," he said reverently. He removed his hat with one hand and slicked back his greasy hair with the other. Whatever her response, it must have been enjoyable, for he grinned like a dazed mule.

"You go talk to my men now. See to it that you let them buy you a drink," she told him as she handed him back the shotgun. "You'll see soon enough it doesn't matter they fought for Lee."

"Yes, ma'am."

Old Charlie bowed his head as he shuffled around her

toward the bar. Without the lure of blood, the crowd outside began to disperse.

I too felt like a mule that'd just been whopped between the eyes. How'd she manage to . . .

She turned to face me. That took all the mystery out of why Old Charlie had buckled. Honey always did work better than vinegar.

This woman had eyes the blue of a mountain lake. Against the luxurious blond of her thick swept-back hair, those eyes were startlingly wide and innocent, as if you had just kissed her and she'd been surprised to find how much she liked it. Her lips had that look, too, the pout of a woman ready to enjoy another kiss, and her teeth gleamed white with shininess, as if she had just moistened them in promise of what the next kiss could be.

After the shock of the seductive force of those eyes, a flawless complexion was unnecessary, but it was there. Along with perfect symmetry of cheekbones and delicate nose and chin.

She wore a black shirt. Her jeans were black, too, unusual in two regards—because women rarely wore pants, and somewhere, she had dyed the jeans or had them dyed. The overall picture was stunning, and she managed to stand in a way that suggested innocence, yet was more provocative than any of the women in the saloon paintings around us.

She smiled as she noted my observation of her, and the smile matched the devilish arch of her eyebrows.

"Marshal Keaton, I believe," she said. Her voice was honey, and she let her tongue work over the words in a Southern drawl that hinted at smoldering hot Georgia summer nights. "That's what folks were saying on the sidewalk."

I tipped my hat. Were we on the street, I'd have removed it. But this was a saloon. And I'm stubborn about wagging my tail when expected.

She extended her hand. "Dehlia Christopher."

I wasn't sure whether she wanted me to kiss the back of

her hand or to shake it. I chose to shake it. Her grip was firm and cool.

"Dee-lee-a," I said, pronouncing it as she had. "Samuel Keaton. I appreciate your help with Charlie."

"Sometimes a woman's touch can make considerable difference in . . ." She smiled in triumph. ". . . delicate points of a discussion."

"I just finished offering thanks. You want it again? Or in writing?"

Her eyes narrowed as she reconsidered me. "Perhaps instead you might buy me a beer."

I did; she was an intriguing mix of Southern belle and forthright woman.

That's how I found myself a few minutes later, sitting at a table, watching this woman gulp with enjoyment the first half of her mug of beer. When she set the glass down on the green cloth of the table, she had no need to wipe her mouth. She'd drunk without spilling across her lips.

"You mentioned your men at the bar," I said. "But I don't see enough dust on you to figure you're leading a herd over trail."

"Is that curiosity, Marshal Keaton?"

"Yes, ma'am."

"Does it pain you to have to admit curiosity in me?" She smiled like a man holding four aces.

I gave her a neutral smile in return. "Hardly. The curiosity is a professional need. This town pays me to keep it clear of trouble. And your men ain't dressed in Sunday-go-to-meeting attire."

Her eyes narrowed again. I understood this to mean she was accustomed to plenty of tail-wagging. Which made me that much more determined not to give her the reaction she expected.

Not that it was difficult to react. Her face was remarkable in its beauty, and the slim necklace that glittered at her throat could hardly compete for attention.

Throat.

It hit me.

The rancher's dead body in the bank vault. And Harper's suit jacket, so small on the other dead body.

Throat.

I knew in that flash why I hadn't been able to shake the nagging feeling that the double murder in the bank vault had not been as simple as it appeared.

I slammed my mug down so hard that beer sloshed over the sides. I stood so quickly that I banged my knees on the table.

"You'll excuse me, ma'am."

She looked upward at me in disbelief.

I didn't explain myself further.

Seconds later, I was on the street, half walking, half sprinting in the direction of the undertaker's.

CHAPTER *10*

Doc Harper was asleep at his desk, bent forward in an awkward position, head on his arms, legs beneath his chair. His spindled limbs reminded me of a stick insect. Yet there was a touching vulnerability about the exhaustion that would allow him to sleep in such a position, and I was reluctant to wake him.

So I stepped back from his open doorway and took a seat in his waiting room. The undertaker had already confirmed what I needed to know, and the luxury of working for the already dead is that they are in no hurry.

He must have heard the slight noises I made, for barely seconds after I had leaned back, webbed my fingers behind my head, and stretched my legs, Doc Harper appeared in the office doorway. He'd found a brown jacket to replace the one used as a shroud for Calhoun, and this one fit his long arms as badly as the previous one.

I smiled a greeting.

He stared down at me with no expression across his gaunt face.

"Afternoon," I said and rose to my feet.

He grunted. Pressure lines from the weight of his head on his arms were angry red across the skin of his forehead.

"I'll return," I said. "Might be there's a better time to—"

"Speak your piece," he said. "You didn't make two trips here in one day to ask about the weather."

"I surely did not," I said. If he wanted abruptness, I could match him. "Why'd you show up so soon to look at Nichols and Calhoun in the First National vault?"

"None of your business."

I smiled. I could afford to. His crustiness fared poorly compared to the threat of an old drunk with a shotgun.

"Why'd you move them?"

"None of your business."

"What'd you find?"

"None of—"

"Turtle," I said.

He blinked. Twice.

"I knew a woman once," I told Doc Harper. "She had this saying. See a turtle sitting on top a fence post, you may not know how it got there, but you could be good and sure it had help."

He mulled that over. Permitted himself a tight smile. "I heard you already declared their deaths solved."

"Nichols pulls a gun on Calhoun at the boardinghouse," I said, nodding. "Forces him to open the vault. Gets most of the money on his horse just outside the bank. Returns to the vault, either to finish off Calhoun or to take more money, and Calhoun surprises him with a gun. They shoot each other dead. The horse wanders off. Gold is returned when the horse is found. Same with most of the money, except what the breeze blew away." I paused. "That the way you heard it?"

Doc Harper nodded. His eyes did not move with his head,

though. Just stared straight through me.

"Good. 'Cause that's the way I told it. No loose ends. Something folks will believe."

"You don't."

"I see a turtle, belly flat atop that fence post, legs pushing at air."

"So what got you thinking that turtle hadn't figured a way to climb up there itself?"

"You tell me," I said. "By all indications, you saw that turtle first and from a ways off."

"I might get around to it. Convince me you aren't in Mayor Crawford's pocket."

My face must have reflected the surprise I felt, because Doc Harper sighed. "You wouldn't be here asking," he said, more to himself. "You'd be in some alley waiting for me to pass by. And I got my doubts it's Crawford anyway. He doesn't have the guts."

"Doc, all of a sudden I'm seeing this turtle covered with whitewash, like not only it's had help but been places I ain't considered." I remembered some of Crawford's twitchiness in his office during my first questions. "You telling me you know something about Crawford that has a bearing on this?"

Doc shifted his weight from one leg to the other. It seemed to cause him pain, but bent like he'd been to sleep, that didn't surprise me.

"I'm telling you that Lorne Calhoun and I were close friends. And he'd mentioned a couple of worries about the First National. Now Calhoun is dead."

He hesitated, then continued with certainty. "Samuel, Nichols didn't kill him."

I didn't expect it, the small piece of pleasure I took to hear Doc Harper soften and call me by my first name. A man gets accustomed to traveling alone.

"Don't let this upset you too much, Doc. But maybe we're whistling the same tune. Because I know Calhoun didn't kill Nichols. And I can prove it."

I'll agree with temperance people any day. Whiskey is not a cure. Any man who drinks it expecting as much only has to wait until the next morning to find out how badly he fooled himself.

Yet—and the temperance people don't seem to cut slack in return—there is a measure of quiet peace in sitting across the table from a friend, sipping whiskey slow and sharing considered words at the same pace.

Which is one reason I'd asked Doc Harper to join me at the Red Rose instead of continuing our conversation in his waiting room. Doc had eased up on me, and somehow it had made me want to stand straighter—like I'd enjoyed the pat on the head. That was unusual because most often when I'm pushed, I close my eyes and push right back, no matter what direction that pushing takes me. Maybe it was because I sensed Doc had no favorites, that he pushed himself just as hard as he pushed anyone else.

After some thought, he'd agreed to meet me at the Red Rose, and had paused in his office only to leave a note directing patients to the saloon should they need him.

I sat with a shot glass of whiskey in front of me.

Doc had his long gnarled fingers wrapped around a mug of black coffee.

It was closing in on dusk now, and the saloon was half full—quiet enough that Doc and I could speak in low tones. The four Rebs still sat at the bar and had nodded hello as Doc and I walked in. Old Charlie was sitting to the left of Josh, nodding and waving his hands in animation, probably happy to have a new audience for his timeworn stories.

I took my first sip of whiskey, enjoyed the burn of its warmth, and set the shot glass down.

Doc stared at my whiskey, then raised his coffee to his lips. He winced at the taste.

"More than one spoon's melted in that acid, Doc. Sure you won't join me and paint your tonsils?"

He shook his head. "What's your proof that Calhoun didn't shoot Nichols?"

"It was your jacket that you laid across Calhoun that got me thinking, Doc."

He closed his eyes briefly. Pain, again, poorly hidden. I realized how deeply that grimace had etched lines into his old face. "Seems a poor thing that all I could offer him was that jacket."

I cussed myself. Just because Doc didn't show grief didn't mean it wasn't there. And I'd thrown it at him casual. I could've just as easy told him Dehlia's lovely throat had sent me running to the undertaker.

"Doc, I'm sorry."

He smiled his tight smile. "What'd you get to thinking?"

"Calhoun was a tall man," I replied without hesitation. We'd both pretend our conversation wasn't about a dead friend. "As tall as you."

Doc nodded. He had himself reined in now.

"And Nichols was shot in the throat," I continued. "He was a shorter man than Calhoun, but, as the undertaker will confirm, that slug took out the back of Nichols' skull."

I remembered too much of the dead man in the coffin and reached for my whiskey as some of the blood feelings came back to haunt me about my brother. Doc Harper watched the shot glass all the way to my mouth, then swallowed a gulp of his coffee.

"It doesn't make sense," I said after a deep breath. "The bullet was going upward when it hit Nichols. Yet Calhoun was the taller man. I just can't see that Calhoun was on his knees when he shot and was shot."

Doc frowned in concentration. "Why not?"

"First reason's a slug mark," I said. "The bullet from Nichols' gun hit the vault door chest high to Calhoun. How could Nichols take a shot in the throat, then live long enough for Calhoun to get to his feet before shooting him?"

I rolled another sip of whiskey over my tongue. By Harper's envious look, I was tempted to offer him his own, but I'd already asked.

Doc frowned again. "A smart lawyer would say different. That Calhoun was standing and shot Nichols from the hip. Bullet would be rising then."

"Except for reason number two. The other slug mark— the bullet that hit Nichols. Back side of the vault. It was shoulder height. *Not* the mark of a bullet that was rising after it hit Nichols."

Before Doc could reply, Suzanne stopped at our table. She sat on the edge of the table, adjusted her shoulder strap, and crossed her legs.

"Marshal Keaton and Doc Harper," she purred. "If I didn't know better, I'd say the both of you were plotting evil deeds."

Doc pulled at his necktie. Her perfume did have some power. And those black stockings did contrast nice with the green cloth of our table.

"We are," I said sourly. "I was hoping Doc could prescribe some medicine that would keep Brother Lewis quiet in that jail cell."

Suzanne ran her closest hand across my shoulder and tickled my throat with the tip of her fingernail. Where was *this* coming from?

Doc Harper grinned. At my discomfort? Or the thought of finding a way to quiet Brother Lewis, a subject of mutual dislike we had discussed as we walked to the saloon?

"Marshal," she said, "I hear you met someone in the saloon this afternoon while I was at the jail waiting for the Chinaman."

"Yup. Old Charlie. And he didn't smell near as nice as you."

"I didn't mean Old Charlie," she said, not amused. "I heard you met the woman sitting at the bar with those four men."

I looked up in time to catch Dehlia looking away. I hadn't noticed her join them.

"Her," I said. And forgot to wipe the slow smile from my face.

Suzanne stood and sniffed disdain. "*She* wears pants."

Suzanne marched to another table before I could reply.

Doc smiled. "For a man who was able to think through those slug marks, you show an amazing lack of perception."

I ignored that. "How'd you know that Nichols didn't shoot Calhoun?"

That put the frown back on his face. "Chicken feathers."

"Chicken feathers?"

The saloon doors banged open.

"Doc!" It came from a man in coveralls. Short, stocky, wild-eyed.

Doc rose.

"Doc! It's worse now! Whatever's giving her that bad throat is closing up now. Betty's blue, she's breathing so bad. She won't even open her eyes no more."

"All right, Abe. She back at the homestead?"

Abe shook his head. "I brung her in with me. That's how blue she is. Doc, you gotta do something."

The harsh lines on Doc's face transformed into gentleness I would not have believed this tall, rigid man could possess.

"Samuel," Doc Harper said. "I don't care how far it takes you, how hard you got to run to get them, and how bad the light is this time of the afternoon, but don't return to my office unless you have a couple of sandburs."

I wasn't sure I'd heard him correctly. "Burs? Big prickly seed-type of burs? Out in the grass type of—"

"Exactly. And each breath you waste now is one less breath left for her."

CHAPTER 11

IN THE LIGHT of the oil lamps and what-ever sun still came through the window, I could see on Doc Harper's desk a needle, a scalpel, a short length of leather cord, a small jar, and a can of lard. I set three sharply barbed sandburs—dry, hard, each the size of a small pea—alongside the lard.

Abe's wife, Betty, was stretched on her back on the long low table on the opposite side of Doc's office. She wore a gingham dress that had seen many washings, and the dress lay like a drape across her and the table. Her breathing fluttered along with her eyelids, and by the white-blue of her round face, I dreaded the moment that even the fluttering would cease.

"Abe, you'll step into the waiting room."

Doc spoke tenderly, but it was said in a way that brooked no disagreement.

Doc shut the door behind Abe.

"You'll have to hold her," he said. "Abe doesn't have the height and muscle you do. And what I've got to do is nothing a man should see his wife go through."

Doc didn't wait for me to agree.

He moved to his desk and lifted the scalpel. With fine, precise movements from those ungainly fingers, movement that surprised me as much as had his gentleness, Doc Harper began to slice a narrow thread of leather off the cord.

"Cloth thread breaks too easily," he explained without looking up.

He took the needle and poked a hole through the center of one of the sandburs. That complete, he threaded the sinew through the hole and tied a knot at one end, so that when he lifted the thread, the sandbur dangled below like a ball.

With quick, sure movements, he scooped lard onto his other palm and rolled the sandbur through it. A grunt of satisfaction, and he looked at me.

"Lift her off the table. Hold her from behind. Reach beneath her armpits and around so that you can squeeze tight and stop her from moving."

I did as directed. The faint smell of soap reached me from her dress. Sick or not, she, or Abe, had determined she would be wearing her best to meet the doctor. Or death.

"Let her head fall back against you," Doc said.

There was no panic in his voice, and I understood how easy it would be for worried patients to remain calm around him. She was a heavy woman, and I had to heft her and let her sag to get her head lolling against my shoulder.

"Good," Doc said. He pried her mouth open, and with a splint of wood in one hand and the leather thread in the other, he pushed the bur far down her throat.

She gagged and twisted, and I had to brace my legs to keep from falling.

"Nearly there," Doc soothed.

To her? Or me? He pulled the sandbur loose.

"It's caked pretty bad," Doc said. "Get ready for another try."

He repeated the process. She bucked against me.

"Once more," Doc said.

I took a breath and readied myself. She kicked again, like a frightened calf straining away from a branding iron.

Doc pulled the sandbur out again and smiled at the results. With the splint, he scraped some hard white matter off her tongue. He walked to his desk with the splint and tapped it on the edge of the open jar, so that the hard matter fell into the jar. Doc replaced the lid, then turned to me.

"Lay her back on the table," he said. "It's clear enough she can breathe. If she's over the worst of the infection, it won't grow back."

As I was leaning over her to set her down easy, her eyes opened and flared with surprise.

I found myself grinning as I set her down. "Sorry to disappoint you, ma'am. This ain't heaven. And I ain't no angel."

Doc Harper snorted from behind me. "Samuel, instead of wagging your tongue, you might want to fetch the lady a glass of water."

After Abe and Betty had left, I reminded Doc Harper that he owed me a story about chicken feathers. He declined my invitation to return to the saloon to discharge that obligation.

"I'm tired," he told me. "I must have made twenty miles today in my buggy, and these bones can't take the punishment they could three decades ago."

I thought of the inscription I had inadvertently read in the front of the book I had borrowed from Doc Harper's shelf earlier in the day. *To Cornelius, from your loving wife, Sarah. Christmas '46.*

"Thirty years is a long time, Doc." While I was curious, that was as close as I'd get to asking him what roads he'd taken to get here in Laramie and what had led him to his bachelor life, away from his loving wife.

Doc closed his eyes. "Thirty years ago, I was your age. I'd have accepted your offer to return to the Red Rose."

He opened his eyes, an almost owlish movement, and stared briefly at me. "I hope you know a lot more than I did then."

I could think of no answer, only more questions, so I said nothing.

"Chicken feathers," he said after a few moments. Heaviness had crept into his voice, and he sagged in his chair. Had I not wanted to hear so badly what he knew, I would have insisted on leaving to give him his rest. "Proof of something I suspected anyway. Proof of something I was going to find no matter what the law said about it."

I nodded encouragement.

"Calhoun was a good man," Doc Harper said. "You can't know that. You haven't been in Laramie long enough, and you might hear different from others who didn't look beyond what they saw when he walked back and forth from his boardinghouse to the bank. Calhoun was quiet, scared much of the time, but this was a man who cared about people. His friendship made my life bearable."

Doc sighed. "If he had a weakness, it was his obsession for order. I believe that was his way to make up for his fear."

"Fear? Of Mayor Crawford?"

Doc shook his head. "Nerves. That's how I first met him." Doc waved a weary hand toward his office door. "Pull up a chair from the waiting room."

When I returned, Doc spoke as if I hadn't left.

"Realize I'm only telling you this because the poor man has passed on. I believe a doctor has a moral obligation to keep secret what happens between him and a patient. A practical reason, too. Patients would stop visiting if they knew the doctor made their business public."

He ran his fingers across the top of his head, looking for energy to continue.

"Calhoun came to me because of nerves," Doc said slowly. "Wanted a potion that would stop his hands from shaking, let him walk the streets without worrying about runaway horses, let him work without fearing a bank robbery."

"Give him whiskey?"

"Not funny," Doc said sharply. "This man's fear ate at him. I did what I could. Just listened. Sometimes that's all a doctor can do."

Instead of offering a comment to lighten the mood, I took Doc's advice.

"Calhoun was afraid of the world," Doc said. "The big wide world with all the things beyond his control. His way of getting around it, I believe, was to regulate everything that he could control."

An ironic smile. "I used to be like that, too. Most blessed thing about faith for me was letting go of that control. I'll work hard at what's set in front of me and let God worry about the rest."

Another ironic smile. "Banking was perfect for him. Gave him a sense of control. Ledger numbers on paper. Black and white. No grays. Work the numbers right, and there are no mistakes."

"He found some," I guessed. "Worried at them like a dog on a bone."

"Until Crawford told him to set the bone aside."

"Calhoun told you that?"

"Yup." Doc took a deep breath. "I told him to disregard Crawford's order. If it was looking for the sense behind those numbers that got him shot, it was my advice that killed him. That's why my first thought was murder."

He held his hands out, the action of a helpless man. "I told him that because I knew he'd get no rest until the numbers made sense. I thought that finding the courage to disobey Crawford would help him realize the world wasn't so frightening." Doc dropped his voice to a whisper. "I should have stayed with pills and potions."

"Did you pull the trigger?"

Doc didn't answer.

"Doc, unless you pulled the trigger, it ain't fair, you trying to shoulder the load for the same world Calhoun had enough sense to know you can't control. Your advice seems solid to me, and beyond that, there's no saying Calhoun was killed over those numbers."

I remembered something Doc had said earlier. "Besides, you told me you didn't figure Crawford was behind this."

"Someone was behind it." Doc had straightened, and by the strength in his voice, I knew anger was taking him. "The same someone who used a pillow to muffle the sound of the shot. The same someone who took his time to clean up after. Someone who wanted the rest of us to think only two people had been involved."

"The feathers," I said.

"When I cleaned up the entry wound, I was low to the ground, and I found something in the blood between the two bodies. Bits of feather stuck in the blood. Like feathers from a pillow."

Doc stood, then set his hands on the top of the chair back to lean forward. It brought his face directly to my level. He stared into me.

"Samuel, all I can figure is someone pressed a pillow into Calhoun and looked him in the eye. Just like I'm doing to you right now. And both of them knew why the gun was pressed into that pillow."

Now Doc's face was granite. "Calhoun, the one person most afraid of fear, had the time to look right back and know what was coming. Those seconds for him would have been an eternity of hell."

Doc put his right hand on my shoulder. I doubt he even knew he was doing it, or that his hand dug into me like an eagle's talon.

"Samuel, find that man."

CHAPTER 12

MOST OFTEN ON THE PLAINS, a man learns news through gossip and stories, and a smart man will discount half of what he hears. But I was there at Fort Robinson in Nebraska that summer afternoon a few years earlier and have only my eyes to blame for any of the times I may have mistold the story when it came my turn at trail campfires or saloons.

I have always begun the story by asking if anyone around me would hesitate to reach into a pail of water for a handful of silver dollars. When asked why a body would not, I generally smile.

For I *had* reached into that pail of water. It was set up near the entrance to the officers' messroom at Fort Robinson, and I did not recognize the apparatus set up nearby that pail. Captain John Bourke, aide-de-camp to General George Crook, had invited me to supper and then, at the door, to help myself to the coins magnified so shiny at the bottom of the clear water.

"Go ahead," he told me. "You need an excuse to wash your hands anyway. Busting horses all day is dirty work."

I agreed with both his comments. While I knew something must be wrong with his invitation—nothing in life worth having comes without a price, and Bourke's reputation as a practical joker was as widespread as the military—I saw no harm in amusing him. After all, he was the man who was purchasing my horses for the cavalry troops.

I plunged my hand in and nearly jumped from my boots. The water had bitten me with such savagery that it felt as if bobcats had attached themselves to my fingers. My hand jerked and spasmed to those invisible bobcats for what seemed like two minutes before I managed to pull loose.

"Well, sir," I said as calmly as I could, hoping to appear unfazed, "I prefer a mean horse."

It was the best I could think, yet nothing would have forestalled his laughter. The shock was plain on me, and the other officers in the mess, who had watched expectantly, were slapping their thighs with glee.

"Electricity," he said when he caught his breath.

I peered into the water to find the source of its painful bite.

That filled him with more mirth. "It's nothing you can see," he told me. "Think of it as tiny lightning bolts, ready to grab your hand."

He caught my sour glance at the other officers. "They're laughing double hard because each and every one suffered the same fate."

Bourke went on to explain that the apparatus hooked by wire to the pail consisted of a revolving handle that generated volts of this electricity that were stored in the square block that he called a battery, not to be confused with the military term for cannon or mortar stations.

I thanked him for expanding my knowledge in a way I'd never forget, and over the meal he explained further that this joke had provided many hours of entertainment, especially during visits by the Indian chiefs who lived on agencies near the fort.

For them, Bourke called it his medicine box. It hadn't taken long for word to get around that it held medicine so powerful even Spotted Tail and Dull Knife had been unable to overcome it. Fact was, Bourke told me, more than a couple medicine men from Sioux and Cheyenne tribes had come in from days away to prove their medicine stronger than his. All, of course, had failed. None had received Bourke's explanation for the source of his medicine.

I had originally intended to stay at Fort Robinson for a few days, long enough for the quartermaster to approve of the twenty horses I'd brought in. Long enough to enjoy what civilized pleasures could be found at the fort. Bourke that night informed me that he—along with several chiding Cheyenne women—had finally convinced High Wolf to attempt to overcome the medicine box that had defeated all other medicine men within a hundred miles of Fort Robinson. As High Wolf was the most renowned medicine man among the Cheyenne, it didn't take much for me to decide this showdown would be worth the wait. And it wasn't as if I had anywhere pressing to go anyway.

Three days later, High Wolf appeared. He drew a considerable crowd of Indians and soldiers as they made room for him to face the medicine box in the middle of the barracks grounds. For this great occasion, some of the more confident officers smiled broad triumph and openly dropped more silver and gold dollars into the bottom of the pail.

High Wolf had painted himself as if possessed. His leggings were decorated profusely with bright beads in ornate patterns. He wore eagle feathers and fox fur across his shoulders.

Captain Bourke stood nearby in full uniform.

High Wolf reached into his medicine bundle and withdrew some fresh stems of sweet grass. Captain Bourke saluted the pail of water.

Then High Wolf became serious about his foe, the medicine box. High Wolf balled the sweet grass around a small stone taken from his medicine bundle and held it high and proclaimed it to be a magic object. He placed the wrapped stone in his mouth, made obeisance to the sun and four winds, and began to hum a medicine song.

Captain Bourke responded with his own seriousness. He began to spin the handle of the battery's generator.

In the half hour that passed, no person in the crowd stirred or made noise as High Wolf gradually increased the volume of his humming. Captain Bourke increased the tempo of his handle-cranking.

High Wolf could hum no louder and still had difficulty overcoming the noise of that spinning handle, so he broke into a chant. Bourke replied to this new power by dancing as he cranked and launched into a rendition of the ballad "Pat Malloy."

Finally, High Wolf stopped abruptly and Bourke respectfully stilled his own voice.

In the silence broken only by wind sweeping across all of us, High Wolf moved close to the pail and raised his arms to the sun. Without warning, he plunged his brawny forearms into the water.

I can only guess at how many thousands of volts Bourke had cranked into his battery. While I'd hopped and cussed at the bite the water gave me earlier, High Wolf convulsed as if hanging on to a grizzly's tail. That medicine man proved his mother should have named him Iron Mule, for only one animal could have matched him that moment for the strength and stubbornness and kicking ability he displayed as he bravely held his hands deep in the water.

High Wolf bounced in a tight circle around that pail, legs smashing in all directions as he kicked like a Texas congressman, and still he managed to keep his hands in the water. By the time all those bolts of lightning finally threw him free of the pail, he had smashed the rickety battery to pieces.

To all our surprise, High Wolf showed neither humiliation nor defeat as he pushed himself up from the ground. He shook his head, spit out shreds of grass and the medicine stone that had failed him so badly, panted until he'd gotten his breath, and requested a second try, something that Bourke could not honorably refuse.

The captain put his contraption back together, but High Wolf's desperate flailing had done its damage. No amount of cranking could produce enough volts to deter a man as motivated by reputation and crowd as High Wolf. Minutes later, High Wolf easily fished the silver and gold loose from the pail and held it high to the whoops and cheers of all the Cheyenne and enlisted men gathered around.

That was the story that went through my mind as I rode alone southwest on a trail that ran alongside the Laramie River. I had two destinations this morning. First the Bar X Bar, which I'd been told sat on the edge of the riverbank, then a few hours' ride later, the Rocking N.

This double murder was that pail of water, at first deceptively clear and still. I knew as much about murder and finding murderers as High Wolf had known about electricity. And I would have preferred the bite of electricity. Someone had been able to coldly kill and had the brains to coolly attempt to disguise those deaths as a sudden shoot-out. In the open, that someone would be a formidable opponent, and I didn't even have the edge of knowing who he was and from where he might come shooting.

And I'd be plunging my hands into that pail by fishing around with no real sense of what to ask when I got to those ranches. And all I'd be able to do is hang on as long as possible if my questions became as dangerous as the ones that had killed Calhoun. Did I have the choice of pulling my hands loose? High Wolf had the crowd and his reputation to drive him. I had the memory of the look of pain and anger and anguish on Doc's face as he told me to find the killer.

I just prayed that if something knocked me down as badly as High Wolf had first fallen that I'd have the chance and courage to get up again and return to the pail.

CHAPTER 13

I SAW THE TOP of the windmill first—store-bought—mounted on a wooden derrick easily as tall as the Pacific Railroad Hotel. The blades whirred and swung in the wind, and steady creaking told my ears it was in full use, pumping the hundreds of gallons a day that would be used for drinking, cooking, and washing.

When I broke out of a gully, I saw the rest of the spread from the top of my horse. Wood corral fences stretched in one direction, outbuildings in another. The ranch house was nearly a mansion. It had gray stone walls, a wide sloping roof that led down to a veranda the width of the house, and the most telling luxury of all, large windows set in every side.

In one of the far corrals, I saw dust and commotion as a cowboy cut loose on a green bronco, and against the haze and the sun, I could make out the figures of other cowboys leaning on the fence to add whoops and cat-calls to the lone rider.

I smiled. It had been a while since I'd

fought a tornado of fury in the same way. There was an exhilaration in surviving, feeling the horse quiet to a standstill, nodding casually at the spectating cowboys as if the task had been nothing at all. Yet not once had I swung off such a horse without walking stiff-legged in agony, and rarely had I finished a day of breaking horses without passing blood when I watered. At five dollars a bronco, the pay was good, and riders with less brains than guts could make a month of cowboy's wages in a single day, but few could put three days of that kind of work together without suffering an injury that kept them out of the saddle for weeks.

Someone touched my leg and took me from my recollections.

I looked down to see a dipper of water extended to me by an older woman in a bonnet.

"Thank you, ma'am," I said as I dropped down from my saddle and removed my hat for her. "I look that dusty?"

"I was in the garden when you rode in," she said. She pointed at a small square corral on the other side of the windmill where I would not have noticed her without looking hard. Between the horizontal wood posts of the corral, I saw several baskets, filled with, I guessed, potatoes.

"Begging your pardon, ma'am, but are you Mrs. Ford?"

She looked down at her plain dark dress and her soiled hands and shook her head. "Not dressed like this, mister."

I didn't understand until the screen door banged open several seconds later and another woman moved onto the veranda. Although the porch roof screened her from the sun, she shaded her hands to scan the yard, a theatrical movement that served sufficient notice of her curiosity.

"That'd be the mistress of the ranch, Mrs. Ford," the woman said. "I'd best get back to the garden."

She scurried away with the dipper, lifting her dress from her ankles to miss some of the horse apples scattered in the main yard. I took my horse's reins and led it toward the ranch house.

"Morning, Mrs. Ford," I said as soon as I was close enough not to have to raise my voice. "My name's Samuel Keaton. I'm the marshal over to Laramie."

She nodded without leaving the veranda. "Come into the shade. I'll see that someone takes care of your horse."

"Obliged, ma'am," I said. I looped the horse's reins over a nearby rail. "But I doubt I'll be here long. I'm on my way to the Rocking N and thought I'd swing by to see if I could talk to one of your men."

She moved to the edge of the veranda to look down on me. My hat was already in my right hand, and I used the excuse of running my other hand through my hair to study her in return.

She was petite with a tight-fitting dress that showed it. Her dark hair was drawn back in a tight bun. She had a remarkable face, barely creased with wrinkles, and her dark brown eyes regarded me with seriousness but no real interest.

"You'll at least sit," she said.

I saw no chairs on the veranda. I decided that told me something about Mrs. Ford and her husband. Faced southwest as this veranda was, with the rounded tops of the Medicine Bow Mountains rising against the horizon, a man would be hard pressed to find a prettier or more peaceful view, especially with the sun setting in the cool of an evening. No better place to sit and relax and enjoy a cup of coffee at the end of a day. Yet they kept themselves inside.

I dusted my hat by slapping it against my thigh and followed her into the ranch house.

What drew my eyes first was the fireplace. An ox could roast comfortably in there. The wood floor was smoothed and varnished, covered here and there by rug or, in the far corner, by a bear fur, its head snarling a silent protest against such a captivity. The furniture gleamed. Paintings filled the walls.

There were knickknacks in all directions. I'd seen houses like this before, but only in St. Louis, affordable only to the wealthy there. It strained my mind to imagine how much it would cost here, what with the need to ship everything by rail and transport it the dozen or so miles from Laramie.

"Have you had breakfast?" The words were friendly but sounded aloof, as if she knew she was obliged to ask.

"Yes, ma'am."

"You'll take tea?"

"If it's no trouble."

She lifted a bell from a nearby table and tinkled it twice. That didn't appear to be much trouble.

"It will be a few minutes," she said. "Please, sit down."

I declined the stuffed armchair. It looked as if I'd sink deep, putting me in the position of a child peering upward at the adult world. I was also conscious of my jeans, dusty from the ride here, and how horsehairs would cling to the material of the armchair. I chose instead a chair at the dining table.

She sat at the other corner of the table and waited for me to speak.

"A redheaded fellow," I said. "By the name of Clayton Barnes. He worked for you long?"

She bit her lower lip. "I can't really say. Our foreman does the hiring."

I should have known. The rail that had made it possible to ship materials for a house like this was also the rail that had suddenly made it possible to ship cattle east. Big-time ranchers were growing rich by letting cattle graze the wide-open government land, and easterners and Europeans were investing millions in this new industry.

Mrs. Ford was not pioneer stock, someone who had stood at a man's side and built this ranch up from nothing. Pioneer stock didn't spend this money on a house, didn't have servants to respond to tinkles. Pioneer stock was too afraid of the next drought or grass fire or long winter to spend profits this freely.

Maybe—and it was an unkind thought—with her face and figure Mrs. Ford had married into eastern money. She was here, I speculated, because she'd have no choice if she wanted to stay attached to that money. As a prisoner of that money, doing her best to create an oasis of civilization around her, she would have little idea of the day-to-day operations of the ranch.

"Has this Clayton Barnes done something wrong, Marshal?"

"No, ma'am. It appears he did something right. Turned in a saddlebag full of bank notes."

Her eyes widened. "I hadn't heard."

"More to it than that, ma'am. Two men were found dead in the First National."

If it were possible, her eyes widened more. Her hand started moving toward her throat, but she stopped herself, and her voice came out as a gasp. "Two men? First National?"

"It's sad news, and what takes me out to the Rocking N . . ." I tried to keep the words soft, as if that would lessen the brutal truth. "Bob Nichols. Lorne Calhoun."

She became more rigid.

"Did you know him?" I asked. "Bob Nichols?"

"Not possible," she breathed. "He can't, it isn't . . ."

"Afraid so. A couple of nights back. Appears as if they shot each other."

"I . . . I'll see what's taking the cook."

She rose abruptly and left me in the wake of her perfume. It felt like I was missing something about our conversation, but I couldn't pin exactly what.

She returned on the heels of the cook, a matronly woman with a grim face who served the tea from a bone-white china pot, cups and saucers to match. The cook gave me a final glare and departed. I hid a smile of amusement to be drinking from an object that would take me a month of marshaling to pay for should I drop it.

"It feels like I'm stumbling in the dark, ma'am." I raised my eyes to Mrs. Ford's face, now more composed, but still white. "Got no idea what questions to ask or where to start. Now if you know anything about why Bob Nichols might be in a bank vault after midnight . . ."

She shook her head. Took another sip of tea. Her cup clattered slightly as she set it down.

"Was he close as a neighbor?" I asked. "You knew him well?"

"Actually, only by sight, Marshal." Those were the first words she'd spoken in a few minutes. "And in terms of hearsay, well, I keep pretty much to myself."

I reflected on how that would make these wide-open plains even lonelier.

"Perhaps your husband, ma'am. Or the ranch foreman. Would I be able to find them nearby?"

I was wasting my time here in the house, but maybe a half hour's extra time on the Bar X Bar might give me something, anything to point where next to look.

Again, she shook her head. "The foreman is out"—she waved her hand vaguely—"somewhere on fall roundup. Along with most of the men."

That left me thousands of acres to cover.

"Your husband out there, too?"

"Sometimes." That surprised me. I had a picture of another easterner, wiping his hands with a silk handkerchief as he totaled another column of numbers on his ledger. "Today, however, Cyrus is in Cheyenne. He . . . he travels frequently on business."

I nodded politely. "Perhaps, ma'am, I'll return another day."

"Certainly." She seemed to be holding something back,

and I waited. It became a strained silence, and at last I gulped back my tea and smiled.

"Thanks for your hospitality, ma'am."

"Yes. Of course."

She accompanied me to the veranda.

As I turned my horse to ride away, she called out.

"Marshal Keaton?"

I turned back to her. She looked even smaller, seen from the height of my saddle.

"Mrs. Ford."

"Lorne Calhoun. Did he . . ." She had a handkerchief in her hands, and she squeezed and twisted it as she spoke. "Was his death . . . did he . . ." She took a breath, one that seemed to heave her entire small body. "Did he suffer?"

I thought of the pillow pressed against his chest and how Lorne Calhoun would have looked into the killer's eyes as they both knew the trigger would be squeezed in a cold-blooded execution.

"No, ma'am," I said, "it hit him fast, hard and out of nowhere. A man couldn't have died easier."

And as I rode, I realized this brief side trip might well have been worthwhile. Her disbelief at the news of the two dead men had not been over the murder of Bob Nichols, but Lorne Calhoun. Had I not stopped here at the Bar X Bar, I would not have seen how she squeezed and twisted that hand-kerchief in grief over a quiet and gentle man who had died for figures that wouldn't add up.

CHAPTER *14*

UNLIKE MRS. FORD, Helen Nichols was pioneer stock. She fixed me with eyes red and swollen from tears and stood with her arms crossed over a massive bosom.

"Marshal, say a single word against my man, and I'll skin every strip of hide offen your body."

I didn't disbelieve her intentions nor her ability to deliver on the threat.

Her bosom matched the rest of her thick body. Her formless red dress was short-sleeved, and while those crossed arms didn't ripple with muscle, each was solid and thick. I sat on my horse ten feet away from her but from that distance could easily see the nicks and cuts on her fingers, damage done to hands that never ceased work.

The scowl that darkened her face seemed capable of turning away an unarmed man, and considering her bulk, I did feel better that my Colt rested in plain sight on my hip.

"You hear me? I'll strip every inch of hide. And I'll do it slow, too."

"Mrs. Nichols, I ain't even down from my horse."

"You might as well set right there and turn around if you're here to throw dirt on a good man."

"Wasn't my intention, ma'am."

"Didn't take you long to inform me about your badge."

"It does seem curious that he'd be found in a bank vault, ma'am. You can't blame a lawman for the need to ask questions in this sort of situation."

"That sounds an awful lot like an accusation, Marshal."

Now what? I'd have a better chance of moving a mountain range than this woman.

I noticed that three small boys stood behind her, huddled in the doorway of their soddy as they stared at me with bewilderment. I reminded myself that, despite the bulldog set to her face, her eyes were swollen from grief. I realized with sudden shared sorrow that this woman's anger was not directed at me.

"Mrs. Nichols, I'm here because I have a good idea your husband did no wrong. And if I can, I'd like for him to be able to leave his boys a good name."

Her scowl broke into a grimace of anguish. As if something inside her had busted, tears rolled across her leathery face. She tried to maintain the toughness of her widespread stance and the crossed arms, but she buckled to her pain and hid her face in her hands.

I rode past her and found a place to tie my horse. I doubted her fierce dignity would allow comfort from any source, especially a lawman, and it seemed a good time to let her find her previous composure.

"Howdy, boys," I said to the three in the doorway as I walked toward them. Their faces were troubled as they watched their mother behind me shake with silent tears, head bowed in her hands. "Boys, did you catch a peek at the bear I was chasing this way?"

They looked away from their mother to me, and their mouths dropped.

"Yes, sir," I said. "'Bout as big as a buffalo. You're funnin' me, right? About not seeing him? He must have come stampeding through here faster than a horse in a tornado."

They shook their heads in grave unison. I didn't know much about kids, but I guessed the oldest to be less than eight. Give them a few years, and the soddy they shared would be shaking dirt every time they stretched.

"How about the snortin'?" I asked. "Surely you boys heard him bellerin' and snortin' as he passed by."

Again, grave denial.

I jingled the coins in my pocket. "I can't understand that, boys, because old mister bear was some kind of mad. We'd been wrestling about a half hour before I finally got his mouth open."

"You fought a b'ar?" the oldest said. His chunky face and dark hair showed he took after his ma.

"I peeled from my clothes to go for a swim in the river. Soon as I turned my back, he began to snuffle in my pants," I said. "Weren't right, him taking my money."

The three took small steps away from the protection of the shade of the soddy, unable to resist my story.

"Money?" the oldest asked, wanting to believe.

"You betcha," I said. "Money. Slipped all my coins under his tongue and tried running off. But I grabbed his tail and swung him back right smart. Then after a lot of huffin' and puffin', I finally pried his mouth apart. And I'm here to tell you that few things smell worse than a bear's breath."

Shy grins.

I held out my hand. "Got all my money back from him, too."

I opened my hand and showed them the coins. They

peered in earnestness. "You think you're smarter than a dumb old bear?"

They nodded.

"Meaner?"

They shrugged.

"We'll see," I said. "You take a coin each. Don't be placing it in your mouth, though, not after the bear had his licks at them. Go round back the house and hide yourselves. If I can't find you, I guess you keep what you got. If I do find you, well, we'll see if you can wrestle better than that old bear."

They were gone with the money in a heated footrace before I managed to place myself on a crooked wooden stool in front of the soddy.

Mrs. Nichols still hadn't moved.

I surveyed the homestead: this sod house and two bunkhouses made of sawed lumber. One small corral. Windmill.

A thousand head of cattle, Crawford had told me. Nichols would be paying off his note on the sale of a thousand head. No man by himself runs that much cattle, and those two bunkhouses showed me where the hired men stayed.

Most times, a cowboy's biggest complaint was the bunkhouse, except more often than not, they called them lice cages. I worked one ranch where any man who picked one of them graybacks from his blankets or clothes and threw it to the floor without first killing it was fined ten cents for each offense. Ironclad rule. Bunkhouses were cold and drafty in the winter, sweltering in the summer, and they stank of boots crusted with cow manure, unwashed bodies, and clothes that hadn't seen soap or river for months.

It said something to the cowboys that Bob Nichols would first spend cash on the sawed lumber for their bunkhouses before replacing the sod structure where he kept his family. Soddies—and this one was no exception—were made of thick bricks of sod, maybe a foot wide and two feet long, stacked to form walls that were sturdy enough to last six or seven years against any weather, even a tornado. Soddies were fireproof, cool in the summer, warm in the winter, easy to build, and unless a man spent five dollars on the luxury of glass windows and a wood door, they were free for the taking.

But soddies leaked in any rain, drizzled earth crumbs when dry, and more than once I've heard about folks who woke to snakes that had slipped off the roof and fallen into their beds. Helen Nichols was a good woman if she supported her husband's decision to save their new house for later.

I waited for Helen Nichols to compose herself.

Ahead of me, in the dirt just ahead of my feet, bluebottle flies collected in a frenzy around blood that had dripped from recently butchered chickens. I snorted in irony at my keen sense of observation. Scattered feathers ground into the soil. Blackened clumps of clotted blood. And a lone chicken claw. I was quite the marshal, able to put something like that together.

If only this double murder would fall into place so easily.

What did I have for certain? The what, where, and when. Two men dead in a bank vault, killed sometime during the early hours of the morning.

Even those facts led to questions, for each man had died in a stranger manner than I'd first suspected, their deaths disguised for reasons I couldn't even begin to guess.

What did I have to add to those uncertainties? Who had killed them. And why.

All I could know about the killer was that he had joined the men he intended to kill sometime after Nichols had knocked on Calhoun's door at the boardinghouse.

As for why, again I floundered. There was no apparent link between Calhoun and Nichols, other than both had ties to the First National Bank. The only third party I could find who had something in common with both was Crawford, and my instinct told me he was not the man. Against all likelihood, if

Crawford was the murderer, I still did not know why. Without that, I doubted I could prove anything that would stick in a trial.

Finally, there was the returned money. All I could decide was that the killer had hoped the double murder would appear as a shoot-out between the two men—that it had been an expensive gamble, then, to make it seem as if the horse had wandered away before Nichols could return.

Knowing I had so little, and seeing this widow in her grief, made my waiting all that much more miserable.

CHAPTER 15

FIVE MINUTES PASSED before she walked back to me. Tears had softened her face, and much to my surprise, I noticed she was a young woman, and that without the twisted anger on her features, she carried her own kind of beauty.

"Marshal, you'll forgive me? It's just that already I heard folks say it served Bob right for his transgression. And I know he didn't do it. No matter what it looks like, I know he didn't do it."

"I believe there's more to it than what meets the eye, ma'am. That's why I'm here."

"Helen. No need to be fancy." She tried a smile and sniffled. Watch a woman that big sniffle, and you'll know it's not a funny sight, but one that can break your heart.

"Helen, then. Most call me Samuel. Unless they've taken a dislike to me."

She sniffled again and wiped a large forearm across her eyes.

"My boys," she said. "How'd you get

them out? The sight of strangers tends to send them packing right back inside."

"Lied to 'em. Then bribed 'em."

"And you wear a badge." A throaty chuckle. "Let me fetch you some water. You've been riding awhile."

The water did clear the dust that dried my mouth. She refilled my mug from a pitcher of water and offered me late lunch. I protested, but not strongly, and within minutes, she returned with thick ham sandwiches, slathered with mustard.

She lowered herself onto a stool beside mine, and I tore into the first sandwich. This woman knew how to bake bread.

"Bob liked these," she said. "I was standing there just now as I cut the ham, thinking how much he liked these. Seems that everything I do now reminds me of him. Lord, I miss that man."

She bit her lower lip. "Seems me and the Lord are on a first-name basis now. I can't imagine how any person would get through this without knowing there's a home beyond."

A tear rolled down her wide cheek. Some women might have daintily wiped it with a handkerchief or with their finger-tips. She simply leaned her face into her shoulder and rubbed.

She looked up. "Don't worry, Marshal. I won't cry no more whilst you're here. I know how tears bother a man."

I took my time swallowing the food, then more water. I had no idea how to proceed.

"Marshal," she said, refilling my mug again, "I expect you got a whole slew of questions, what with you thinking you can clear my man's name. You jest get started, and I'll answer best as possible."

I looked straight into her square face. "Do you have any guesses as to why he'd be in that bank vault?"

She did not flinch. "Since they brought me news of it yesterday, I've worked my brain into knots over that. Bob was a good man, a fair man. No matter how bad it's been, he'd never consider taking a penny offen another man."

I must have waited too long to speak, for her voice took on some fierceness again.

"Marshal, you can think what you like. So can the rest. But one thing for sure, and no woman would disagree, when you live close with a man and you rise with him in the morning and hold him at night and you listen to his fears and share what good comes along, you learn a man inside and out; and even if you cain't put it into words, your heart knows him. Bob Nichols was as good a man as could be found on God's green earth."

She stopped for breath. "If you found Bob Nichols in that bank vault, someone must have forced him there. That's all I can say as to why he was there."

It was not the time to mention that a witness had seen him knock on the door of Lorne Calhoun. Nor to mention that I believed Doc Harper when he spoke for Calhoun, making it unlikely that Calhoun had been the one forcing the two of them into that vault.

Fortunately, Helen had given me something else to establish.

"Things been bad?"

Helen lowered her eyes and dusted imaginary crumbs off her lap. "Cash-wise, yes, sir." She lifted her head, and her chin was stubborn with pride. "We arrived with what we hauled in a wagon and established this homestead by the Land Grant Act. Lots of folks done the same and quit halfway through. Not Bob."

Live five years on the land, government said, and you owned it clear title. If I remembered right from what Crawford had told me, they had only a year left.

"In four years, Helen, you built up your herd to a thousand head?"

She gave me that sharp, fierce scowl. "Who told you?"

"Crawford. Like I said, ma'am, I wanted to start somewhere to find the truth behind all of this."

She spat. "Crawford."

I waited.

"Sweet as pie when things looked good," she told me. "That's how we built the herd. Bob borrowed some each year, sold cattle in the fall, and borrowed more the next year. Worked good, too. We only claimed this quarter, but all the rest of the wide open land fattened our cattle."

I nodded. This was common enough. The Land Grant Act had been set up by easterners, who were familiar not with these arid lands, but with fertile soil and abundant rainfall, and thus failed to understand that a quarter section here could not provide sustenance for a family.

"Then comes along big operations like the Bar X Bar, and it gets tougher to find sweet grass and water." She stopped to point a finger at me, stabbing it in the air to emphasize her words. "But we were still making it. Bob's got a good crew of men, and he always found ways to profit."

"Until . . ."

"Nothing here changed," she said and spat. "Crawford did. Last three years he didn't mind holding our notes till the cattle were shipped."

"This year . . ."

"Bob rode in to town a couple weeks ago. We wanted a little extra cash for payroll. First time ever, he didn't give Bob none. Our—"

"Was it Crawford that Bob spoke to? Not Calhoun?"

"Crawford, Marshal. Bob cussed that man out again and again as he stomped back and forth of where we sit."

There went my obvious link between Nichols and Calhoun.

"Our crew decided they'd wait for their payroll until the cattle shipped," she continued as if I hadn't interrupted. "Otherwise we might have lost plumb everything."

I thought that through. Crawford hadn't told me any of this. What was he hiding?

"Marshal?" she prompted me.

"Cattle shipped now?" I wanted to know that Nichols hadn't needed cash badly enough to kill Calhoun. Hearing that the hands had decided to wait for payroll helped.

"Our boys are moving 'em to the rails as we set."

"That must take a load off."

"My man is dead, Marshal. Ain't nothing gonna take that load off." The tears welled in her eyes again.

I found myself taking her hand from her lap and squeezing it in mine. Her palm was callused, skin on the back of her hand raw. We sat there in silence until she sighed and slowly withdrew her hand.

"Don't mind me," she said. "Get on with your questions. I won't rest until you've cleared him."

I felt helpless. Doc wanted me to avenge one man, she wanted me for another reason, and I'd be unable to ignore the memory of those three bewildered boys in the doorway and how it might be for them to grow up thinking their pappy died robbing a bank. Yet I still had little idea how to proceed.

I tried putting myself in Bob Nichols' boots, and that led me to another question. "Just before he left, did Bob tell you anything that seemed strange?"

She shook her head. "Marshal, I told you, I've worked my brain into a knot. He left one morning, no different than any other when he went to ride the range. Four days later—yesterday—One-Arm Wilson stopped by with Bob's horse and told me as gentle as he could why Bob wasn't coming back himself. Jake's a good man."

Jake was. I'd been dreading the prospect that I'd be the one breaking it to her.

"Four days?" I asked. "That didn't seem strange for him to be gone so long?"

"Not for a man riding range. Lots of times he'd pack a mess of grub—" She stopped and squinted puzzlement. "Marshal, he didn't pack grub that morning."

"Without fail," I said, "he'd pack grub if he figured on riding range for more than a day?"

"More than a half day," she said firmly. "He hated to miss a meal. And he weren't fussy about chuck-wagon cooking."

I nodded agreement. Good cooks on the range were treated like kings, simply because so few were good.

"Anything else strike you as strange?"

She shook her head.

"In the months before, did he ever leave for a few days without taking grub?" Maybe that would point me to where he'd gone. I had a strong feeling now that if I could explain his absence, I'd be a lot closer to the killer.

She shook her head again, now slowly, as if she were giving it more thought. "Strictly speaking," she said after a pause, "there was his trip to Denver. He didn't pack no grub for that."

I seized on it. "Any chance he went there four days ago?"

"None."

"You sound certain."

"I most certainly am. Iffen he was headed for Denver, he'd have told me. Just like the first time. No, Marshal, when he left this time, he didn't have no bag packed."

I kept my thoughts to myself. Could be he had unfinished business in Denver, business he'd been reluctant to share with her, especially if that business involved something that had led to his death.

I kept my voice casual. "How long ago was that?"

"August," she said. "His brother passed on there. Bob had to settle some papers. Spent time with a lawyer fellow by the name of Leakey. I remember that. Bob and I had a lot of fun with that name."

"Must have been important, going to Denver," I said, letting my eyes wander across the horizon as if it mattered little whether she answered or not.

She smiled. A defeated smile. "We thought so, Marshal.

Those papers were some mine claims. Each one turned out as useless as Bob's visit. Worse, cash poor as we was, it didn't help none, paying for rail tickets and hotel."

"Where'd he stay?" I asked. I hoped I wouldn't have to go to Denver. But asking now would save me a trip this way again, should I ever need the information.

"The Broadway Hotel," she said without hesitation. "Overlooks Cherry Creek. I remember because he went on and on about how things were in Denver. How he'd take me there and show me all the fine things as soon as we could afford it."

Sudden silence. I swung my eyes back to her.

The tears had begun to roll again, and her face held a helplessness that tore at my heart.

"I'm sorry, Marshal. I promised not to cry. But thinking of how he dreamed for the both of us, and now ain't nothing gonna bring him back so that we'd ever get to Denver the two of us . . ."

She fought for breath. "Maybe I'm about done with this kind of conversation. It's hurting too bad."

I stood.

She remained on the stool.

"I'll do my best," I said.

I doubt she heard me. She continued to stare at the ground as I walked to my horse.

Her sadness stayed with me as I rode back to Laramie. In the loneliness of the sage and brush and wide-open sky, there was nothing to distract me from thoughts of love and death.

Because Helen had loved her man so deeply, his death was that much greater a loss to her. And if he had lived? Every year for ten, twenty, forty, however many years, their love would have built to its final tragedy, that one or the other must die. Was this not plain, that the greater the temporary triumph of love, the more crushing its inevitable defeat?

I took a path through some tumbleweed, and a jackrabbit

spurted dust as it kicked away from the hooves of my horse.

I watched until its white tail stopped bobbing in the distance and realized it might pass the bones and pieces of hide of a dozen of its kin, yet would never understand that it, too, was as mortal as all other jackrabbits who had lived before. No, of all the creatures, only we faced such a curse, able to know as we lived that death someday would steal from us everything we had learned, remove from us our greatest loves.

The blackness of that futility settled heavy on me, and despite my best efforts, my mind turned again and again to the woman I'd sworn to return to come spring. I had no certainty of where our love might lead, and like Helen, I was discovering that the sweeter the love, the more the pain. That only worsened my loneliness and made the last miles into Laramie a long, haunted trip against the darkening of the sky.

I wasn't able to maintain a hold on my self-pity, for waiting in front of the marshal's office was a man named Benjamin Guthrie, who demanded that I hunt down and shoot the Rebs who had broken his left arm sometime in the previous hour.

CHAPTER 16

"STEP INSIDE," I said to calm this man's rantings. "Tell me about it."

I began to unlock the office door.

From the street, Benjamin Guthrie raged at my back. "Marshal, this is no time for talk! I demand immediate justice."

As I pushed the door open, Brother Lewis sprang from his bed behind the jail bars. "Marshal, it's been noon since I was fed. Dogs get treated better. I demand you release—"

I shut the door on him and turned back to face Benjamin Guthrie, the lesser of two evils.

The sun was nearly gone now, so that both of us stood in the long shadows of early evening. I didn't have to see him clearly to know him. More than once since I'd taken the job here as marshal, we'd passed each other on the street and nodded acquaintance.

Guthrie was a big man, taller than I was by an inch or so, probably heavier by twenty pounds. Full beard, touches of gray in the black of his hair. As usual, he wore a suit and vest, befitting his occupation as proprietor of Guthrie Dry Goods and Clothing, one of the larger stores on Main Street. This time, however, the left sleeve of his jacket was pinned to the suit, and his left arm stuck out, supported by a sling.

"Don't stand and gawk at Doc Harper's handiwork," he told me. "Do your job."

"Which is?"

"To protect the folks of Laramie. Respectable folks who work hard and pay your wages." He winced as he shifted.

It had been a long day of riding. I wanted a small shot glass of whiskey and enough quiet and peace to drink it slow. Then I wanted sleep. And no dreams. I did not want, at this moment, yet more action to protect the folks of Laramie, especially ones who seemed to think that bullying was the best way to prod me.

Yet, despite my natural stubbornness at being pushed, I had to agree with Benjamin Guthrie. I'd taken a job.

"You said Rebs," I sighed.

"That's right," he blustered. "Who else?"

I did not like what his question meant. "You mean," I started slowly, "you're making a guess?"

"No guesswork. Who else in this town would attack one of Laramie's respected businessmen?"

"Listen close," I said with as much patience as I could find. "Did *you* eyeball the man who did it?"

"How'd that be possible?" His voice did not lose any of its petulant rage. "They threw a sack over my head first and roped me like a steer."

"Someone else witnessed it. Right?" My plea was wasted in the thunder of his indignation.

"If I had a sack over my head, how'd I know if anyone was around to witness?"

I closed my eyes. "Backtrack some. Just tell me what happened."

"I just did! Now get to work!"

"Humor me."

He shook his head at my incompetence, then winced again at the pain caused by his slight movement. "I stepped out of the Red Rose just before dinner."

"Time?"

"Five-twenty. Dinner's always at five-thirty. Mabel knows dinner's at five-thirty. And Mabel knows it ain't to be served a minute later. Five-twenty gives me time to stop at the store and amble on home, just like I always do."

Mabel had my sympathy.

"Five-twenty then. You step out of the Red Rose."

"Where, I might add," he lectured, "them Rebs was sitting and able to watch me leave."

"Right."

"Like always, I first stop at the store for a final check to make sure the door's locked. That's probably what gave them time to sneak outside."

"Right."

"I turn back to go home. I pass the Red Rose again, and there's a gap there between it and the building next to it. That's where it happened. Sack's thrown over my head. A rope cinches my arms tight against me. Them Rebs musta been waiting to pull me back into the shadows there. Then something whacks me hard against my arm. I knew right then it was busted. I about passed out from the pain."

"You robbed?"

"No."

"You have an argument with any of them in the Red Rose?"

"No."

"Without a witness and without reason . . ."

"Marshal, I demand justice. This arm didn't get busted by itself."

"Mr. Guthrie, I can't arrest someone just on your say-so. Maybe there's someone else in town who carries a grudge."

"Not a soul. I do business square." His face broke into an ugly, taunting grin. "We hired you on because we heard you were fast and tough. You suddenly afraid of gunplay?"

"Always have been. Only a fool ain't. What's your point?"

"What I came here for!" He almost bellowed it. "Justice!"

I nodded. He'd expelled enough of a lungful that I could smell beer on his breath, even with the wind that blew down the street between us.

I thought of my advice to Old Charlie, when I'd told him to turn in the bank notes unless he wanted Crawford to keep gnawing on him. Guthrie would do the same to me unless I at least made it appear as if I was doing something.

"I'll have a talk with them Rebs," I told him. "And I'll ask around to see if anyone saw them follow you from the Red Rose."

"That's it?"

"The best I can do," I said. "Unless you want the badge."

I guessed he was glaring at me, but the effect was lost in the shadows that separated us. And I was too tired to care anyway.

———

No gray jackets occupied the Red Rose. Nor the Comique Dance Hall. Nor the Laramie Saloon.

I began to check the hotels. Not because I believed they were behind the attack on Guthrie. Two days earlier, they'd handled Old Charlie with a calmness that led me to believe they weren't the sort to jump someone from hiding. As to who and why Guthrie had been attacked, that was too puzzling for me to try to figure this late in the day.

No, I wanted to find those gray jackets to let them know how Guthrie was spreading the word against them. If I could clear them quick of Guthrie's accusations, it might save ugly trouble later. I didn't need more grief, not with my mind on a killer who probably hadn't left Laramie.

Naturally—considering the state of my feet—it wasn't until I walked to the registration desk of the last hotel on my list that I found where they'd chosen to reside in Laramie.

The Union Pacific Hotel.

"Yup," the clerk mumbled. "Three rooms they took. The brothers split two rooms. Miss Christopher took the third."

"Obliged," I said and tried to read his guest list upside down from where I stood. "Four brothers?"

He protected his list. Amazing. The less power a person had, the more jealous of it he'd be.

"I've had a long day," I said. "Help me out."

He looked out from a skinny face that didn't crack into a smile.

"Someday you might need me," I said with the same weariness. "A Colt .44-40 will probably do you more good than the names will do for me."

He thought it through, as if we were actually bargaining. Probably the only reason I wasn't forcing him was because I still smelled the stink of the bullying tactics of Benjamin Guthrie.

"Ike. Peter. Josh. Wiley."

"Last name?"

"Christopher."

He said it as if I should have known they carried the same last name as Dehlia.

"How long they booked for?" I asked.

He hesitated again. Which was once more too often for my state of mind.

I walked around the desk.

He huffed at my trespass.

I ignored it and swept him aside as if he were a bedsheet draped over a clothesline.

"Don't put me in a worse mood," I said.

He stayed put.

The register showed they had prepaid for three weeks. Not only that, but they had taken three suites on the top floor. A pricy stay.

I moved away from the desk and smiled at the clerk, who was smoothing his hair back with one hand and wiping lint off his shoulder with the other. Obviously, I'd contaminated him.

"Don't worry about me," I said. "I'll find my own way up."

———

The red carpet of the long hallway absorbed the sound of my boots, and because of that, I heard the indistinct murmur of voices as I approached the rooms on the top floor of the hotel.

The register had shown that Pete and Wiley occupied suite 205, and the voices came from behind that door, so I decided to start there. I knocked softly.

Immediate silence. I could imagine the reaction of gunslingers at an unexpected knock, and I decided not to light any fuses.

"Nothing to be alarmed about," I said to the door. "Marshal Keaton paying a friendly visit."

Some thumping. Footsteps that creaked toward the door. It opened, not to show Pete or Wiley, but Dehlia Christopher. Same black jeans as when we'd met the day before. Now a red shirt, sleeves rolled halfway up her forearms. She probably knew the effect of that red against the rich blond of her hair. I certainly did.

"Marshal Keaton," she said. She remained in the doorway.

I removed my hat and held it in my left hand. "Didn't expect it to be you," I said. "I was looking for some of your brothers."

"What a shame."

She said it so flatly that I could not decide if it had been sarcasm.

"If they've got the door covered, ma'am, you'd be welcome to let them know my hands are empty."

"Marshal, I'm surprised you'd make an assumption like that. Unless you've had reason to cover one or two doors in your past."

In the Red Rose the day before, her voice had been playful, seductive. Now it was slightly tense, as if the banter was forced.

"If you're through with the games, I wouldn't mind getting down to business."

She shrugged and invited me inside.

The suite was a double room, lit by oil lamps trimmed to a dull glow. One side held a large bed. The other side held assorted pieces of furniture—writing desk and cane chair, tall wardrobe, low armchair. A throw rug covered most of the floor between.

Almost in the middle was a small table. The two older brothers sat beside it, one on each side, ashtray between them, smoke curling upward from a lit cigarette. On the left sat the man who had spoken first to me. And opposite him, the one who had pulled Josh back down to his chair. Each made it plain they had no intention of lowering their revolvers until it was obvious I indeed had empty hands as I walked in.

"Gentlemen," I said politely. My hat remained in my left hand, and my right hand stayed clear of my holster.

They did not rise nor lower their guns.

Guthrie. The clerk. Dehlia. Now them. None of it was improving my mood.

"Was I looking for a fight," I said, "it wouldn't be here. No. I'd arm myself with a posse and wait for a little more distance between me and your guns."

"What *are* you looking for?" This from the oldest. I felt

tension but couldn't understand why. These men had enough experience to know that a gunfight was not brewing.

"You Pete?"

He gave a slow nod. Still kept his gun trained on my stomach.

"Pete, I'm looking for a quiet, restful spot to put my feet up. I'm looking to forget this badge keeps putting me where I don't want to be. But before I get to that quiet, restful spot, I'm looking to make sure it stays quiet and restful enough in other places in Laramie that I can enjoy my own quiet, restful spot. What's standing between me and that quiet, restful spot is you and those guns and a bad attitude. Something I'd like changed before I forget I came here with peaceful intentions."

Pete grinned. "You sound meaner than a grizzly with a sore tooth."

He set his gun on the table. Wiley did the same.

"Whatever brought you to Laramie is your business," I said. "I ain't asking. And I won't, unless it involves the law. You go your way, and I go mine. Trouble is, those gray jackets bring hard feelings to some folks. Like tonight. I've got a man who swears up and down you boys ambushed him outside the Red Rose."

"We didn't," Wiley said. "That's the biggest lie—"

"Do you see a posse with me? I'm not here to accuse you." I took a deep breath. "Nothing about you boys smells of stupid, and my guess is you'd find a lot smarter way to bushwhack someone."

"Why, Marshal," Dehlia began from behind me. "We'd never even consider—"

"Be nice if you had someone to witness that you all stayed in the Red Rose long past six o'clock." I cut Dehlia short without letting her build her mock hurt. "That way Guthrie won't be able to stir up trouble against you."

I waited, but neither Pete nor Wiley volunteered any information. Something about the two of them was bothering me, but I couldn't place it.

"Were you playing cards?" I asked. "Spending time with a dance-hall girl?"

Silent shakes of the heads. Then Wiley spoke. "Truth was, Marshal, Pete and me did leave about then. Josh and Ike, they did stay behind for some billiards."

"It'd be nice if you had someone to attest to your whereabouts."

Wiley looked at Pete for approval.

"Nope," Pete said, as if he were answering a silent question from Wiley.

"Too bad," I told them. I was curious, but if they weren't going to volunteer, I wasn't going to force it. After all, if they didn't want me to know, it wouldn't be difficult to lie.

I watched them a few moments longer, taking advantage of the silence to search for the cause of the troublesome nagging in my mind.

Then I saw it.

The smoldering cigarette.

Neither brother had taken a puff during our entire conversation. Moreover, it was obvious by a bulge in their cheeks that each carried a chaw in his mouth.

Who owned the cigarette? Dehlia? Or was someone else hiding somewhere in the room?

Dehlia moved beside me and placed her hand softly on my arm.

"If that's all your business, Marshal, perhaps . . ."

"Perhaps I'll be on my way?" Why was she so sweet? And why the distracting touch on my arm?

"Yes," she said, "on your way. May I presume this time you'll wish me good-bye instead of dashing through the door like a madman?"

I nodded absently but didn't reply. I hadn't forgotten that sprint to the undertaker's, but my mind was more on where a person could hide quickly in this suite. Under the bed?

I turned to leave and let my left hand swing around to lightly brush against her hip, a movement that knocked my hat loose. I stooped to pick it up and used that excuse to sweep a glance low along the floor.

"Marshal." It was Pete.

I straightened.

"You stood us a round of drinks the other day. Never came back to collect yours. It'll be waiting for you. Stop by."

I put my hat on my head and tipped it in his direction.

Dehlia guided me by my elbow to the door. "You won't be offended, Marshal, if I offer to continue our conversation when you stop by for that drink? You do intrigue me some."

"Be happy to oblige, ma'am." I gave her my best bashful grin, as if the thought of sitting nearby to her got my heart thumping like a dog's tail.

She smiled in return, then quietly closed the door in my face. I stood there in the hallway for a moment, staring at the dull white paint of the door.

As if I didn't have enough questions to occupy myself. Because I knew it wasn't her cigarette that had been left to burn into ashes. Not when someone with pale snakeskin boots was standing behind the wardrobe on the other side of the suite.

CHAPTER 17

"Mawshaw," the Chinaman said in his rapid-fire rhythm, "mow sih-shoo-taw coffee." The Chinaman poured into my half-empty mug with a broad grin, bowed slightly, added coffee to Doc's mug, and walked to the next tables. His long braided ponytail swung with each of his quick steps.

"Mow sih-shoo-taw?" Doc asked. "Sih-shoo-taw coffee?"

"More six-shooter coffee. I do my best to teach him how to say it proper. But whenever I ask him why he can't spit out a single decent 'r,' he asks me to pronounce his name. In Chinese. First time I tried, he giggled so bad he nearly dropped the coffeepot."

Doc mopped his plate with a piece of toast to collect the last of spilled egg yolk. "I'd heard folks grumble that you spend too much time and money here," he said. "Guess it's worth something, now that he's named his coffee in honor of your Colt."

This was the cleanest eatery in town.

Grease didn't cling to the tables and chairs. The food arrived hot with no imbedded hairs or insect shells. The price was right. Yet of the seven tables he had set up here, never more than three were occupied. Not because it was tucked in a small building away from Main Street. But for the same reason no one had let him rent space in a better location.

That was on my mind as I spoke to Doc. "Folks that think all Chinamen should work on the railroad ain't seen how many die to dynamite. Bothers me that they won't look past the color of his skin. And you discovered how good he does breakfast."

Doc wiped a fleck of toast from the corner of his mouth. "Yup. Think I come here enough, he'll name something on the menu after my scalpel?"

I slugged back a mouthful of coffee, swished it visibly, then swallowed with a grimace. "Doc, it's a joke he likes. One day I told the Chinaman this stuff was so strong it could float a six-shooter. I thought he'd choke himself, he laughed so hard."

Doc smiled. He forked the last of his eggs into his mouth, scraped his chair back to give his legs some room, and cradled his mug of coffee in his hands. "I can see how a man gets into this breakfast habit," Doc said. "Beats hitching my horses and riding a half day into the countryside to watch someone die."

"Don't be hard on yourself, Doc. You done fine with Betty the other night. I'd never seen nor heard of that sand-bur trick."

"That's because I stole the idea from a Blackfoot medicine man."

I raised my eyebrows. "That probably ain't something you'd take back East and share at college."

"I won't ever go back East."

That hung there between us, the way he said it dampening the mood. Again, I thought of the inscription in his book from his loving wife, Sarah.

As if he realized the turn our conversation had taken, Doc made an effort to smile. He sipped at his coffee, grimaced in agreement at my assessment of its potency, and began to ramble.

"I try to keep up," he said. "Manuals, reports, things like that from the East. Doctoring is becoming more and more of a science. Someday folks might even call doctoring a profession."

Another sip of coffee. "You won't hear many doctors say this, but the more we learn, the more that's a mystery."

"Why's that, Doc?" Around Doc, it was easy to slip into the role of listener.

"I read considerably," he said as introduction. "My interest happens to lie in what can't be seen with the naked eye. In fact, I've got a microscope in my office so I can try some of the same experiments I read about."

"Doc," I said. "Pardon my ignorance. A microscope? Some scouts I've met carry pocket telescopes. . . ."

He smiled. "Think of a microscope as a telescope that magnifies things real close to you, instead of things far away. Someday, you get bored, we'll take a clear drop of water. With the microscope, you'll see creatures wriggling around—so small that a hundred of them could fit on the head of a pin."

I remembered the brass urn object in Doc's office. I remembered, too, what Doc had done with the stuff scraped from the woman's tongue. "Betty's throat—you wanted to look at what came from it, too?"

"You're a quick study, Samuel. See, some forty years ago, this European fellow, Christian Gottfried, he wrote up papers about what he called bacterion, tiny critters that live everywhere, even on the inside of Betty's throat."

Doc caught the skeptical look on my face. "Samuel, when you sneeze, you're probably getting rid of a whole country's worth of them critters." Doc was serious, too. "I know," he continued, "I've looked at the results of my own sneezing.

The critters appear as tiny rods. More than a person can count."

"Doc, you got me curious now. I'd like to look for myself."

"Fair enough," he said. "But what I was getting at is that we do our best to convince ourselves that we know something, anything, when we really don't have a clue about this world."

"Doc, I know we're both sitting in the Chinaman's restaurant."

"You don't know how to pronounce the Chinaman's name. You're sitting across from me, and you don't know how I spent the first fifty years of my life. You don't know what was on this very same spot a hundred years ago, let alone a thousand years ago. You don't know what will be here a hundred years from now. You don't know how that coffee is spreading through your body, you don't know what causes your hair and fingernails to grow, and you don't even know if you or I will still be alive by the time the sun sets."

I put my hands up to fend off his attack. "I think I understand where you're leading me, Doc."

He took a breath. "And I was just getting started with my list."

"Talk about Abe's wife, Betty, is what got you started."

"Then take Betty," Doc said. "She's one of seven sharing their farmhouse. Whatever it was that started choking the inside of her windpipe could have just as easy done it to someone else. But it only struck her. It's a mystery, Samuel, just like everything in life."

He shook his head. "Same with epidemics. Why's one person get hit and not the next? No, Samuel, doctors don't have near the control they wish they did. Fact is, the older I get, the more I realize the best we can do is offer comfort."

A memory crossed his face and he grinned. "Comfort and the odd bit of common sense."

Doc had to pull in his legs to give the Chinaman room as he stopped by to pour more coffee. With a full mug again, he leaned forward and rested his bony elbows squarely on the table.

"Yup. Common sense. You notice hardly any women here in Laramie wearing layers and layers of skirts like in some towns?"

I thought that through. "Now that you mention it . . ."

"I've been here almost since the railroad," Doc said. "About a year after setting up office, a preacher's wife stopped by. Complained about her backache. Said she'd been suffering for years. Been to a dozen doctors, tried all their cures."

"And?"

"I told her to go home, change into something else, and bring back what she was wearing during the first visit. She did. We weighed it. Twenty pounds. I then suggested, no matter what folks expected the preacher's wife to wear, that she try hooped skirts, as they were lighter. Three weeks later, she was free of backaches. It caught on with the other womenfolk."

I nodded appreciation. Then it seemed like my turn to continue the flow of talk.

"Ever prescribe turpentine for piles?" I asked.

He thunked his coffee cup down. "No!" Doc said in disbelief. That brief animation brightened his face, and he seemed a decade younger.

"I swear by it," I said. "Heard it from an old colonel. Never believed him till it got so bad once, I couldn't hardly ride. That night, I was so desperate I made application before going to bed."

Doc shook his head in sympathy.

"The application sure made me prance some," I agreed. "Sleep didn't come easy neither. But by morning, it felt better, and sure enough, day by day, they finally disappeared."

Doc snorted laughter. "Any other tricks you can teach this old dog?"

"I'm fond of the whiskey and lemon cure," I said, recalling the advice of a Texas rancher. "To shake the worst of colds, one quart of whiskey and a dozen lemons."

"Yes?" There was wariness in Doc's voice. He knew I was setting him up.

"Yup. Cure comes with directions, too."

"I'm waiting."

"Throw the lemons at a fence post and drink the whiskey."

Doc groaned.

I shrugged. "At least it didn't matter none whether you hit the post."

We were the only ones left in the eatery now. The Chinaman had slipped away to the kitchen area. With nothing for either of us to say at this point, it was so quiet we would have plainly heard the buzzing of flies had there been any banging into the window that overlooked the street. Which was another thing I liked about the Chinaman's place. His constant war with flies.

Doc cleared his throat. "Was this breakfast just a friendly invitation? You don't strike me as the kind that needs company just for the sake of company."

"Company's been worse, Doc. Anytime you want to share coffee and eggs, just holler." I tilted my hat back. "I was hoping today to run a few speculations past you on these murders."

"My ears are open."

I summed up for Doc what little I had learned by riding out to the ranches. Crawford had refused to lend Nichols money this year, when he had done it all other years. Crawford had also failed to mention that fact to me—and I couldn't decide if it was because the lending issue was significant or just the opposite, so insignificant it had nothing to do with anything.

I also told Doc about the strange good-bye from Mrs.

Ford, and how I interpreted it as meaning she knew Calhoun better than should be expected.

Finally, I told Doc that Nichols had left the ranch four days before his death, but he hadn't packed grub, and how I thought that meant it was safe to assume he wasn't riding range. I mentioned Denver as a possibility for where he'd been and explained my theory that maybe something had happened there during his August visit that had drawn him back.

Lastly, I told Doc that I intended to revisit the Bar X Bar to ask Clayton Barnes about the horse he'd found and returned to Jake Wilson. Little as that was to work on, with all the rest, I still had hardly anything and needed to grasp as many straws as possible.

Doc absorbed it all and closed his eyes in thought.

He remained silent for so long, I wondered if—at his age and with a full belly—he'd managed to overcome the effects of the Chinaman's coffee and against all odds had fallen asleep.

Doc opened his eyes and gave me an owlish squint.

"Samuel Keaton, you want more from this breakfast than my listening ear." He wagged his finger at the silent protest of my upraised hands.

"Doc!" I tried indignation but couldn't hide my grin.

"Son, don't forget I've got thirty years on you. When a stubborn independent cuss like you sits down to ask for advice, I start listening for what he really wants. What I heard was that you're going to visit Crawford and lean on him for answers. You'll go to Denver if you have to. And you don't need me to help you talk to that Barnes fellow. All of that's straightforward. You don't need help with those speculations, 'cause all it will take to confirm or deny those speculations is legwork."

Doc steepled his fingers and stared at them for a few moments. A smile played at the edges of his mouth. "You drew up a pretty list, threw in all that smoke, and what's left when it clears is Lorne Calhoun. I'm the one who told you no one else knew him. So who else can you dog for information on him and Eleanor Ford? You sat me down not for advice, but to see if I knew anything about the two of them."

"It did happen to cross my mind that he might have mentioned her name in passing."

Doc pursed his lips with satisfaction at the accuracy of his assumption. "I told you earlier," he said, "that I believe a doctor has a moral obligation to hold secret what he learns from a patient. I've seen how loose talk destroys a reputation. Doctor or patient."

"That notion struck me as sensible," I said. "It also struck me that in a town this small, there's not much you don't know about folks here or on nearby ranches."

Doc started to say something, but I wagged my finger at him in the exact manner he'd done to me minutes earlier. "I'm not suggesting you give me dirt to help me do my job, Doc."

He relaxed.

"What I'm asking you is for anything Calhoun might have said away from the doctor's office. As a friend, not a patient."

"About Eleanor Ford?"

"Yes," I said.

"Nothing. Calhoun was a gentleman. She was a married woman. It is inconceivable that he would have had the opportunity or desire to do anything that might endanger her reputation. Nor would he talk about it. To anyone."

"But they knew each other."

"I believe yes."

I studied Doc. "You're holding something back."

He didn't disagree. Nor was he now relaxed.

It dawned on me why he couldn't tell me what he knew. "Eleanor Ford is a patient of yours."

He didn't disagree.

I realized if he did have something to tell me, it would tear at him, the choice. Duty. Or avenging a friend's death.

I wouldn't have wanted to face that dilemma and decided to try to ease him from it. "Doc, you were only half right when you accused me of throwing smoke around. I truly did want whatever thoughts you might have on Crawford, or Barnes, or Denver."

Doc's shoulder's dropped slightly, and the tension in his face eased. "I'll study on it," he said. "Remember, I want the killer hung as bad as anyone."

"I know that."

Doc pulled his watch loose from a vest pocket. I took the hint, pushed my hat brim low, and stood.

He rose with me.

As we reached the door, Doc stopped. His voice had the tone of an afterthought. "Benjamin Guthrie track you down last night?"

"Howling a storm."

"Took a half hour to set his arm. He probably told you that."

"He was more concerned that I gun down every stranger in town."

"Any ideas who jumped him?"

"Not yet," I said. "I'd forgotten about it till now."

Doc pushed through the door. He stumbled slightly, and I wondered if I heard a groan.

"Don't ignore Guthrie," Doc advised from ahead of me. I caught up to him and matched him, slow stride for slow stride. "He's not a man you want against you."

"One of the town fathers, I've gathered."

Doc turned his head to me and gave another of those owl-ish gazes. "You can warm your socks in the oven, but that don't make them biscuits."

"You mean he shows pretty good," I said. "Big, good looking, well dressed. But . . ."

"He's not a man you want with you, either."

"I'll remember that, Doc. Thanks."

We reached the corner. Nearly nine o'clock. The day was warming. Another glorious blue sky above. Indian summer in Wyoming was as pleasant and gentle as the blizzards that followed were vicious.

I bid Doc good-bye and headed down the street to open the marshal's office and face what was becoming a morning ritual of revivalist hell. I wished the circuit judge would get here soon. Even if I did have to charge a man with something as ridiculous as attempted murder by snake-throwing.

"Samuel," Doc called from behind me.

I retraced my steps back to him.

"Denver," Doc said.

It was a place I preferred not to make a homecoming. But he didn't have to know that.

"Denver," I repeated.

"Think about Nichols' trip in August. How's a man get to Denver from here?" he asked.

"Train. Union Pacific to Cheyenne. From there, the Denver Pacific south."

"Samuel, would any rancher walk into Laramie?"

"He'd rather be without boots than his horse."

"So if you rode in from the Rocking N, where would you leave your horse? That is, if again you were headed out of Laramie by train?"

I snapped my fingers. "Jake Wilson."

CHAPTER 18

As I waited for Jake Wilson in the coolness of the interior of his livery, Doc's words echoed in my mind. *"It's a mystery, Samuel, just like everything in life."*

At the Chinaman's, I'd stopped Doc's list of what I didn't know because I wanted to get on to asking him about Calhoun and Eleanor Ford. Here, however, in the silence broken only by the occasional horse's snort, or by a rustling of straw as a horse shifted positions in one of the stalls, I could not push away Doc's words.

"It's a mystery, Samuel, just like everything in life."

Everything?

I told myself to amuse Doc in his supposition, to look hard at the sparrow that had just flown in through the gap of the livery doors. I'd seen hundreds before. It was a sparrow. A brown sparrow. What more was there to know and how could there be mystery in a sparrow?

I could hear Doc asking me what caused it to fly.

I could hear myself telling Doc that I was a marshal, a tough man with guns, capable of riding for days without rest, and not only that, I was in pursuit of someone who had killed two people in a bank vault. Why should I waste my time on something as meaningless as what caused a sparrow to fly?

I could see Doc shrug as if I had to decide for myself the answer to my lack of curiosity.

And, against my will, I began to wonder what caused that stupid bird to fly.

Feeling ridiculous, and glad to be alone, I took several steps and picked up a fallen feather among several that rested on the dirt floor of the livery.

I could not look into the sunlight, so I turned my back to the gap between the doors and held the feather high so it would not be lost in the shadow of my head. I looked at the feather closely, then eased apart its softness.

The feather was a marvel.

Its strands had released with reluctance, and I saw how silky smooth and tough each of those tiny strands was, how wonderfully made to be able to cling to the strand beside it. No matter where I looked at it close, I could not see where one color of the pigment began or ended. Yet when held at arm's length, I saw again the mottled brown and black of a feather. So strong and tough, yet so light it almost did not exist. And how was a feather grown and constructed from the seeds and water that went into the sparrow? I could not conceive how something so perfectly made could be so common. And if something this common held so much mystery and wonder . . .

"Marshal, my bet is that it fell from a bird."

I dropped it and spun around.

"Blast it, Jake! Decent men knock to announce themselves."

"Not at their own livery. Not when they can't figure out

why the town marshal's holding a feather above his head and mumbling to hisself."

I glared at him. "If you'd be here like any other man doing an honest day's work, I wouldn't have to look for ways to entertain myself while I waited."

Jake laughed. "Now *I* gotta explain my whereabouts?"

He didn't wait for me to answer but instead threw the double doors open wide.

I saw where he'd been. Loading feed onto the wagon that stood directly outside.

Jake unhitched his horse from the wagon and led it into a stall. He returned to the rear of the wagon and began to push it inside. I moved beside him and threw my weight against the wagon. It took several minutes to reach the back of the livery, and I could feel sweat begin to trickle down between my shoulder blades.

Jake grinned at my hard breathing. He reached for the top of the wagon with his good hand, and with a single smooth hop, he pulled himself up to the top of the wagon wheel and from there sprung onto the bags of feed.

He pointed me to stand nearby a small pile of feed bags.

I did.

Without warning, he reached down with that good arm, hoisted a feed bag into the crook of his arm, juggled it to get a grip, then threw it at me.

I barely managed to hold my grunt inside at the impact of that bag. I set it atop the pile beside me. By the time I turned, another bag was already in midair.

It continued that way for the next quarter hour, and as Jake threw down the last bag of feed, I was huffing bad and blowing sweat spray with every breath.

"You were saying something about an honest day's work, Marshal?"

"As I recall," I managed to say, "I was asking about water."

Jake returned a minute later with a jar of cool water.

"I appreciate your help," Jake said. "Usually I have to walk it over. Throwing bags down with no one to catch busts them open."

I wiped my face with my bandanna. "Help's no problem. Beats sitting in the office and listening to Brother Lewis. I got a feeling the man talks so good about hell because he has a firsthand acquaintance with the devil."

"That explains why you didn't mind wasting time with a feather? That you'd rather be anywhere but there?"

I gave him a look as if I'd just tasted sour milk. *Feather.* Jake, it appeared, liked throwing as much rile as possible into the people around him.

I didn't mention that my other reason for waiting was that I had little stomach for the others I needed to visit—Crawford, for one, Benjamin Guthrie later in the day, for another. I didn't mention I'd been hoping that Jake might be able to tell me something to give me an excuse to delay both those visits.

Jake continued as if my worst look had been a benevolent smile. "So how long you intend to keep that preacher man in your jail?"

"Until the circuit judge comes by."

"Some folks say you oughta let him go. Some say you oughta arrest Doc. He was the one that caused it."

"Some folks say a lot." I favored Jake with another sour glance. "How often do *you* listen to them?"

Jake grinned. "Not often. Like about them Rebs. Guthrie's started a whispering campaign. Rumors about them being trouble, and why isn't the marshal doing something about it."

"Enough folks believe those Rebs are trouble," I said without blinking, "they *will* be trouble."

Jake grinned again. "And you've got them in town for at least a couple weeks."

"Glad you find it amusing." I frowned. "How'd you know, anyway?"

"Got their horses stabled here. Paid in advance. And they ride some fine horseflesh, Marshal. Expensive new saddles, too. Tooled by Pete Marlo, and if he ain't the best saddle-maker in Colorado, he's certainly the best in Denver. These boys ain't had to keep the same pair of boots so long they's down on their heels."

I gulped some more water. Tried not to think about all the little bugs that Doc had promised were swimming in it.

"Jake," I said between gulps. "You're a fountain of infor-mation. You oughta be a deputy sheriff."

He grinned more. It was a catching grin. "So, Marshal, what else do you want to know? You didn't come here to get your horse, otherwise you'd have saddled and gone already." A pause and a widening of his grin. "And you can find feath-ers lots of other places."

"Nichols." I refused to let Jake enjoy any reaction to his feather remark. "What was your read on him?"

"Good man," Jake said without hesitation. "Honest. Square. Always paid his way. And I'm not saying that just to speak good of the dead. Ask anyone in town. They'll tell you the same."

"That's what I heard. I also heard he went to Denver in August. He leave his horse here?"

"That was just before the town hired you on, Marshal. And yup, he did leave his horse with me."

I took another gulp of water. Tried to ease into the next question casual-like. "How about a few days before he died. He leave his horse here then?"

Jake's grin turned into a squint of speculation. "I heard you and Crawford already decided it was the two of them shooting each other dead."

I shrugged.

"You're playing this hand close to the chest, Marshal."

"You volunteering for a deputy badge?"

"Nope."

I smiled.

It didn't take him long to understand. "Right, Marshal," he laughed. "No badge. No deal."

I continued to smile.

"We'll do it your way," he sighed. "No, Nichols did not leave his horse here in the week before he died."

My slumped shoulders must have shown disappointment. So this was a dead end.

"Sorry," Jake added. "And August was the last time I seen him, when he returned from Denver and took his horse here from the stable."

I nodded. I hadn't really expected anything about this double killing to be simple.

"For what it's worth, Marshal, Nichols did seem different somehow that day."

"Yeah?" I wasn't hoping for much.

"Well, I joshed him about not seeming in a hurry. Folks knew he doted on his wife. I commented that a man without his woman for as long as he'd been gone should be in an all-fired hurry to stampede back to the ranch."

"I have noticed you do like sticking the knife," I said mildly. "And twisting it."

He grinned as if I had complimented him. "Feathers?"

I nodded.

"That's why it sorely disappointed me that I couldn't get Nichols' goat. A few other times, I mention how much woman she must be, he fairly busted, not knowing whether to be proud or whop me upside the head."

"And the day he returned from Denver?"

"He hardly heard what I said. He mumbled something about Eleanor Ford. I asked him what he'd meant, and he just shook his head."

Eleanor Ford? Why was another line of the web pointing back to her?

"You sure you didn't hear what Nichols said?"

Jake scratched his chin. "Maybe something like he didn't know whether or not he should stop at the Bar X Bar to see her first. That's the closest I can guess. And I wouldn't swear to it."

"Thanks, Jake."

He walked me into the sunshine. Instead of shaking my hand in farewell, he faced me squarely, good hand on his hip, the other arm dangling loose.

"Marshal, I've been having my fun with you. Passing on how folks talk, seeing how you'd take it."

I looked him in the eyes. And listened.

"Thanks to Guthrie—Lewis the preacher man, too— there's been more than a few whispers about you. Worse, for folks in a small town like this, no one knows much about you. All they know is you killed the marshal you then replaced. It appears like you're taking Brother Lewis personal, when lots others who enjoyed his revival don't see that he done too much wrong."

Jake wasn't grinning now, and he kept on going. "Suzie, well, she's one of the best dance-hall girls in town, and more than one in town is upset how she don't show interest in them no more and how she moons over you all the time. But word goes around you appear to have your mind fixed on a half-breed Sioux, which don't do no good among the sizeable camp of folks who figure Injuns oughta be poisoned just like wolves, 'specially now that treaty trouble's on the horizon. Guthrie says you're not man enough to face down the Rebs— and of course you already took their side against Old Charlie, even when folks can't figure why you treat Old Charlie so good instead of throwing cold water on him whenever he gets too much into the snake poison."

Jake shook his head. "And atop of all this, you're friends

with a Chinaman, for crying out loud."

"You keeping notes for a newspaper article?"

His grin returned. "Relax, Marshal. You asked me earlier, do I listen to other folks. The answer is no, I don't. I listen to what's behind their talk and decide things for myself."

He stuck out his good arm, waiting for me to shake his hand.

"What I'm saying is," he finished, "were you serious about ever needing a deputy, and you don't mind someone who can only draw one gun at a time, I'm your man."

CHAPTER 19

Mayor Charles William George Benedict Crawford was my next destination. Even that disagreeable task could not dim the whistling mood that had taken me as a result of Jake's offer. Except on my way to the First National, I made the mistake of walking Main Street on the same side as Guthrie Dry Goods and Clothing.

My good spirits lasted exactly ten steps past that storefront.

"Marshal," Benjamin Guthrie called from his doorway before I could complete the eleventh step, "Marshal Keaton, I want words with you."

I took on a good case of deafness and lengthened my stride.

"Keaton!" Guthrie hurried along the sidewalk, calling so loudly that I could no longer ignore him.

I stopped but did not turn.

He reached me and glared. "Marshal, you've made no arrests."

He wore a different suit today, just as fine as any others I'd seen him wear. His shoes were polished black, his derby brushed and clean. A broken arm hadn't slowed his grooming at all.

"Furthermore," he continued in the same demanding tone, "you did not report back to me."

"Hardly appears to be a need," I said almost with a drawl, "what with you knowing everything already."

He lifted his free hand and made a move to jab me in the shoulder with his forefinger to emphasize his next words.

I'd expected something by the way his face had darkened in immediate fury to be backtalked, so I was ready. I did it simply and cleanly. Drew my Colt in a sweeping motion so that before his finger had made contact with my shoulder, the revolver barrel was jammed firmly into his stomach.

He froze as the hammer clicked back.

His face whitened and his hand dropped away from me. We both looked down at the revolver, then back up at each other. I withheld the information that my firing pin was poised above the empty chamber I always kept that way to cut the odds of an accidental shooting.

We stayed like that for a couple of heartbeats. Long enough for me to make my point. Not so long he'd realize how much I was enjoying this.

I then smiled apology and withdrew the barrel.

"Sorry, Mr. Guthrie. Bad nerves." I slid the Colt back into my holster and eased the hammer down. "It just happens that way when I'm surprised by sudden movement."

He removed a hanky from an inner pocket and delicately wiped his brow.

I took advantage of his silence. "I'm still asking around, Mr. Guthrie. You'll be the first to know if I learn anything new."

Color began to return to his face, and to reestablish the authority he thought due to him, he searched for a way to continue to bluster. "Yesterday it was me that got hurt," he said. "Who next? One of the womenfolk? How much asking do you have to do? Those Rebs are easy to find."

His hand moved reflexively upward, and I wondered how often he jabbed people as he forced his words on them. It gave me satisfaction that he stopped his attempted jab and stared at his finger, then dropped his hand back down to his side.

"Mr. Guthrie, my promise remains. I'll keep asking until I run into the person or persons that bushwhacked you. So far it don't appear as if those Rebs had much to do with it."

"But . . ." His mouth worked as he struggled to find more words to use as bludgeons. "This . . . this is . . ."

I stopped listening, for I had noticed the approach of a brougham carriage—and a double-suspension one at that—pulled by a two-horse team of matching whites, each groomed as neatly as any boy readied for a Sunday picnic. Had there not been dust on the carriage, the wood paneling of the passenger compartment would have gleamed with the richness due to a carriage worth nearly five years of a cowboy's wages. I was not the only one watching in admiration as it moved down the street.

A hired hand was up front to handle the reins as the brougham passed. I saw the outline of a woman passenger who sat alone, hands in her lap, in the compartment behind him. Sunlight flashed across the woman's face, and I knew I should know her.

"Marshal, are you paying attention to me?"

"Nope."

The brougham had stopped in front of the First National Bank, so close to the sidewalk that its shadow darkened Crawford's office window. The hired man stepped down from the brougham and walked around to assist the woman as she disembarked.

"Marshal!"

The bonnet kept her face hidden, but from the trimness of her figure and the wealth shown by the brougham, I believed I could make a guess as to her identity.

"Guthrie," I said without taking my eyes from her, "I'll stop by your house later. Probably after you've had your supper."

"I don't see why we have to take something this sordid into my home."

Crawford was hurrying through the doors of the First National, stepping onto the sidewalk to bow to the woman.

Eleanor Ford.

Interesting, I told myself, that toad Crawford had probably jumped before the brougham's shadow had stopped moving across his window.

"Marshal!"

"Later, Guthrie." I answered without looking at the store owner.

"I'm a man of considerable influence," he insisted. "Treat me this way for long, you won't wear that badge."

I didn't answer. I was already on my way back to Jake's stable. I wanted two fast horses. One saddled and one to follow behind so I could switch when the first one tired.

CHAPTER 20

RUN A HORSE FULL OUT, you'll get maybe ten minutes of gallop. Much longer, and it'll be played out so bad you might not be able to run it again for a day. Much longer after that, and chances are good you'll be falling from a horse whose heart has just exploded.

While I was tempted to run that hard anyway, I forced myself to keep the horses to a brisk canter. Even with one cord tethered behind, a canter was pushing them both plenty hard if I intended to keep that pace for the entire distance to the Bar X Bar. I felt that urgency because I wanted as much time as possible there before Eleanor Ford and her hired hand returned to the ranch in the brougham, and I had no assurances that she'd be long with Crawford or that she had further business in town to keep her away from the ranch.

Eleanor Ford.

In the few days since the double murder, I had already connected her three times in three different ways to the men involved. Once, by her own admission to Lorne Calhoun. Once, by hearsay through Jake, to Bob Nichols. And once, by my own eyes, to Mayor Crawford. It had to be more than coincidence.

But how could I follow all the strands to the core of the web I suspected her of weaving? Doc, for the moment, had chosen to remain silent about her. I wasn't yet prepared to tip my hand by asking around town, for as Jake had shown me, word moved quickly through Laramie.

That left me the ranch itself. At the least, I was hoping this might kick something loose to give me an excuse not to go to Denver.

I would ride up and politely ask after Eleanor Ford, show suitable surprise at her absence, and express my disappoint-ment at the same. Depending on who informed me of her absence, all it would take after that was easing into questions about her in such a way that it didn't appear I was asking those questions. As long as I could figure what to ask before I reached the Bar X Bar.

"Howdy." I doffed my hat, gave my friendliest grin. Here along the garden, I had to speak loudly above the creaking of the windmill. "This time 'round, I won't be calling you Mrs. Ford."

My grin was rewarded with a curtsey from the same older woman who had offered me water on my first visit to the Bar X Bar. This visit, however, no horse-breaking activities filled the far corrals. It appeared we were alone among the array of ranch buildings.

I swung down from my horse. Groaned. Stretched. Slapped my hat clear of dust.

"Mrs. Ford isn't here," the woman informed me. She still held a small spade that she'd been using to dig in the garden on my approach. Piles of potatoes littered the broken ground in the small corral behind her.

No sense in waiting to ease into my questions. I showed mock surprise and grinned again. "How'd you know I wasn't here just to visit you?"

"Mister," she pointed at my horse and the one tethered behind, "it's been twenty-five years since someone lathered their horses that bad for the chance to see me."

I looked her up and down, letting her see me do it. She wore another plain dress, one that bulged out in lumps across her coarsened body. Despite her timeworn appearance, she'd spoken with a sauciness that let me understand she enjoyed banter.

"Naw," I said, giving her a final study, "I'd never believe twenty-five years since a man came calling."

She rolled her eyeballs at my blatant flattery.

"Twenty-four, maybe," I finished. "But not twenty-five."

A broad grin bunched her cheeks and deepened the cracks of her weathered face. "Mister, you said that just like Mr. Springer would have, bless his departed soul. He always knew how to catch me unexpected. It's why I ended up accepting his proposal. I wasn't expecting it."

She leaned the spade against the corral fence. "That's me. Emma Springer."

"Samuel Keaton," I said. "Pleased to make your acquaintance."

She put her hands on her hips and studied me in the same deliberate manner I'd looked at her.

"Samuel Keaton, you say. Why's that name familiar?"

"I'm the marshal, out of Laramie."

"Married?"

"No, ma'am."

Emma Springer gave me a sharp look. "It's business that brought you here to see Mrs. Ford twice in the same week?"

"You're not shy with questions, ma'am."

"At my age, ain't much time to waste."

"It's business," I conceded. "But now you got me curious. Why might you think it'd be anything but business?"

She shrugged. "A woman shouldn't gossip."

I'd long since figured out a declaration of that statement always meant the opposite.

I invited her to find us some shade. We moved to a bench at the side of a bunkhouse.

"I wouldn't consider it gossip," I told her as we eased ourselves onto the bench. "More like background. Two men are dead, and I'm trying to find out who was behind it."

"The bank vault murders? Nichols and a town fella? I heard they had a falling-out and shot each other."

I nodded. "Maybe, maybe not. Fact is, there's three little boys down the road who just watched their mama bury their father. I'm doing my best to make sure they'll at least have a decent memory of him."

She shook her head and chuckled. "Shameless, attempting that sort of blackmail on an old woman. You even managed the right quaver in your voice and all."

I twisted my hat in my hands. Tried to hide a grin of admission.

She patted my knee. "Samuel, we'll get along just fine. I'd forgotten how much fun it is having a fine-looking man this interested in me."

She caught my sharp look in her direction.

"You didn't fool me at all," she said. "Horses lathered that bad, like you was in a hurry, but you made a side stop to visit me before knocking on her door?" She patted my knee again and answered her own question. "Nope, when you came straight to me, I knew right then it wasn't Mrs. Ford you had on your mind. At least, not first on your mind."

What could I say to that?

"So how can I help?" she said with a grin.

I thought that over and gave her a grin in return. "Gossip."

"Background," Emma said firmly.

"Background."

"You don't believe Mrs. Ford had a hand in this."

"Do you?" I responded.

Emma thought for a few seconds. "I believe she's been guilty of poor judgment once or twice. But killing a man? That's a harsh accusation to lay on a body."

You don't have to pull the trigger to be responsible for a man's death, but I didn't say that aloud.

"You let on like I might not be here on business," I said. "That the poor judgment you mean?"

Emma nodded. "People talk. No matter how proper it is when a man sits for tea, if he shows up once every month or so, people talk. Then when Mr. Phillips died . . ."

"Mr. Phillips?"

"Leonard Phillips. A nice man. Much older than Eleanor. He established this ranch. She moved here with him just after the rail reached Laramie. Couple years later, a horse threw him, broke his neck. His body was barely cold when she married the man that had been calling."

I searched my memory. "Cyrus?"

"Cyrus Ford."

"I haven't met him," I said.

"No surprise. The man's away more than he's here."

"In Cheyenne now, as I recall from my last conversation with Mrs. Ford."

"Plenty of financial interests elsewhere, I'm told. Leaves her with too much time on her hands."

"And she's had other callers. . . ." I was thinking of Lorne Calhoun. Maybe Eleanor meets him at the bank one day, they strike up conversation, leads to more than a casual acquaintance, especially if Lorne gets starstruck by the attentions of a beautiful woman like her, and maybe she has a reason for leading him on, a reason that leads to his death. . . .

"Latest caller was a hard-looking man, Marshal."

"Hard-looking?" Death will soften a man's features, take

a lot of mean out of his face. But try as I might, from my memory of Calhoun lying on the floor in the bank vault, I couldn't stretch myself to believe anyone would call him hard-looking.

"Hard-looking?" I repeated. "Maybe in a suit and tie? Like the banker type?"

"No, sir." She shook her head for emphasis. "This man had tied-down guns and wore Rebel gray."

CHAPTER 21

IT SEEMED EVERY TIME I learned something new, it led to more puzzlement.

I had plenty of time to ponder the implications of a Rebel visitor as I headed directly east of the Bar X Bar, trusting Emma Springer's directions on how to find Clayton Barnes and the rest of a small crew working on fall roundup.

With at least five hours of daylight remaining, I enjoyed the slower pace. I imagine the horses did, too. I'd given them the chance to take water at the Bar X Bar, and I'd brushed them down before saddling up again.

A breeze carried the smell of sage and the slight whisperings of bent grass. The sky's infinite blue became pale, almost white at the mountain edges of the horizon. The peace of this aloneness felt good, and I smiled to recall advice I'd received long ago from a gray-bearded, short old cowboy. He'd taken a deep breath on a day just like this and said that when you worked a plow, all you see is a mule's hind end, but working from a horse, no matter how bad the pay, you can see across country for as far as your eye is good.

I wondered what advice he'd give me here.

I couldn't even begin to string together the bits and pieces I'd already learned. Nichols had called on Calhoun and escorted him to the bank. Someone there had been waiting to kill them. This someone couldn't have been a stranger, for Nichols and Calhoun had fallen like sheep, and I couldn't see both of them entering that bank vault and going to their slaughter without a mistaken trust in their executioner. Nichols had gone somewhere for at least three days before knocking on Calhoun's door that fateful night, and this somewhere was not anyplace that he'd anticipated the need for his usual grubstake. Calhoun had been puzzling about accounting errors in the weeks before his death. Nichols and Calhoun had both known Eleanor Ford, for reasons I still didn't know. Crawford, who also knew Ford, had strangely—at Eleanor's request?—denied a loan to Nichols.

And now, as if I needed a whirlwind to come from nowhere and scatter these bits and pieces even further, it appeared one of the Christopher brothers had been visiting Eleanor Ford in the absence of her husband. Worse, as Emma had established for me, this Rebel stranger had visited the Bar X Bar at least three times in the weeks before now renting a suite at the Union Pacific Hotel with the rest of his brothers.

Or had it been another tie-down man in Rebel gray paying visits on Eleanor Ford? Was it mere coincidence that Dehlia had arrived shortly after with her brothers in *their* Rebel gray and tied-down guns? If not a coincidence, what was the significance of a man in snakeskin boots hidden behind a wardrobe? If a coincidence, who was that other Rebel, and why were Dehlia and gang in town? And did the attack on Guthrie figure in any of this, or was that merely another headache arriving at an inopportune time?

I nearly groaned aloud as I spun those bits and pieces through my head.

Finally, I gave up thinking and tried to lose myself in the solitude of my ride. That took a certain concentration that I'd been able to do with ease in the days before meeting the woman who had left me a Moon Basket along with the haunting distraction of her memory.

I settled into the slow ride and focused on what each of my senses brought me. I listened as hard as I could for every sound—crunch of horses' hooves, brush of chaps against tall grass, cry of prairie birds. I breathed deep and took in and sorted every scent, letting my skin tingle with every sensation—the coolness of the breeze across my face, the trickle of sweat on my back, the heat of sun on my shoulders, the sway in my saddle. I opened my eyes and looked, really looked for every detail within range of my vision—the dark green of spruce girdling the mountain, and the edges of those mountains against the sky, the rolling brown and faded green of the land that stretched to mountains, gullies and the draws immediately ahead, the jumble of tumbleweed beneath, the wheeling of an occasional bird across the sky. It was a process that froze the future and past and put me nowhere but in the very moment.

It took some doing to bump all the other thoughts from my mind and concentrate on the simple joy of what it meant to be alive and riding across the plains.

And just when I reached that timelessness, the bawling of cattle reached me.

———————

This appeared no different from dozens of other fall roundups I'd seen. In the bowl of a small valley, hundreds of cattle were milling in a large dusty circle, the result of a week's hard work by a couple dozen ranch hands.

Spring or fall, the roundup process was the same. Ranch

hands fanned out to all points of a compass, gathering steers, bulls, cows, and yearling calves, then driving the cattle in small bunches to this common meeting place.

Once here, when the cattle were moving in a tight circle, the frenzied bawling of the calves and the bellowing of the bulls would subside some, and it only took a few men riding the outer edges of the circle to keep the herd grazing together as more cattle were driven in from the outer edges of the range.

In the spring, it was a time to separate new calves from their mothers for branding, to rope and castrate and dehorn, to sort one ranch's cattle from another. In the fall roundup, the marketable steers were cut from the herd and readied for a drive to the railhead.

As I rode down the small hill into the center of the valley, a maverick yearling broke loose from the herd. Within seconds, a cowhand began to gallop in pursuit, making sure to keep the yearling between his horse and the herd. He matched his horse's speed to the yearling's and galloped alongside, edging closer and closer until it forced the maverick back to the herd. It was something that happened more than occasionally and exhausted not only the horses, but the men.

I looked for the trail boss and decided he was the man sitting on a horse nearby the remuda, the three or four horses per man that the outfit would supply to keep the cowboys on fresh animals. If this man wasn't the boss, he was at least far enough away from the herd that I wouldn't have to chew dust as I talked.

I drew near, and he acknowledged me with a nod of the head.

"Afternoon," I said, speaking loudly to be heard above the bawling of cattle. "You mind directing me to the whereabouts of Clayton Barnes?"

"Not at all," he said. His dirt-smeared face was drawn. Cowboys took what little sleep they could snatch between guard duty, and any foreman worth his salt didn't make exceptions for himself. "You won't mind me asking the reason? I ain't a prying man, but he is part of this outfit, and I can't afford trouble."

"No trouble," I said. "He turned in a dead man's horse a few days ago. As marshal, I'd like to ask him a few questions, is all."

"Marshal?"

I opened my vest and showed him the badge that I had pinned inside.

"You're the snake-shooter," he said. "I heard about it."

"Couple of lucky shots."

He nodded. We'd both said enough on that subject. "Marshal, you'll find Barnes working a draw maybe three miles northeast. It's a tangle of scrub brush, and there's at least a dozen of the wildest cattle of the bunch holed out there."

"Obliged," I said.

"He's a redhead," the foreman said. "Can't miss him. Just a kid with peach fuzz."

I turned my horse, then looked back over my shoulder at the foreman. "I ain't generally a prying man," I said. "But it is part of wearing this badge. This Clayton Barnes, would he deal from the bottom of the deck?"

"Don't think so," the foreman said. "Truth is, he ain't sharp enough. Good man, hard-working. Honest. But not the sharpest."

"Again," I said, "Obliged. Any of your boys ever whoop it up good in Laramie, I'll see they get a fair shake."

The foreman tipped his hat and returned to surveying his herd.

That three-mile ride took longer than I'd expected, as the country got a little wilder, the gullies a little deeper, and the brush a little thicker. I could see how it'd take considerable work to move cattle from this area of the range.

A couple of times my horse snorted and turned its ears in different directions, but it didn't alarm me. The horse tethered behind wasn't showing distress. We were far from Sioux country, and any animals large enough to be danger would have long since cleared the noise of this part of the plains.

A half hour later, I regretted my lack of caution.

I'd hallyhooed Clayton Barnes to get his attention where he was picking his horse along the wide bottom of a dry creek bed. And just as I rode up, someone shot me out of my saddle.

CHAPTER | *22*

I'D BEEN SHOT BEFORE, but then I'd seen the revolver and knew it was coming. The bullet had spun me, merely punched through the light flesh of my arm, then come and gone to leave a burning sensation through the severed nerves and also a hole that eventually leaked enough blood to put me in major trouble.

But when that bullet had hit, I'd known what was happening.

This time, it was an overwhelming shock, much of that shock a result of total bewilderment at the suddenness of events that my mind could not grasp.

I had ridden to within maybe ten feet of Clayton Barnes where he sat on his motionless horse waiting for me. I drew a breath to say hello to Clayton Barnes but got no further with my greeting.

Someone unseen slammed a fence post across the side of my thigh, rocking me with the impact. Before I'd managed to sort through this surprise, I felt the pain of shredded muscle, as if a spike in that fence post were ripping deep into the front of my thigh. Before I could look down to puzzle this, my horse began to rear in panic. Even as I fought to stay in the saddle on a horse pawing air high with its front hooves, a short burst of rolling thunder echoed through the draw.

I finally realized I'd been shot in my left leg.

My horse dropped to all fours, and I clutched at my thigh with a glance over at Clayton Barnes to see if he shared my disbelief. That glance showed me the face of a boy, eyes wide, mouth gaping as he, too, tried to fit together the sights and sounds of a man shot without warning from hidden ambush.

Before either of us could react, dust kicked from Clayton's shirt. Chest high, centered near his buttons. A gush of red filled the hole in the fabric. Another peal of rolling thunder.

He began to tumble from the saddle.

A zinging whine past my ear. Delayed thunder again.

I realized I was a target still high and visible atop my horse. I pushed off and dove into the soft sand, letting myself tumble away from the dancing of both my horses' hooves.

A geyser of sand inches from my head. Then that echoing thunder.

I was exposed in this dry creek bed. No boulders. No trees. Just sand and tufts of grass.

I rolled twice more, until my horse was nearly above me, screaming its panic. The horse tethered behind was pulling against its rope in equal panic. For that moment, as each horse pulled against the other, I had a screen between me and the unseen sniper.

I tried to stand to jump for my horse, maybe clutch its neck and hold on long enough for it to gallop to the gully walls just past some cottonwoods. But I crumpled at half stride. My leg had collapsed.

Another zinging whine. That dreaded thunder.

Barnes was dangling from his horse, his left boot caught

in a stirrup, his head and shoulders dragging on the ground. If that horse bolted, he'd be pounded to mash. If he was dead already, what happened next to his body wouldn't matter anyway. But it did matter to me that his horse stay with us.

From where I had fallen, I reached down to my right hip, drew the Colt, and fired upward.

It did not need to be a lucky shot, nor skillful. Clayton and his horse were so close they were blocking me from the sun, and my bullet hit exactly where I'd aimed: just beneath the horse's jaw, driving the lead upward into its skull. Almost gently, the horse went to its knees and, in a slow sway, fell to its side.

I scrabbled past Barnes and took cover behind the fallen horse.

In that time lapse, both my horses finally turned in the same direction. The extra noise and smell of blood only served to upset them more, and both dropped their heads and began to gallop.

It left me alone with a dead horse and probably a dead man, and I was unable to move to other shelter, even if my leg would have permitted such action.

A thud. Then that crack of thunder. A bullet had pounded into the horse's ribs. On my stomach now, and without rising, I reached back and tried to pull Barnes to me in the shadow of the horse's body.

Wasted effort. I could not get enough leverage without exposing myself to the rifle fire. Clayton's body was dead-weight.

Another shot. The shooter had raised his sights to miss the horse, and as my toes were turned downward into the sand, the bullet tore the heel off my boot.

Bad as the situation was, it could have been worse. The horse could have fallen onto the other side and buried the scabbard and stock of Clayton's rifle. Instead, the scabbard was on the upper side of the dead horse's ribs, and I could pull it loose with little risk to myself.

I levered a shell into position and propped the rifle over top of the horse's ribs.

Without lifting myself to aim, I fired.

It was a blind shot, pointed vaguely in the direction where I'd guessed the sniper might be, and I expected no results. I did, however, know it would notify our attacker that I was armed, ready, and not entirely helpless. With luck, it would keep him from riding in.

It discouraged him so much that he waited at least five seconds before firing again. And again. The two shots hit the dead horse with enough force that I could feel the impact from where my shoulder was pressed against its hide.

I'd been waiting for these shots. And I'd counted. The delay between impact and sound reaching my ears had been a one-count.

I levered another shell into the rifle.

One second?

The shooter was definitely not within pistol range. If I dared peek, I'd have to search the edges of the bank where I'd descended earlier to greet Barnes.

I squeezed off a hurried shot, aimed more to the top of the ridge, then ducked again.

Two shots in return. One hit the horse; the other passed over my head with that unmistakable careening whine that belongs only to a bullet.

I took comfort in the shooter's ability to rapid fire. It meant that whoever was firing was using a repeating rifle, a lighter one without the knockdown power of the single-shot buffalo guns that could kill a two-thousand-pound beast over a half mile away. The comfort was that I might still have a leg when all this finished, for a buffalo gun would have torn a hole big enough to fill with my fist.

I levered again. Fired again. Ducked again.

Silence in return.

Was the shooter moving in? If so, I was at a disadvantage. No place to go. And with this dead horse in plain sight of the sniper, he could work around, shoot from a different angle. And I probably wouldn't even have the warning of sound to tell me that another bullet had punched its way into my body. Yet if I lifted my head to scan for movement, I was a dead man, too. The sniper had shown chilling accuracy for someone with a light rifle at least a couple of hundred yards away. I did what I could. Nothing.

My heartbeat seemed to fill my ears, so I thought I misheard the drumming of a horse's hooves. But when I risked another quick glance, I saw a line of dust rising from where the sniper had probably been firing.

A bluff to get me to think he'd left?

Only, I told myself, *if he had two horses and could afford to lose one to finish this.*

And if he had left, why? My last shot had told him I was still alive, and it didn't take much savvy to realize he did want me dead.

Probably not a bluff, I decided to comfort myself with the thought. But how long could I wait to decide?

I waited anyway. That was my only choice.

My leg began to throb. I allowed myself to look down. Blood welled from two holes in my jeans. The bullet had entered and exited the muscle near the top of my thigh.

I curled into a ball and lay on my side so that I remained protected by the dead horse. I pulled at my belt and finally slid it loose. I cinched the belt above the bullet holes. Tied it as tight as I could. Anything to stop as much bleeding as possible.

No shots. No sounds.

Maybe he *had* left.

Now that time had slowed again and the fight heat was gone, my leg began to make itself felt. The throbs rocked me.

No shots. No sounds.

Dizziness began to replace the throbbing, began to blur my vision.

I fought the waves of darkness, but they whispered to me, promised me peace, and a final swell took me away.

CHAPTER 23

I WOKE CUSSING AND SCREAMING at the panther that clawed at my leg. Trouble was, I couldn't even swing at it or grab its neck to pull it away.

It took a half second of focus to realize that the shadowy figure crouched over my lower body was not a panther, but Doc Harper, lit from behind by the oil lamps on the shelves of his office wall.

He straightened. "Don't fight it, Sam. I've got you tied down."

Hands, arms, legs, and feet. Even my head was strapped onto the low table where only days before I'd so gently placed Betty in her gingham dress.

Doc pressed something into my leg. I found myself arched in agony, a direct response to the liquid fire that tore into my muscle. The smell of freshly branded hide filled my nostrils.

He stepped back. From what I could see without moving my head, he held a long, thin bar. Glowing red at one end. The end he'd pulled from my leg.

It took effort, but I managed to fill my lungs with air. "You lop-eared, lantern-jawed, half-bred, pox-eaten dog. If you do that again, I'll—"

He shook his head at me. Stepped forward. The fire ripped through my leg again, a pain so fierce I couldn't even scream.

He stepped back again. It took me even longer to find air. "Mangy, skunk-loving, scabby, flea-infested—"

Doc grabbed a rag and shoved it in my mouth.

"Civil War," he said as he walked from the office into his waiting room. Seconds later, he walked back into the office. His hand was behind his back, but it didn't fool me. I'd heard the banging of his potbellied stove lid. He'd grabbed another iron.

"That's right. The War Between the States," he said as if he hadn't interrupted himself, and as if my muffled protests into the rag were polite requests for him to continue. "Back then, a leg like this would only take me forty-five seconds. The time it took for two orderlies to put you on the table, for me to saw through, for the leg to hit the ground, and for the orderlies to move you to a bed where they'd bandage the stump. With no guarantees that you'd live for the price you just paid. We didn't have time for these niceties back then. No, sir. Bullet in the leg almost always meant get rid of the leg. Count yourself fortunate."

He bent over my leg to approach it from the other side with an iron glowing red-hot, and he used it to ram more fire into me. I screamed anger into the rag. I'd never felt pain so bad, and I didn't care how well intentioned Doc might be or how fortunate it was that he didn't have a bloodied hacksaw in his hand.

"If it's a consolation," Doc said, "this might be all it takes to keep the gangrene away. Any luck, you'll be walking with a cane tomorrow."

He brought an oil lamp close to my leg and examined my exposed thigh in its yellow light. Doc clucked a few times and nodded to himself, then bandaged me with his usual efficiency.

"I'll cut you loose now," he said.

He pulled the rag from my mouth, but I was soaked with my sweat, too spent to continue my diatribe. The best I could do was flex my wrists and hands in their new freedom as he wrapped my leg in bandages.

That finished, he helped me into a sitting position. My right pant leg had not been touched, but my left pant leg was cut off almost at crotch level, and the bandages were startlingly white against the flesh of my thigh.

"I've got crutches for you," Doc said. "But don't stand until you're ready."

I waited until the spots stopped swimming in my eyes. By then, Doc had returned with the crutches and a flask of water. I gulped with greed.

When I nodded, Doc took the flask and placed the crutches in front of me. As I leaned onto them, Doc kept a careful guiding hand on my elbow.

He noticed I was shivering.

"Follow me," he said.

I did, at a turtle's pace. It had been my left boot with the heel shot away, leaving me to hobble on a whole boot on my right foot. Small mercy.

I followed Doc out of the office, through the waiting room, and down the hallway to another door, this one locked.

I leaned forward on my crutches and panted as Doc fumbled with the key.

I followed him inside and waited in the darkness.

Doc scratched a match into flame and lit an oil lamp. As its light grew, I saw that this was his living quarters. Throw rug in the middle. A couple of paintings that showed no detail in the dim light. Bookshelves along two of the walls. A small writing desk. And a large stuffed armchair.

Doc pointed me to the chair.

I eased forward and sank into it. My shivers didn't stop.

Doc returned from another room with a straight-backed chair in one hand, a blanket in the other.

He tossed the blanket at me. "You can go ahead and wrap yourself," he said. "I'd hate you to get the idea I care."

He set the chair nearby and slowly lowered himself into it.

"Long day," I said. My voice croaked. I still shivered beneath the blanket.

"Long day," he agreed.

"Whiskey'd be nice," I said.

"Yup," he said. But he made no move to get some, so I let that idea slide.

"Who found me?"

"Bar X Bar boys," Doc replied. "They'd heard the shots. Knew it was trouble. Said it sounded like a range war."

"It was."

"Gathered that. The kid was dead by the time they got there." Doc's voice was sad.

We both stayed with our thoughts on that. A couple minutes passed before Doc spoke again. His voice was sad, but not empty sad, as if he were trying to shake us both from our mood.

"You're a fickle man," he told me.

"Fickle?"

"When you outgunned Harrison a few months back and tried to outrun the posse, I was the one that patched your arm."

That escape attempt had failed because I'd passed out. I'd woken in a jail cell, arm in a sling, weak, and facing the noose. Back then, of course, I wouldn't have known who'd done the doctoring, and till now I'd not given it much thought. Not with all what had happened after. It made sense, of course, that it had been Doc who'd fixed me.

"I'll thank you for it now," I said. "But what's my arm have to do with fickle?"

Doc chuckled softly. "Twice I've had occasion to observe that you mumble a lot when you're unconscious."

"Doc . . ."

"Few months back, only one word came out that made sense. Clara, Clara, Clara. This time round, you kept calling out Rebecca, Rebecca, Rebecca. That strikes me as fickle enough."

"If you're asking, Doc, I'll explain. But not tonight. How's that?"

"That's probably the same answer I'd have given had you asked me about Sarah. And from that book you went through, I've wondered if you'd ever get around to it."

He waved away my reply. "So few people in this town care for books. That's why I was able to spot how the dust had been disturbed. Fact is, I took your curiosity in book learning as a good sign. And your discretion as a better one."

We lapsed into another friendly silence. My shivering lessened, and my eyes grew accustomed to the darkness. I could tell that Doc kept his living quarters as neat as his office.

"Pondering on the shooter?" Doc eventually asked.

"Yup. I can't believe it's unrelated to the bank vault murders. If that's so, I'm just thinking it means somewhere, somehow, I pulled on a bear's tail without knowing it."

Doc nodded. "Like someone thinks you're close to finding the truth."

"Something like that. What's frustrating is I don't even know enough to know when I pulled on the bear's tail."

"Run through the list of where you asked questions."

"Been doing it. Eleanor Ford. Helen Nichols. You. Jake Wilson. Crawford. That's it." I shook my head. "No, that's not it. Emma Springer."

"She's a tough one," Doc said. "Outlived a husband and two sons. And will probably outlive her next husband if she ever marries again."

"I told her you were sweet on her, Doc. Her eyes lit right up."

He groaned. Served him right for tweaking me with Clara and Rebecca.

Silence again as we retreated to our own thoughts.

Then Doc shuffled out of his chair. He left the room. When he returned, he held an envelope.

"I got to thinking about Eleanor Ford and Lorne Calhoun," Doc said. "I'd decided if I could find you anything that another person might have been able to get outside of being a doctor, that it'd be fair to pass it along."

He extended the envelope to me. "So I used my privilege as an old friend. I went through everything in his room at the boardinghouse. I was hoping for a diary," Doc said. "Tried to convince myself that Lorne wouldn't mind, since we're both set on finding the same answers that I suspect he died looking for."

I took the envelope. It was thin. Didn't have much in it.

"It's only a letter," Doc told me. "Ticket stubs. A telegram. I searched for two hours. That's all I found that was of interest."

"Why of interest?" I tucked the letter beneath my vest in my shirt pocket.

"No," Doc said. "You read it first. I'd like you to come up with your own opinion without me coloring it first."

"All right." A spasm of pain shook my leg, and I couldn't hold back the groan.

"It'll hurt," Doc said. "For more than a couple days. But it could have been worse. The bullet only took muscle. And it passed clear through. The boys got you back into town quick enough. I washed it good, cleared it of sand and dirt. Then cauterized it. You're strong, healthy. Tomorrow, maybe the day after, a cane should be all you need."

I thought of the dust that had kicked from the shirt of Clayton Barnes. Thought of how Doc had said we'd didn't know from day to day if we'd live to see the sunset. "Give me the pain any day, Doc. Beats a coffin."

Doc agreed but did not sit.

It probably had been a long day for him. He wasn't young. And somehow, he was seeming more frail. He was probably aching to rest.

I struggled to my feet, then grinned at the effort it took, because it was effort that reminded me my bed tonight would be a bed, not a coffin.

"You'll watch yourself," Doc said. "Whoever did the shooting was serious about his intentions."

"I'll watch myself," I agreed. "But right now, I'm more worried about walking half-naked through town. You didn't leave me much for pants when you got at my leg."

"Keep the blanket," Doc said. "Return it tomorrow."

Doc walked me down to the street and nodded goodnight.

I stumped it back toward my rented house, glad for the darkness of the streets and the lack of passersby. It was awkward to use the crutches, more awkward to keep the blanket around myself. I made progress only after I decided practicality took precedence over modesty and slung the blanket over my shoulder. Even at that pace, it took nearly fifteen minutes to reach the small house at the back edge of town.

I wasn't looking forward to the rest of the night.

Usually, tiredness was all the cure I needed to get through the dark of night. Enough tiredness that when my head touched the pillow, I'd be asleep.

I knew tonight, by the pounding throbs of my left thigh, I'd be lucky to catch a catnap before morning. Which meant I'd be alone with the thoughts of Rebecca and how she as

Evening Star was building a life apart from me among the Sioux.

I was right about the lack of sleep. But wrong about being alone.

I dropped the blanket at the door and fumbled with a box of matches that I kept near the solitary lamp in the small front room of the house. When the burning wick flared light into the small front room of the house, Dehlia Christopher called my name from the shadows where she sat on a corner chair.

CHAPTER 24

I LEANED AGAINST the left crutch, dropped the one in my right hand, and drew my Colt. Leveled it at her head. Cocked the hammer.

I sighed. Pointed the Colt at the floor. Eased the hammer back. Holstered the revolver.

"You'll excuse me for jumpiness," I said. "The afternoon did not treat me kindly."

"You don't consider me dangerous?" Her voice was a teasing pout.

"Extremely," I said. "But if you—or maybe brothers nearby—wanted me dead, it would have happened as I lit the lamp."

"Why would anyone want you dead, Marshal?"

"You tell me."

"I should know the reason?"

"Admirable habit, Dehlia. Answering with questions. Like you're working hard to keep a man on edge."

No response.

With the help of my remaining crutch, I

moved ahead to the small bedroom just beyond her chair.

"If you don't mind actually receiving an invitation, feel welcome to make yourself at home as you wait," I said as I passed her. "It'll take me a few minutes get a fresh pair of pants."

She stayed. Her brothers were not hidden in the bedroom. As it was the only bedroom in this small wood-frame house, and as the small kitchen was in plain view of the front parlor, I concluded she was here alone.

As I struggled out of my torn pants, then into the next pair, I broke into a sweat again. The drops felt like blood on my forehead. In short, no matter how good Dehlia looked, and she did look very good in the soft yellow light of a room that had been barren of any woman since I'd moved in, I was not predisposed to light conversation when I returned to the parlor and took a chair opposite her.

"I heard," she said, "that you'd been shot."

I let my grunt of pain as I sat serve as an answer.

She stood from her chair, crossed the short distance between us, and placed her hand on my shoulder. "That's why I took the chance of coming here."

"Not my boyish charm? Or my wonderful manners?" I did my best to keep my voice surly. It bothered me that I was so conscious of her light touch and of the waft of perfume and of the slimness of her body.

She smiled as she looked down on me. "In your way, you have considerable boyish charm. And manners that intrigue me."

She sat on her haunches and smiled again as she stared upward into my face. "Truly, Marshal, I'd like to know more about you."

The tilt of her flawless face and gleam of teeth from parted lips and slow, lazy smile combined to make a good painkiller, for I barely knew my bandaged leg existed.

"I'd like to know where you got that scar." She traced its

lines along my cheek with the fingernail of her other hand.

There was that medicine bundle in my bedroom to remind me of Rebecca. This woman was beautiful, but I loved another. I pushed her hand away.

"As I reckon this is just a game to you," I said, "perhaps you'll cut to the chase?"

That lazy smile only grew lazier as she stood. "I like a horse that doesn't take easy to the bit. Shows spirit."

"It's a real shame you hold that what passes between a man and a woman is a matter of who's got the reins," I replied after a moment. "Situation like that, you can honey the bit all you want, but it don't hide the taste of steel."

She laughed. Low and teasing. "A philosopher lurks within all that brawn."

"If you say so. I'll remind you that whoever lurks there is tired. Gunshot and real tired. So if you don't mind . . ."

"I don't mind." She became intent. "The bank vault murders. I'm here to save your life. Drop the search."

My turn to smile lazy triumph. "Which brother you trying to protect?"

She paced several steps. I liked that. She had to pause for an answer.

"Ignorant fool," she said without passion. "You have no idea. That's what's going to get you killed."

"I have an idea now," I said. "You gambled you could turn me away. Gambled that against what I might do with what I learned from your visit tonight. And what I learned is that you and your brothers are tied in to the killing."

She shook her head. Those full lips were tight in frustration. "Think what you like, Marshal. You have no idea what's happening."

"It's a gamble you lost," I said.

"Listen." Her voice was urgent. I almost believed she wasn't acting. "Just wait a week. That's all I'm asking."

"One week. Then what?"

"Then I'll deliver everything. Seven days won't make a difference to the dead men."

"Why not now?" I persisted.

"I've risked everything just to warn you."

I snorted sarcasm. "Because of my pretty face, no doubt."

"Listen to yourself. Arrogant, insufferable. So centered on yourself that you need to somehow believe I'm here because of you."

She spun on her heel and pointed at me. "Chew this. Just happened that I did think it'd be a pleasure to try honey as a way to make my request. But I'm here for me. Two men already dead, three including the cowboy that died out there with you today. I don't want it on my conscience that a fourth followed, and I don't care if that fourth is old, young, ugly, fat, or stupid."

She stopped to draw a breath, then raged on. "Instead, with that smirk on your face, right now's when I start praying the next person dead is you."

She stomped past me.

I clamped her wrist. She was mad enough, she almost pulled me from the chair.

"You know the murderer," I said, equally fierce. "Tell me who it is. Whether or not I win your popularity contest."

"Good night," she said.

"You're under arrest."

She laughed. A nasty laugh, this time. "Under arrest for what?"

"Accomplice to the murder."

"You have a witness to swear I told you anything I did? Or do you want me to start screaming for help right now?"

I dropped her wrist.

She reached the door. Smiled sweet venom at me. Then slammed it shut with a force that made me grateful not to have paintings on the wall.

As I lay in the dark, my mind worked through all the implications of Dehlia's words. She'd as much as admitted that she knew the murderer and why the men had been murdered. She'd gone as far as accepting some of the blame for their deaths.

Couldn't I somehow tie that in with the scattered pieces of information I'd managed to glean over the last few days?

I didn't make the attempt.

Whenever I managed to think beyond the pain of my leg, my mind returned instead to my worry and fear and love for Rebecca. Every night here in Laramie I counted the time that would pass until I reached her next spring, took out and polished every memory I had of her, and fell asleep filled with mingled sadness and hope.

I could not sleep.

I threw the covers back and hobbled to the uncurtained window of the bedroom.

The cool air of the open window did little to ease my frustration. Dehlia had made it clear a kiss was there for the taking, and it had led me to wonder if Rebecca had faced the same temptations as Evening Star among the Sioux. What if I was being the fool here while she gave her love to others there?

Jealousy flitted close.

I told myself I was being irrational. I told myself that I was working myself into a frenzy. I told myself to sleep.

But when dawn broke and gray began to fill the bedroom, I was still sitting on my bed, legs in front to ease the pain, exhaustion not even enough to shut out my thoughts.

Next spring seemed too far away.

CHAPTER 25

AT SOME POINT, I did doze.

When I woke, mouth dry, knives of pain in my leg, I remembered what I had intended to do until the powerful distraction of Dehlia's presence—read the contents of Doc's envelope, tucked into the back pocket of my torn pants.

I went for the jug in the kitchen first, splashing cold water against my face to remove the chalky exhaustion that hurt my eyeballs. I kindled a small fire in the potbelly, set a pot of coffee to brew. Then I drank near a quart of water, which reminded my system of all the water I'd taken in the previous evening, so I hopped and cussed each step to the privy, and hopped and cussed each step back.

The sun was bright by then, and for a moment, I wondered about Brother Lewis. He'd been alone in the marshal's office almost twenty-four hours. I only wondered briefly, for I knew I had more to complain about than he did, and contemplating his suffering improved my mood.

I took my time dressing. Noticed the sweat didn't pop out near as much. Then I tracked down an old set of boots, as I had no urge to continue wearing a set with only one heel.

Coffee was good and strong by the time I had a mug and was able to set myself in the chair that in earlier darkness had supported Dehlia Christopher.

I read the letter first.

August 26, 1874
Dear Mr. Calhoun,

I appreciate your willingness to go above and beyond the normal call of bank duty, especially in light of the suspicions we share.

I have enclosed sufficient, and I hope generous, funds to defray the expenses you might face. Receipts will not be necessary; if I cannot trust you, there is no one I can turn to with any certainty.

I feel the urge to repeat, even after our lengthy discussion, the caution you must use. I have also changed my mind since our discussion—please do not risk being openly seen asking questions.

As to your kind advice, please know that I have changed the will to safeguard myself as you suggested.

Yours sincerely,
Eleanor Ford

The telegram shed no light on this letter. It was dated four days later and simply said: "RETURN AT ONCE STOP." The telegram had been sent from Laramie, and received in Denver, signed for by L. Calhoun.

I reread it.

Denver?

I turned the envelope upside down, shook it. Four train ticket stubs fell into my palm. I knew before I looked what the stubs would tell me. Laramie-Cheyenne, Cheyenne-Denver, Denver-Cheyenne, Cheyenne-Laramie. Lorne Calhoun had gone to Denver from Laramie and back at the request of Eleanor Ford.

Bob Nichols had returned from Denver, anxious not to see his wife, but Eleanor Ford. The Rebels owned new saddles made in Denver, and I had to recall no further than Dehlia's visit hours earlier to understand that these Rebels were involved.

Denver. I could no longer avoid it. Or who might be waiting for me there.

———

Jake Wilson rose from my chair as I hobbled through the doorway of the marshal's office.

"Talked Mayor Crawfish into giving me a spare key late yesterday afternoon when you hadn't made it back," Jake said from behind my desk. "Then I heard from Doc, and we figured you might need some help, what with your leg and all."

I wasn't listening to Jake. I was looking beyond him at the cell and Preacher Lewis.

"Oh that," he said as he noticed the focus of my attention. "Your prisoner tends to aggravate a man. He complained about supper. Same with breakfast. I don't appreciate food thrown at me. And yelling gives me a headache."

I scratched my head. "But a . . ."

"Horse? Does fill the cell, don't it? You'll notice your preacher friend ain't saying much. This horse, as I was careful to explain to him, is about as high-strung as piano wire. Sometimes just a sneeze sets him off. Bucks, kicks, throws himself like he's been possessed. I've seen that horse tear apart a stall in minutes."

I grinned in admiration at the huge black horse that stood in the center of that cramped jail cell.

Pressed against the wall, Brother Lewis had room to stand, but not much. If he wanted to lie down on his mattress, or sit on the end of it, he could do that too. It boggled my mind, however, to imagine how that space would disappear quick if the horse took it into his mind to prance, even a little.

Brother Lewis glared at my grin. He didn't, however, so much as whisper his disapproval.

"I have apologized to your preacher man repeatedly," Jake said. "Last night, one of my fool stable hands fed the horse a goodly portion of cabbage."

Jake shook his head in sympathy. "Fearful, how cabbage will bloat a horse. Why, if that horse weren't able to air itself out every five minutes, it would probably die right there in jail."

Jake waved his hat several times to emphasize exactly how that gas affected him. "Marshal, I consider myself fortunate to be able to step outside when it happens. A well-mannered prisoner might be invited to join me in the fresh air, but I don't hardly see how that might be possible with this preacher man."

"You've shown fine judgment, Jake."

He beamed.

"Except for one thing, Jake."

He squinted.

"Don't you figure a judge might consider this to be cruel and unusual punishment?"

"Well, Samuel, I—"

"After all, Jake, that horse didn't do no wrong."

CHAPTER 26

"TOWN COUNCIL HAS JUST HIRED itself a deputy," I announced to Crawford as I stepped inside his office without knocking and without saying hello. I laid my cane across the edge of his desk and sat down opposite him, also un-asked.

"On whose say-so?" He left the cane where it was.

"Yours."

Crawford capped his fountain pen and set it on top of the papers he'd been reading. His suit jacket hung on a coat hook behind him, and his belly pushed hard at his vest. His sleeves were rolled up, and he left his fat fore-arms on his desk, his hands flat and palms down each side of the papers. He stared at me for a few seconds.

I smiled. Told myself to keep smiling as if I held four aces and was about to show. "It's going to come to light, your doings with Eleanor Ford. Best thing for you is to appear to bend over backward in assisting me."

His hands flopped briefly, like the dying spasm of a beached fish. "Eleanor Ford? She's a customer. There's nothing there to come to light."

His twitchy hands, however, had rewarded my shot in the dark.

"No? I'm sorry to have bothered you, Mayor Crawford."

I pushed myself to my feet, took my cane, and slowly turned. The leg hurt, but Doc had been right in his prediction. Now the wound only felt like a deep, deep bruise.

"Where are you going?" Crawford's voice was tinged with the worry and suspicion that an innocent man would not have shown.

"Newspaper office." I took another slow step.

"Why?" he called to my back.

I stopped in the doorway of his office. Used the cane to make a tottering half-turn so that I faced him again. "Why? Newspapers print news. I figure if you don't want to answer to me here, soon enough you'll have a good chance to do it public."

"Sit down, Marshal."

When I was comfortable in the chair I had just left, he leaned forward. Tried to give me a look of confidence. Didn't work. Not with new sweat shiny on his forehead. Not with his face showing the appearance of a deer held by a lantern's shine.

"Marshal, I'd like the chance to straighten out your confusion."

"You're a considerate man. Tell me about you and Eleanor."

"Tell me what you know."

I began to push myself to my feet.

"This ain't fair, Marshal. In a small town like this, hearsay can kill a bank. Once people lose faith, there's a run on their deposits. Any unsubstantiated rumor—and that's what the newspaper would print—will squeeze the lifeblood from the First National."

I lowered myself again. "You have my sympathy," I said. "Trouble is two men died in your bank, and I think you're hiding something. If that's all I have to take down the street, that's what I'll tell."

He jerked his head in surprise. "Two men dead? I thought you'd solved that. And what does this have to do with my dealings with Eleanor Ford?"

My turn for surprise. Crawford was a poor poker player. If it hadn't occurred to him that there was a connection, what exactly *was* he hiding?

"Crawford, yesterday someone shot me from my horse. That someone hasn't forgotten about the bank vault murders. Which means I won't."

Crawford uncapped his pen. Capped it. Uncapped it again. The light clicks of his movements were the only noise in his office.

"Start with Nichols," I said. "You refused him a loan this summer. Why?"

Click. Click. Click.

"Come on, Crawford. I'm close enough to all this that someone wants me dead. I will get the rest. If I get it without your help, I'll do everything I can to substantiate as many rumors as it takes to shut you down."

Click. Click. Click. He was moving the cap faster. Unaware of it.

I thought back to his nervousness during our first discussion in this office.

"Who else had access to the vault?"

"Just Calhoun." He was too miserable to be believable.

I tried another shot in the dark. "Eleanor Ford?"

He stopped the clicking with his pen cap. Looked down at his desk. Nodded. "But it couldn't be her," Crawford said.

"That's why I didn't tell you. She had no reason to steal any money."

"Anybody could have a reason," I said. "Why is it that she could get into the vault at night?"

"For the same reason she wouldn't steal money from the First National." Crawford raised his head. "She owns most of it."

"What?"

"No one knows. She wants it to stay that way. So do I."

I understood his sentiment. If folks knew he was more an employee than banker, especially employee to a woman, he wouldn't be able to convince them of his importance. It would take a lot of fun out of rolling those five names of his from those fat lips.

"Eleanor Ford owns most of the First National." I was musing aloud, but Crawford took it as doubt.

"Leonard Phillips, her first husband, put most of the money into starting the bank," Crawford said. "When Phillips died, his shares passed on to her."

"She spend much time overlooking your work?"

"No need to," Crawford said quickly. "She doesn't know banking, and I do."

"Convenient, then, that Phillips passed on to give you full reins around here."

"Not for her," Crawford said. I noticed the unspoken implication that it *had* been convenient for him. "She wanted his share in cash. She wanted to move back East."

"Why didn't you oblige?"

"It was impossible."

When I asked why, Crawford explained. He became animated as he spoke, and his sheen of fear evaporated. Whatever he was and however pompous outside of this office, I soon understood that he knew and loved the business of banking, especially because he began by outlining bank history, and much to my surprise, he was able to make it interesting.

He said Congress had established two national banks by charter, one in the late 1700s and one in the early 1800s. Both charters had essentially failed, and without government restraints, many banks had collapsed because of greed, accepting too many risky loans against too little cash reserve. It was in 1863, Crawford told me, that the federal government started a system of chartering banks that required them to back their loan notes by government securities.

It meant that prudence was enforced by law. For every thousand dollars deposited into Crawford's, he could lend no more than nine hundred dollars; if he was caught with less than a ten percent reserve, he would lose his charter.

Crawford went on to tell me that in a town as small as Laramie, nine hundred dollars would be immediately spent at another local business—for why would someone borrow money unless they had a need for it? Whoever received that money would then redeposit the bulk of it at the First National. That would give Crawford a new deposit of, say, eight hundred dollars, of which he could turn around and lend ninety percent, or seven hundred and twenty, immediately spent at another business. He'd expect about six hundred of that to be redeposited, which left him five hundred and forty to lend. And so on. Crawford called it the fractional reserve system.

I allowed as that seemed to mean that the original thousand dollar deposit could—despite the Federal Reserve policy of ten percent—be lent out so many times that he might end up with five or six thousand dollars in loans.

Crawford smiled at that, told me in an ideal world he'd be able to squeeze that original deposit into ten thousand dollars worth of business. Then he frowned and said that competition made it less than ideal, which meant he generally expected the deposit multiplier to be closer to two than ten.

I whistled. "Not bad business. Start a bank with fifty grand and make interest on a hundred grand worth of loans."

"Something like that," he said. Now his smile was the indulgent humor of someone teaching a boy in school the ABCs. "But when Leonard Phillips followed the rail into Laramie, he gambled most of what he owned from the East to start his ranch and charter this bank. It was a good investment, considering what the railroad has done for Laramie."

"How much did he invest in the First National?"

"A quarter million," Crawford said. Cool, as if those kinds of numbers didn't rattle him.

"A quarter million dollars," I repeated slowly. A quarter of a million dollars when a cowhand made only a dollar a day. I could not fathom that much money owned by one man, pooled in one place, nor that much money dispersed in a complicated system of loans, bank accounts, and bookkeeping. And this was Laramie, a dusty town tucked lonely on the plains between two mountain ranges. How much bigger and more complicated in Denver? New York? Washington?

"Folks sit where you sit," Crawford said. "They want one hundred, two hundred dollars. They can't see the picture I do. To them, life's no more than the house they want to build. Cattle they need to buy. They can't understand why I'm so hardhearted. A bank depends on the faith of its depositors. If they lose faith, or if I make too many bad loans, everything collapses. Laramie could weather a failure of the First National, but a lot of people would be hurt bad along the way."

I nodded. It did make it different, trying to see it from Crawford's point of view. I hadn't respected Crawford because he was short, fat, and fearful of most of the things I'd learned to defeat. I hadn't realized in his own territory he was as tough and smart as the best bronc riders and quickest gunmen.

"Crawford," I said, "I'll tell you square right now. If your hands are clean on these bank vault murders, I'll do everything I can to make sure no dirt gets smeared on you or the First National."

He nodded. Vigorously.

"If not," I continued, "I'm going to consider every lie I hear from you as a personal insult. And treat you accordingly."

His Adam's apple bulged as he swallowed. "It's a deal."

"Good. Part of that deal is that my new deputy is Jake Wilson." I couldn't avoid a sheepish grin. "And, Mayor, this time I'm asking, not telling."

"One-Arm Wilson? But he's—"

"*Jake* Wilson's a good man. Could you see to it that Town Council approves his salary? Shouldn't be a problem. Until I got here, they had a petty thief named Smickles for deputy and seemed happy enough to have him around."

"Jake Wilson, then," Crawford said with reluctance. "I hope you know what you're doing."

With Jake, yes. With just about everything else, no. Which is why I needed Crawford to answer the questions he avoided so far.

"Start with Bob Nichols," I suggested. "Why'd you refuse him a loan this year? Why'd you keep that fact from me?"

Crawford took a deep breath. "I'm telling you this because I'm going to trust you. I refused him the loan because the First National was low on cash reserves. I didn't tell you first time around for the same reason I didn't explain my decision to Nichols. Do I want that kind of information getting around town? No. A bank is built on faith and—"

I laughed admiration at Crawford's single-mindedness. "I see where you're leading that herd," I said. "Tell me about Eleanor Ford. Why's she still in Laramie?"

"That original quarter million is buried so deeply in loans, there's no way she can draw it back out. Leonard Phillips's fortune, which turned to her on his death, is cattle and bank shares. Not much cash. I don't have enough money that I can buy her out myself. We've been trying to find a buyer for a couple of years now. And that's another thing. Word gets out she's trying to sell, a lot of folks get nervous, and when they get nervous, they lose faith in the bank, and when that happens . . ."

I waved him silent. He smiled shyly, understanding the humor in my mock disgust.

"How could you find a buyer with that kind of money in Laramie?" I asked. "Or expect to keep it secret?"

"Laramie! I couldn't think of anything worse! Laramie's the last place we'd try to find a major stockholder in the First National."

I remembered the train ticket stubs.

"Don't tell me," I guessed. "Denver."

He gave me a strange look. That told me enough. But he confirmed it anyway.

"Denver? How'd you possibly know?"

I wondered how much I should tell Crawford about what I knew. Maybe he'd be able to shed some light on why Eleanor Ford had directed Calhoun to Denver on her behalf.

On the other hand, I still wasn't sure that Crawford had told me everything. What he had told me, I believed in my bones, was truth. Yet I couldn't shake the feeling there was more. His banking world was a complicated one, and I couldn't hope to understand enough to beat him at that game.

"How'd you possibly guess?" he repeated.

"More than one reason," I replied. I'd just decided to ask Crawford to take me on faith with that answer, when a loud rap of knuckles on the door took both our attentions from the conversation.

It was Jake. "Mayor Crawf—"

"Jake, *Mayor* Crawford has just appointed you deputy." I'd just learned a good lesson about the politics of honey versus vinegar. Jake and I would talk about Mayor Crawfish as soon as convenient. "So whatever business you're reporting is now official."

With his good hand, Jake tipped his hat at Mayor Crawford. He then looked anxiously in my direction.

"Yes, Jake?"

"Marshal . . ." He looked at Crawford again, back at me. He was hopping on his toes so bad, it appeared he wanted to ask permission to visit the privy.

"You'll excuse me?" I asked Crawford.

Crawford nodded.

I led Jake out to the sidewalk in front of the First National.

We both tipped our hats at the two ladies we'd nearly bumped as we stepped into the sunshine.

"Yes, Jake."

"I arranged for extra help to do my chores in the livery. Then I moved the horse out of the cell, like you asked."

"Probably took some work, if it was as lazy as you told me."

"It hasn't kicked in years. Your preacher man don't know that, of course, and I have a good feeling he won't be raising his voice much, not when he knows he can have that horse back with him any time he gets lonely."

"Did you get the photographs, too?" I asked.

"First thing. Just as you figured, Keller keeps all the negatives of his portraits."

"Good. What's the real news?"

He grinned. "This deputy work is real soft. Beats shoveling—"

"Same stuff you're throwing in my direction now. What's the real news?"

"Soft work, like I tried to say. It was a real pleasure keeping an eye on that lady friend of yours."

"And? Quit dragging this out, Jake. You were fit to be busted back in the bank."

"She spent some time in the Red Rose, talking quiet-like to her brothers." He grinned wolfishly. "I put my beer on your account, being as I was there official."

"Sure," I said with little enthusiasm. " 'Cause if you weren't drinking beer, she'd wonder why you were there."

Jake reached into his pocket and pulled out a couple of crumpled bank notes. "Keep your crying hanky in your pocket, Sam. I played poker in there, too, just to blend in as good as possible. Here's half the money I made on a full house, queens high."

He gave me the notes. Caught the surprise on my face. "This ain't charity. Had I lost, you'd have covered the pot."

"Wonderful, Jake."

"I reckon."

Good man, he was, but I'd have to train him to recognize sarcasm.

"Anyway," he continued, "Dehlia's next stop was the train depot. Left her brothers behind and marched right down the street. Easy woman to follow, wearing pants like that. Marshal, there's a certain beauty when all a woman's parts move together that smooth. Why—"

"How much time do I have, Jake?"

"What?"

"No passenger train this morning. She wasn't headed there to find someone. Only reason could be she wants a ticket. And I imagine you inquired as soon as was conven-ient."

I gave him a wolfish grin to match his best. "So when's she leave for Denver?"

Jake shook his head. "Marshal, you know something you ain't let on. Or you're just plain spooky smart. Either way, remind me to stay on your good side."

"This afternoon's train?"

"Yup."

So that was it. Denver. Now I didn't have a choice.

"Jake," I said, "you take care whilst I'm gone."

CHAPTER 27

HAD IT ONLY BEEN two months since I rode this same passenger train from Laramie, east to Cheyenne? Then, I thought a woman was hidden on the train, following me. Now I was hidden, following a woman. Then, the plains that led to the mountain hills were dry, but not burned brown, the tops of the occasional cottonwood a dusty green, not the oranges and reds of fall.

I gazed out the window of my sleeping compartment at the fall colors as the train chugged slowly upward into the divide that would lead down again into Cheyenne.

A sleeping compartment guaranteed me privacy, guaranteed that Dehlia Christopher would not see me either before Cheyenne or before she stepped down onto the train platform in Denver.

What I would do from there, I didn't know with certainty.

I'd wired ahead to Denver to have a Pinkerton man follow Dehlia when she left the train.

I'd visit the lawyer that Helen Nichols had mentioned.

I also had the photos of Nichols and Calhoun that Jake had procured from Keller's Photo Portraits. I'd ask around at hotels on the hope I might meet someone who remembered one or the other. Denver was big, but not that big it would be a hopeless task.

I could not guess what all of this might accomplish. My job until then was to remain unseen in the sleeping compartment.

The train swayed as it clicked along the tracks, and I decided a nap would not be a poor idea. My leg still pained me and it could use the rest. Dehlia would not be leaving the train for some time anyway. And my gritty eyeballs reminded me of how little sleep I'd received the night before.

I stretched out on the cramped bunk. Naturally, with the luxury of so much leisure in front of me, I could not sleep. I ended up thinking about the late-morning conversation I'd had with Mayor Crawford.

It had opened my eyes to a world I'd never considered. It astounded me that—even in Laramie barely beyond its frontier days—money shifted and turned at the demand of a complexity of documents and regulations that reached invisibly all those miles across the Great Plains from Washington. Here a man's life and death still often depended on his brains and guts and quickness, yet unless he lived completely off the land, and whether he acknowledged it or not, the lawmakers two thousand miles east still determined the direction of his life, because the supply of money affected every occupation we used to carve out our livings.

Doc's voice reached me again. I could hear him pointing out how I was a fool to be surprised at my surprise to learn something new.

This time—especially with nothing else to distract me—I gave Doc's voice full respect.

That feather. Sure, I knew lots about it. Came from a sparrow. Small feathers kept the sparrow warm. Big feathers from a wing gave it lift. I could measure that feather, weigh it, maybe even with Doc's microscope look at it close and tell how all the strands fit together. If I worked real hard, I bet I could have come up with a list as long as my arm of things I knew for sure about that feather.

But what about the other list? Things I *didn't* know about that feather.

How'd the first feather ever get made? After all, logic told me that birds could not have existed forever. At some point, no matter how far back you went, birds didn't exist. So how did it come about, that very first bird? Why? Crows had different colored feathers from partridges. Why? Even if I could explain the mechanism that made a feather grow from water and seed into a certain color and a certain shape, could I know the answer to how that mechanism had come into existence? Or why?

When I started to consider those angles about a stupid feather, I felt small.

And that was just a feather. What about leaves of a tree? Stars above. A newborn calf bawling for its mama. Spider stretching its web.

What if I drew up a list of everything I knew? Then compared it to a list of what I didn't know. The second list would be as long as these tracks, maybe, as long as . . .

I shook my head in disgust at where Doc's convoluted logic was taking me.

I couldn't even know how long the list might be. I couldn't comprehend what I didn't know.

That, I reckoned, didn't place me much differently than a baby at the edge of a lake, running his hands in the sand, happy enough, he wouldn't wonder that the water at his feet came from a lake. Nor would the baby understand if you tried pointing out the mountains past the lake. Or try to explain he needed a blanket to shade him from the sun. Nope. With sand to keep him happy, what more could there be?

To this point, all that I knew about surviving on the prairies had been enough knowledge that, like the baby, I hadn't considered there might be something beyond the shoreline at my feet.

What *was* beyond? How infinite was God? Was I as truly incapable of knowing as that baby was ignorant of what lay ahead of his first tottering steps?

I got the edge of that thought, and I decided I didn't like it much, the black gulf of infinity ahead.

It wasn't fair.

Much against my will, a few months back, Rebecca and a host of other questions had led me to a wary belief and understanding that God was the light of love that gave meaning to my life. I didn't want to be called a believer—too many of them ran around spouting verse and chapter and played it like a game with rules—but when I'd searched, I'd been found by a quiet peace and an understanding of a God of love behind this universe.

That's why it didn't seem fair that when I'd thought I had a few answers, there were only more questions. No wonder so many chose to simply cling to church rules and regulations.

Then another thought struck me. And I grinned upward at the wood paneling of the compartment ceiling.

I'd slap Doc with these questions. Give him a taste of the medicine he'd used to dose me. See how he might squirm.

It must have been a comforting thought, for when I closed my eyes, I slept solid until the train lurched to a stop to draw water at the top of the divide. I was asleep again before the train moved on.

If a man wanted to lose himself, Denver was the place. Territory capital of Colorado since '67, fueled in a spreading bonfire of growth by railroad and then a silver mining boom. The saying was if it couldn't be bought, stolen, or borrowed in Denver, then it couldn't be bought, stolen, or borrowed.

Cheyenne, where we'd transferred from the Union Pacific line to the Denver Pacific, had five thousand already and dwarfed Laramie, reflected by a depot crowd that had made it easy to watch and follow Dehlia unobserved as she boarded the southbound train.

Denver in turn dwarfed Cheyenne.

I stayed in my compartment as passengers disembarked at the Denver station. Even from there, I felt crushed by the noise and confusion that bustled outside my window. Boys hawked newspapers, girls hawked cigarettes and cigars, porters hawked luggage service, and men with horse and buggy hawked carriage rides.

I was glad that I'd wired ahead to the Pinkerton agency a description of Dehlia and her expected arrival time. Denver had exploded in size since I'd last visited, and not even with two good legs instead of a hobble could I have expected to stay with Dehlia as she made her way into the crowds, for I would have had to remain in plain view almost beside her to do it.

As it was, I only got a glimpse of her as she stepped off the train and beckoned for a porter to take her luggage. Then she disappeared into the crowds.

I stood to a relaxed stretch. The Pinkerton man would stay with her, for she was an easy target in those black jeans and with the figure and blond hair that snapped heads from all sides.

Halfway through my stretch, I froze.

I hadn't seen his face—he'd stepped down too quickly from the train and was moving away from me, wearing a black full-length coat and a Montana Stetson that gave me a glimpse of thick, wavy dark hair.

But from behind my train window, I did recognize those boots.

Snakeskin.

Unless I missed my guess, those were the same boots I'd seen hidden behind a wardrobe in the Union Pacific Hotel back in Laramie.

CHAPTER *28*

THE BROADWAY HOTEL STOOD, as Helen Nichols had told me earlier, near the bank of Cherry Creek, not far down from the South Platte. Here, the buildings were cramped together on the flat plains that ended abruptly just west of Denver, where the sheer walls of the Rockies stretched to peaks some fourteen thousand feet high.

I could see the pale blue of those mountains from the second-floor veranda outside my room at the Broadway, just as I could look down from that veranda at the wide streets that ran straight furrows between the cramped buildings. Denver was permanent enough that many of the buildings were brick, not wood, but civilization had not encroached so far that the streets were more than mud and dirt.

I leaned on my cane as I walked to the stairs at the south end of the hotel. I was here at the Broadway because Bob Nichols had stayed here, and I was hoping I might see or hear of something that would have been significant to him, a Wyoming rancher.

I'd shown his photo while I was checking in the night before, but the hotel clerk hadn't remembered seeing him. The clerk, however, had been happy to prattle about other things.

Like these stairs. He'd explained how the stairs and this entire end of the hotel had actually overhung the rain-swollen torrents of Cherry Creek as it ate away the bank during the spring flood of '64, with that water just inches from touching the hotel itself. I had—as was obligated with such folklore—expressed admiring disbelief, for Cherry Creek in the fall hardly seemed capable of drowning a trussed cat. The clerk had assured me of the truth of his tale and added that the creek that May had also washed away a sawmill, a church, a newspaper, and several stores, as well as City Hall and all its records, not to mention twenty drowned Denverites, including the mother of the wife of a friend's friend who'd been taken almost from her bed itself and whose death had been the disaster's only silver lining for the surviving in-laws.

I'd departed long before the flood of '64. My last summer in Denver had been '58, at a dance hall belonging to the first and only woman I had loved before meeting Rebecca years later.

On the train ride here, it had been strong in my mind, curiosity about Clara's dance hall.

At the hotel desk, I'd nearly asked the clerk if it still stood near the section of town where the red lights twinkled at dusk's first darkness. I'd managed to refrain from expressing that curiosity, however. Instead, I had contented myself by promising I would allow myself to stroll past it, if given the chance, but that I would definitely not step inside.

I reached the end of the veranda and tested my left leg with a slow step downward onto the stairs. Pain, all right, but an itchy pain, like stretching and testing the leg would feel good. I decided to turn around and leave my cane in the room. The less attention I might draw to myself, the better.

Five minutes later, I was in the smoky eatery next door to the Broadway Hotel. Leather eggs and rock-hard bread made me homesick for the Chinaman, but were a good excuse to eat slow as I waited for Allan Pinkerton's man to deliver word on Dehlia Christopher.

———

Allan Pinkerton's man was thin and old and small and smiled apology from below a gray bushy mustache, as if he expected me to protest that he was thin and old and small.

"You're Keaton," he said as he pulled up a chair to sit at the table. "I know because I was looking for the scar. Desk clerk tipped me on it."

"I'm Keaton." I pushed my plate aside and stood to shake his hand.

"Kels Madden. As you might be able to tell, I've been with the agency since we were one office in Chicago. I get the lighter stuff now. The youngsters get cases like the James Brothers. Suits me fine. I don't need to be a hero."

He removed his hat and set it in his lap as he sat. His hair was as bushy as his mustache, rumpled by sweat. In his dark jacket, he seemed like a cheerful mouse.

"But like I always say," he continued. "There's old bulls and there's young bulls."

"Yeah?" I'd heard it before but didn't have the heart to stop him.

"See, an old bull and a young bull were on a hillside, looking down at a bunch of cows. Young bull says, hey, let's run down and chase with one or two. Old bull says, naw, let's *walk* down and chase them all."

I shook my head and smiled. "I'll remember that," I said. "I hope it didn't take much running to stay with the woman off the train."

"Nope," he said. "She wasn't hard to find. And I blend

in good with crowds. She took a carriage ride, and I followed in one behind. You'll find a receipt, of course."

"Of course."

"From the train station, I spent maybe ten minutes trailing that woman," he said. "That was it. She didn't go no place else but the fancy mansion up on Banker's Row."

"Banker's Row."

"Not the street's real name, but no one calls it anything but Banker's Row. Unless you own a bank or a mine, you don't own a house there. Some of them are bigger than hotels."

I nodded as I absorbed that.

"And she stayed all night," he said.

"You stood outside and waited?" I tried to imagine this man hiding in a tree somewhere nearby, shivering away the night coldness of fall in Colorado.

He shook his head. "Youngster might do that. But how do you cover all the exits from a house that big? I hopped out of the carriage as soon as I could, went round back that mansion, and had a talk with one of the cook's maids. Big black woman. I even sweet-talked her into a cut of fresh bread." He flashed a grin from beneath that bushy mustache. "Bribe helped, too."

Another grin. "Couldn't get a receipt on it, though. You'll have to trust me on that part of your bill."

Any man of Pinkerton's could be trusted. I didn't protest.

"The maid can't be expected to know the comings and goings of visitors."

"Well, Marshal, here's where you get your money's worth. That blond woman, she wasn't no visitor."

"Interesting," I said. And it was. *Dehlia Christopher, the daughter of a banking or mining magnate? Why the brothers in Rebel gray? Why. . . ?*

"You do take the fun out of a surprise," Kels interrupted my thoughts. He brightened. "I got more that oughta draw a flicker from that poker face of your'n."

Difficult to stay uninvolved with the man's sunny disposition. "You're telling me that I'll be happy to pay your bill?" I asked with a smile.

"Yup. I don't know what your game is, but it's obvious you don't know much about her. And it's a big enough game you'd stay with her from Laramie."

"I hope you're not adding this detective work onto the bill."

"Naw. Just feeling around. A hard habit to break."

"So what else did you learn?"

"Dehlia Girard showed up at the front door two months ago. Long lost daughter, the maid told me." He was watching me carefully. "Hah! I knew you'd flinch."

He was right. "Girard?" I could hardly move my mouth, it'd slammed open so wide with surprise.

"Instructions on the telegram hadn't said more than follow, but it hadn't taken much, so I did extra."

I was leaning forward now, my coffee getting cold. "Girard," I repeated. "Dehlia Girard. Not Dehlia Christopher."

"Her father's David Girard—vice president at Denver First." A sly shake of the head. "If you want to believe the story she told when she showed up. And the maid didn't. None of the help do."

"Slow down," I said. "I'm going to buy you breakfast, and you're going to tell me all of it."

He did between mouthfuls.

Late spring it had been when Dehlia Girard appeared at the mansion. She'd waited in the front hall for hours before David appeared in the early evening. She'd run forward and thrown herself into his arms, crying out, "Papa, Papa!"—the first indication to anybody in the mansion about why she had insisted on waiting.

The story came out shortly after, delivered by David Girard himself. Dehlia was the daughter of his first wife, a woman he'd lost to Yankee soldiers early in the Civil War. Dehlia had been taken in by his sister and her husband, then been lost and given up for dead when that family's farm, too, had been overrun. Dehlia had wandered away in a stream of refugees, been adopted by a passing family, and after all these years, had finally tracked down her father.

The story sounded thin to me.

I wasn't the only one. Mrs. Lesley Girard, a few years older than her husband David, found little in the tale to bring her joy. And inviting into her house a beautiful younger woman as a permanent houseguest brought her even less joy. The maid reported that all of the servants felt on a daily basis a considerable tension because of Mrs. Lesley Girard's dislike of the new arrangement.

Kels Madden informed me of even more that I found of interest.

Mrs. Lesley Girard was the moneyed one, part of a line of wealth that had grown each generation since her forefathers had begun the banking industry in Boston. David had married her about five years before, and with the marriage, he had taken on the title of vice president at Denver First.

When I asked why Mrs. Girard tolerated such a story, Kels Madden grinned and told me he'd asked the same thing.

It was of vast amusement to the servants, he said, Mrs. Lesley Girard's infatuation with David Girard. She was a granite-hearted town leader, society pillar, and shrewd businesswoman, yet she simpered and cooed around her darling husband.

I asked if there had been rumors about David and his so-called daughter.

Kels nodded appreciation at that obvious question and told me that no, there'd been nothing to point to more than her claimed story. Except for two things, as the maid had archly mentioned. One, David Girard and Dehlia Girard made it appear frosty between them at the mansion, as if they were working extra hard to dispel any notion of romance. And two, David Girard did spend a lot of time away from the mansion. On business in Cheyenne, he always explained.

That was all that Kels Madden had for me.

I counted out bank notes to pay his bill and then asked as casual as I could. "If a fellow was looking for fun, would you recommend the Gold Slipper?"

He looked at me strange. "Gold Slipper. How'd you know about the Gold Slipper?"

"Dance hall, right?"

"Sure," he said, "but it burned down over ten years ago."

"Oh." I wasn't going to ask about—

"Clara Johnson," he said, another smile lighting his wizened face. "You can't know about her. You're too much of a pup. And it's been near twenty years. She was a legend here. Broke all our hearts when she went respectable on us."

"Just heard about her once in passing," I said. "At a campfire, from an old cowboy on the trail."

"Well, son," Kels said. "You tell that old cowboy that Clara Johnson is now Clara Lanigan. And she and her husband run the best restaurant in Denver, by the name of the English House."

"Sure," I said. "I'll pass that on."

He stood, spry for someone so thin and small and old. He tipped his hat, gave me a final grin, and left me alone at my table.

The English House. I'd walk by. Maybe. But I wouldn't take a meal there. Not a chance.

CHAPTER 29

A. L. LEAKEY HAD THE CORNER OFFICE of the second floor. Directly below him was the funeral home that belonged to an undertaker by the name of Frank Morgen. I knew, because I'd had to walk through it to find the stairs that led to Leakey's office. By the considerable industry at the undertaker's, and by the lawyer's own admission, Leakey was in the wrong profession.

I sat in the chair opposite a scarred, unvarnished desk in Leakey's cramped office. He stood at his office window, hands behind his back, shoulders slumped, staring down on the street.

"It's not so much that the undertaker will never run out of clients," Leakey said glumly. "It's that he gets his money up front and gets to stiff the clients—good one, huh, *stiff* them?—when they're so upset or guilty or"— Leakey turned to me and shook his head— "happy, maybe with a big inheritance, that no one complains at his prices. Worse, some days it stinks so bad up here, with what he uses to pickle the bodies, that I can hardly breathe."

Leakey was blond, thin haired, of medium height and medium build. With his dark vest and suit, he was remarkable only for the dark gravy stains on his tie and a waxed handlebar mustache that he now twirled between the thumb and forefinger of his right hand.

"Can't be all that bad," I offered. "I noticed your sign below where folks couldn't miss. 'Wills contested, no up-front fee.'"

"It does bring in some business," Leakey agreed. He'd missed the dryness in my voice and taken my comment as encouragement. I wasn't surprised. Nothing about this man suggested intelligence. "I'd like the sign bigger, but Morgen says not. As if he should care. The best move he made was buying land for a cemetery. The way Denver's busting at the seams, it now costs as much for a grave as it cost five years ago for a house plot. It galls me to no end, sitting in my office, smelling his pickle juices, and knowing he's making so much money that—"

"Bob Nichols," I said. "Mining papers that belonged to his brother. Remember him?"

Leakey's mouth snapped shut and his lips disappeared in a tight line. "Yes, I do. And he's long past making a claim now. He signed everything a month ago, and legally it makes no difference what's been found since. So if you're here to—"

"Nichols is dead."

"Oh." Leakey brightened. "Oh."

Leakey smiled and extended his hand. "Who'd you say you were?"

I hadn't. Leakey'd done all the talking since I'd walked into his office.

"Samuel Keaton." I had an urge to wash my hand after Leakey released his grip—and I could recall not having that same urge once after being elbow deep in a cow to pull loose a calf.

I smiled through my distaste, reminding myself how I'd learned with Crawford that honey works better than vinegar. I spoke through that smile. "I'm here to ask you about when you saw Nichols last."

"Because . . ." Leakey's smile turned into a frown of suspicion.

Because I've got time to kill, have no real idea of what to do next, and I prefer to grasp at straws, even if the straw is a third-rate lawyer with no clients. But I didn't say that.

"Because," I said, "his wife said he learned something in this office that got him killed."

That wasn't true, of course, but I had a suspicion Leakey wouldn't tell me anything unless he saw something in it for him. Since I wasn't offering money, maybe he'd be willing to help if he thought it could avoid him trouble.

He stared at me. Evidently, I was wrong to think that the prospect of trouble would worry him at all.

"Look," I said, "I'll give you half of what she's paying me." Which, with a copper piece, would buy him no more than a cup of coffee.

He smiled a Congressman's smile. I felt dirty.

"I can't recall that anything unusual was said here," Leakey said. He shook his head several times for emphasis. "Nothing at all. We spent maybe ten minutes together here."

"Ten minutes? That's it."

"Ten minutes *here*. Going over his brother's papers."

"Where else did you spend time together?" I couldn't see Nichols anywhere else with Leakey.

"The bank," Leakey said. "To get his brother's papers from a safety deposit box. I told him it would be best to have a witness when he did it."

"So you went with him."

Leakey nodded. "He didn't seem nervous or anything.

Not like something would get him killed."

"That was all?" I asked. "You saw him here and at the bank. Nothing seemed unusual."

"Here and at Denver First," Leakey agreed. "Nothing unusual."

"Denver First." I wanted to make sure I'd heard right. It could not be coincidence. Not when I knew that Dehlia knew the killer. Not when Dehlia was linked to that bank through David Girard.

"Sure. Three-story brick building. Couple streets over— where Larimer crosses E Street."

"Obliged," I said. I put my hat on and turned back to the door.

"Was that worth anything?" Leakey asked. "I mean, money-wise."

"If I find out later that it was, I promise I'll get you your half." I tried to return his slimy politician's grin. The effort hurt. "You look like you know a thing or two. 'Specially about working angles that a lot of those mealymouthed do-gooders can't understand."

He shrugged pride.

"And I'm not saying I might be on the wrong side of the law," I continued. "You understand that. Right? I'm just asking a what-if kind of question."

"Sure," Leakey said with a broad wink. Were I closer, he probably would have nudged me in the ribs at the same time.

"So what I'm asking is this. Say a man—and you know it's not me—saw some trouble headed his way and had enough money to fight it with the best in Denver. Who would you pick as a partner to help me—I mean the man—beat any other lawyers in town?"

He didn't think long. "Scott. Brian Scott. No one's sharper or more expensive."

Leakey winked again. "Scott tends to play it too straight for my liking, but I'd be able to offer you—I mean 'the man'—proper kind of advice on the side, if Scott and I were working together."

"Obliged again," I said. I took another step, then stopped and turned once more.

"By the way." I said it casual, but I had a feeling Leakey wouldn't take it that way. "Those silver mines that Nichols signed away. What'd you say they were called?"

"Why are you asking?" Suspicion had clouded his face again.

"Get the papers together," I advised. "All of them. On behalf of Helen Nichols, my lawyer will be going through them with a fine-tooth comb."

"*Your* lawyer?"

"Fella by the name of Scott," I said. "Brian Scott. Maybe you've heard of him."

CHAPTER 30

A COUPLE OF STREETS barely took five minutes of walking, even with a stiffened leg.

I was impressed by the changes that had taken place in Denver. Some of the buildings were three, four stories tall. Brick or stone. Massive structures that reminded me of photographs I'd seen of New York or Boston.

People walked with purpose, the wood sidewalks filled with the hustle of men in suits and women in long dresses and carrying umbrellas they did not need. The streets, while still dirt in most places, were crowded with men on horses and carriages of all sizes. I enjoyed the walk, mostly I think because it was so different from the memories of Denver that had held me captive since I'd left.

Along the way, I had to ask for directions once and was pointed out the bank just ahead of me along the street.

Leakey had been correct in his description of the First Denver Bank. It was a big building. What Leakey had failed to mention, however, were the marble columns and marble steps that led up to the bank doors. Lesley Girard certainly knew how to spend the Boston family money that the Pinkerton man had mentioned.

The interior of the bank lived up to the promise of the marble columns.

Where the First National in Laramie had smooth planks—whitewashed and carefully nailed into place to serve as finished walls, the Denver First had plastered walls—gleaming white, with scrolled woodwork at the edgings of the ceiling.

Where the First National had room for a half-dozen customers and as many spittoons, Denver First was a ballroom, no spittoons in sight. Two, maybe three more First Nationals could have fit in the area behind the wickets.

The First National in Laramie had two wickets; this one seven. And each wicket had at least three customers in line—not many of them in old jeans, shirt, vest, and dusty hat like me. None, I was willing to bet, had limped into the bank because of a recent gunshot wound from an unseen and unknown sniper.

I tried to hide that limp as I walked to the nearest line.

When my turn arrived, I doffed my hat and grinned like I was Davy Crockett trying to scare a possum from a tree. "Morning, sir. Say a man had a pocketful of gold and wanted to keep it safe. Got a place you can rent in your vault?"

To his credit, he didn't look me up and down. Maybe in Denver money wore any kind of clothing.

"A deposit box, you mean," the teller replied.

"Yes, sir." I leaned forward. "You don't mind if I have a look-see first. A man can't be too sure about hard-earned gold."

"Not at all." He pointed to the far end of the bank. "There's a man in the office there. He'll assist you."

"Thank you kindly." My grin was starting to hurt me.

From that office, I was assisted by a tall, thin man into a vault that dwarfed the First National's. He explained how the deposit box system worked, informed me of the bank charges, and asked if I might care to open an account instead so that my goldpoke could earn interest for me.

I was tempted to ask him how much my gold would add to his fractional reserve system and to speculate on the deposit multiplier in a town this size, but I decided while he had been friendly enough, he showed little humor. I declined both the temptation and his offer and requested an appointment with David Girard.

"Mr. Girard?" The teller's eyebrows moved up slightly, something I gathered was an action of significance in this rarefied air.

"Yes. Good ol' Dave," I said. "A few of the boys have spoke highly of him. I figure it's all the whiskey he gives them up at his mansion the boys are always telling me about, but if he's good enough to drink with them, he's good enough for me."

The teller didn't hesitate. He escorted me to an easy chair outside the vault, insisted I relax and wait for a cup of coffee, and promised to do the best he could.

Five minutes later, I was in David Girard's office.

He stood behind his desk and shook my hand with a firm grip.

"A pleasure, Mr . . ."

"Keaton, Samuel Keaton."

"Please, sit down."

He spoke warmly, as if we'd been friends for years, and managed to do it without sounding smarmy. If I hadn't my suspicions—mainly because of his as yet undetermined involvement with Dehlia and because of the coincidence of Bob Nichols' involvement with Denver First—he would have impressed me favorably.

David Girard was big, broad shouldered, trim, fit, good-looking, well dressed, and had a smile and deep blue eyes that would have done a choirboy proud. All this on a man easily ten years my senior, who in other light than the daylight that poured in through his office window could have easily appeared ten years my junior.

And even in the few movements he'd made since I had entered his office, he'd shown an easy confidence and the relaxed strength of a panther in its prime.

I understood how Mrs. Lesley Girard would enjoy keeping this panther on the leash of matrimony and a vice presidency at her bank.

He spoke as soon as I sat. "Samuel Keaton," he mused. "I apologize. The name doesn't ring any bells. And my assistant had spoken of mutual acquaintances and mining interests."

"I lied about both," I said.

He smiled the tolerant smile of a benevolent ruler enjoying the harmless prank of a favored subject. "You lied well, then."

"I'm here on marshal business," I said. "I didn't think you'd appreciate it if I announced it that way. Banks are built on faith, I've heard."

His smile didn't waver. "You certainly heard correctly, Mr. Keaton. And I appreciate your concern." The smile lessened somewhat as his eyebrows furrowed. "A misplaced concern, however. Rumor can only grow on fertile soil, and nothing at the Denver First would support that growth."

I would have believed him, but it was too difficult to forget Dehlia.

I fished in my pocket for a photo of Bob Nichols. On my walk here, I had decided to be as blunt as possible, to beat the bushes with whatever sticks at hand. I had no idea of what was happening here and barely any idea of the players involved. I wanted to see if I could flush anything loose.

"This man," I said. "Seen him before?"

David Girard took the photo and studied it.

I, in turn, studied David's face. And learned nothing.

After enough time to show he'd been genuine in his efforts, Girard returned my photo.

"I'm sorry," he said with a rueful shake of his head and a hint of that winning grin. "Can't recall the face."

Girard gave me another boyish grin. "And I'm sorry to have to ask you this. But what marshal business? And by whose authority? I want to help as much as possible, but I hope you understand that an institution with our reputation can't afford to discuss any confidential matters—if we get to that—with just anyone. And you have, um, shown the capacity to, um, deceive. . . ."

He'd said it so apologetically, there was no way a reasonable man could have taken offense.

"Laramie," I told him. I wondered if he knew that Dehlia was spending time in Laramie. I wondered if he knew why she was there, something I dearly wanted to know myself. "I'm marshaling in the town of Laramie, and this man was recently murdered."

I held open my vest and showed him the badge. "Anyone can have a badge made. And you'd be welcome to have my position confirmed by wiring to Laramie. But it appears that there's not much left I have to ask you. Not if you haven't seen the man before."

Girard gave me a thoughtful nod. "Why, Marshal, are you all the way here from Laramie?"

"I wish I knew," I said.

He smiled. "And why Denver First?"

"Nichols was in to get his brother's papers from a safety deposit box. It was a long shot, stopping here, but the best I had."

Another thoughtful, manly nod. "If you like, Marshal, I can show this photograph to the tellers. They might recall the face."

I thought that through. On one hand, if he was somehow involved, I'd want my presence here to alarm him and force his hand. If I told him not to bother now, he might well realize that *he* had been my target this visit. Extra pressure.

On the other hand, if he were involved and I played this as if I had no idea of that fact, he would be less on guard around me, and I might learn something new that way.

Staring me in the face was the third possibility. That David Girard had no involvement whatsoever, and that I was making as big a fool of myself as I deserved.

What decided it for me was realizing that one of the tellers might recognize Bob Nichols from the photograph. Any scrap that a teller might remember about Nichols' visit might be a scrap to guide me to my next step here in Denver.

"I'd like that, Mr. Girard."

He rose again and let me walk ahead of him out of his office.

I moved to the waiting area and that easy chair while David Girard made his discreet way from teller to teller, pulling each man aside briefly, speaking in a low voice, and with his back turned to the wickets, taking a few seconds to show the photo of Bob Nichols.

Several minutes later, David Girard approached me across the open wideness of the bank's interior.

When he stood close enough to speak in a low voice, he looked directly into my eyes and favored me with the frankness of a longtime friend.

"I'm sorry, Samuel," he said. "None of them remember this man, either."

I tipped my hat. "You've been more than accommodating," I said. "Especially to a man who lied his way into your office."

"My pleasure." He grinned and shook my hand.

He escorted me to the main doors of the Denver First and shook my hand again, informing me to stop by again if he could help in any way.

I thanked him again and told him he had been as much help as possible already.

And he had.

Because when he'd walked across the open wideness of the bank's interior to let me know the results of his question among the clerks, I had seen something that I could not have noticed when he was sitting behind his desk and something I had not noticed as I had been walking ahead of him earlier.

His boots.

Those snakeskins again.

CHAPTER 31

BY EVENING, MY CONFUSION and frustration had lessened not at all.

I'd shown the photos of Calhoun and Nichols to every bartender within walking distance of the Denver train station. This in itself was a considerable feat; Denver had five times as many saloons as churches.

I had not hoped much from those efforts. Yet there seemed little else to attempt. There was an off chance that Calhoun or Nichols might be remembered somewhere, and short of saloons, I could not think of any other places where menfolk gathered so publicly, especially the type of menfolk who would lead to trouble, here or in Laramie.

The results of my attempt had been as meager as my hopes, save for a renewed throbbing of my overworked leg, a throbbing that not even a large mug of beer at the last saloon could ease. I had nothing left to do.

Doc had not been able to supply me with the reason for Lorne Calhoun's visit to Denver, giving me no tracks to pursue for his half of the double murder. For Nichols, I'd already asked around at the Broadway Hotel. Visited his lawyer. Then the bank that his lawyer had mentioned.

What I'd learned at the bank added to my confusion and frustration. Yes, chances were high that David Girard was indeed the man who had been hidden behind the wardrobe at the Pacific Union in Laramie, the same man who had stepped down from the train here in Denver.

Knowing that, however, gave me no clue as to why. All I knew about David Girard was that he'd married into money and had a doubtful relationship as father to Dehlia.

Neither that nor Dehlia's presence here seemed to have connection to the deaths of two men in a bank vault in Laramie.

I did believe something in Denver had caused either or both of those deaths. I was willing to believe further that something here in Denver had led Bob Nichols to the desperation that would force him to join Calhoun in Laramie's First National Bank vault.

But what here could have driven Bob Nichols to such a thing? And was it something linked to Lorne's visit here?

Yet even if I could somehow puzzle the answers to those questions, nothing seemed to bring me closer to the identity of the third man in the vault, the man who had shot Nichols and Calhoun in cold blood and tried to make it appear as a shoot-out between the two. And was that third man the man who had shot my leg?

I felt like a kitten wrapped in a ball of yarn.

Those thoughts tormented me as evening brought dusk upon Denver, and gloom settled upon me where I stood on the hotel veranda and stared without focus at the mountains.

Because the gloom of the night air matched so closely my thoughts, I told myself there was just cause to walk past the English House. After all, it was the only curiosity it appeared

I could satisfy in Denver. To further justify a need to walk past the English House, I reminded myself that I would not go so far as to take a meal inside. Definitely not.

From where I sat in the English House, I was able to survey all the tables and the comings and goings of all the waiters and customers. The corner was dim and gave me comfort that shadow would hide enough of my face to keep me from her notice.

As well, I told myself, for so many years had passed that she would not recognize me anyway. I'd been nineteen, our last night together. Now I'd be a passing stranger.

I tried to escape my thoughts by losing myself in the exquisite tastes of the meal. Roast baby duck. An orange glaze sauce. Tender boiled potatoes spiced with something I couldn't identify that tasted so good I asked for seconds despite the half-raised eyebrow of the waiter. Half bottle of wine. Then heavy coffee and chocolate cake with fresh-whipped cream.

It didn't surprise me that Clara knew what she was doing. She always had.

I looked plenty around the restaurant as I ate. Watched people come and go in the dim glow of the oil lamps that seemed to burnish the dark wood of the tables. I studied the waiters, imagined conversations they had with Clara. I ate in silence and memorized everything I could about the inside of the restaurant.

Yet of Clara Lanigan, I had seen no sign.

I tempted fate by remaining as long as possible, drinking coffee after coffee, musing through memories of Clara, paining myself by comparing them to memories of Rebecca, and in short, making myself as miserable as a man can be alone in a city of thousands.

When I finally pushed away from the table and creaked my

aching leg to an upright position, I was among the last of the restaurant patrons. The last among three, if I were to count, for two men shared a table at the opposite side of the restaurant, and save for them, all tables were empty.

So much for self-discipline.

Not only had I walked past the English House a half dozen times, not only had I finally taken myself inside for a meal, I had waited almost the entire evening just for a glimpse of Clara.

I looked for whatever virtue in my actions that I could and decided I could appease myself that I had at least not fallen so far as to inquire after her.

Once that occurred to me, I looked for a way to fall further. Except the restaurant was now so empty that I could engage no one in conversation as I slowly walked to the door. I even waited there for a few minutes on the chance that a waiter might stray among the tables, but the evening had ended. I left the other two men to the silence of the English House and stepped outside to be braced by the cool September air.

Here the streets were not as wide as the main streets of the business district. Nor as filled with people.

Barely a hundred yards from the English House, I turned onto an even narrower and quieter side street. Minutes later, I realized that I was no longer alone. The two men from the restaurant were behind me, speaking to each other in low tones that carried through the night air.

I thought nothing of it until I noticed that they had split, so that one walked each side of the street as they followed.

I quickened my pace as much as my game leg would allow, and they quickened with me.

I turned once, twice, and a third time so that I was almost headed back to the English House.

They stayed with me.

What had been my thoughts before my visit to David Girard at the Denver First? Beat the bushes with whatever sticks were at hand. It now appeared I had flushed loose not prey, but hunters.

Unfortunately, I did not know the streets of Denver well. Had it been possible, I would have let them follow to a spot of my choosing, then confronted them. As it was, I had stupidly led them to one of the quieter, darker streets. And I doubted I could outrun them.

I considered what action I might best take, until they made the decision for me.

"Stop right there!" one hailed.

They were within pistol-shooting distance. If I didn't stop, I might easily get a bullet in the back. All I could do was turn to face them.

Here on this quiet street the gas lamps were spread much farther apart. Lights from the windows of nearby buildings were barely more than a glow. The men became advancing shadows.

They'd made an impression on me at the restaurant—mainly because of size, each hunched over his plate with shoulders as wide as the table. I remembered the greased-back hair, the unshaven faces of men too lazy to shave regularly but too vain for beards, and I remembered how their jackets had ridden up their massive bodies as they leaned forward, showing clearly the ivory-handled revolvers at their hips.

The first man's voice matched my remembered impressions. Like a boulder rumbling down a rocky mountain creek bed.

"Boy," he said as they moved closer, "it's some dark here, but I can see your hands real good. Back off that six-shooter."

I did not.

"Ever see a shoulder-slung shotgun?" the second man asked.

They were five steps away now, and I could make out a glint of polished wood stock inside the jacket he held open for my inspection. "The holster swivels real good." He opened it wider to let me look into a sawed-down barrel with its twin black holes of death. "Fact is, all I got to do is pull the trigger, and pieces of you make it as far as the edge of town."

I eased my hand back.

A horse and buggy approached, the clatter of hooves an echo on the night-quieted street.

"Not that, boy," the first man said, catching my quick glance in that direction. "Make a move or yell, and you're dead."

I *had* been tensed to jump and roll.

The buggy passed. My tension and fear did not.

"You show considerable sense," the first man said. He moved to within striking distance and stopped, big enough that I was in his shadow. He faced me with his feet apart, hands on hips, and a disturbing amount of confidence. It probably aided him, knowing he had at his elbow a partner with that shotgun swiveled to point directly at my heart.

If they wanted me dead here, I was. No time to draw. No place to hide. No place to run, even if I could with my bum leg.

Still, I intended to do my best to make him pay if he wished to work me over. I watched the first man's shoulders. My first signal of that intention would come not from his hands, but from a shifting of those larger muscles.

He said nothing for a few moments.

Distant shouts reached us, as if somewhere a fight had spilled from a saloon.

I said nothing back. I was scared plenty—the two of them together seemed like they'd outweigh a bull buffalo. If that weren't enough reason to be scared, I could remind myself that buffaloes, at least, were stupid and didn't carry enough firepower to blow holes through brick walls.

Fear, however, usually leads me to anger. I hate fear and

anything that brings it upon me. As they watched me and breathed deep breaths of anticipation and satisfaction, I began to rage at how I'd been backed into a corner of their making.

"Cat got your tongue?" the first man finally asked.

I measured the distance between him and me. I almost hoped he'd make a move. Anything to block the shotgun.

"Hey, boy, cat got your tongue?" he said.

"Don't appear that talking will do me much good," I said. "And sooner or later you'll get around to the whyfors of stopping a stranger on the streets."

"Stranger?" the first one snorted. "Samuel Keaton, you ain't no stranger. Not the marshal that guns snakes out of midair." He laughed, then continued. "That's why we's paying you the compliment of such close attention now."

"That's right," the second man said. He motioned with the shotgun. "Real close attention. So move slow when we tell you to turn around. Move too quick, you're dead where you stand."

"Take my billfold here and now," I said, "it'll save us both a pile of grief."

I moved to reach for it. Froze at the click of a revolver's hammer drawn back.

He'd drawn plenty fast, the man without the shotgun. His revolver was almost lost in that giant hand, and what I saw of the weapon told me I couldn't do anything more ill-considered than continue to reach for my billfold.

Frozen, I watched too for the muzzle flash, as if my mind could actually register it before a half-inch chunk of lead tore out my guts and my life. A couple of heartbeats later, I realized the bullet would not arrive. I allowed myself a breath. Wondered how loud it sounded to these two.

I could certainly pat myself on the back if I chose to believe that this was progress, staring into a revolver and a shotgun on a dark street somewhere in the heart of Denver. His lack of interest in my bank notes confirmed for me that the day's stick-beating had indeed flushed something loose.

I guessed, too, they did not want me dead. At least not in a hurry. Otherwise it would have happened by now.

"Did Leakey send you?" I asked. "Is he sore 'cause I got Brian Scott searching the deeds to the mine?"

"My friend told you to move on, slow." This, a growl of impatience from the first man.

"Not Leakey? How about Girard?"

The man without the shotgun sighed. A deliberate theatrical sigh, somewhat ridiculous for someone his size. I kept that opinion to myself.

He holstered his revolver as he paced several steps away from me. He reached behind his back with his right hand. When his hand reappeared, it held something that in the darkness I decided was the handle and coiled leather of a bullwhip.

"Easy money ain't ever easy, is it, Red?" the man with the bullwhip said.

Red laughed, a taunt of evil delight. "Hardly ever at all. It appears this might get you in a sweat after all."

My own sweat grew that much colder. Bullwhackers never actually strike their teams, for the violence of exploding air above the oxen is sufficient in its promise—a man who knows how to snap a bullwhip is capable of tearing leather off the hide of an ox. A flick of the wrist is all that is needed for a bullwhacker to rip an eye loose from man or beast.

Neither would it be accidental or lucky for the end of the whip to strike that eye. A bullwhacker's favorite pastime at rest stops or campfires—especially with greenhorns new to the trail—is to set a stake loosely in the ground. The coin to be gambled is placed on top of the stake. If the bullwhacker can use the whip to knock the coin off without disturbing the stake, the bullwhacker wins the bet. If the stake moves, the bullwhacker loses the bet. Most often, I've seen the greenhorns lose.

Watching him raise his hand, I grimly realized one other

thing. He didn't have a need to be that accurate to inflict punishment. As with a bullet, anywhere on the body, or near the body for that matter, is close enough to get plenty of attention.

Another carriage and team reached the edge of my vision as it approached from the far end of the street. I could not have said whether it was a one-horse team or eight. I had eyes only for the snapping of the man's wrist and arm. Air exploded within inches of my ear.

The second man laughed again. He'd seen this before.

Another crack of torn air. This on the other side of my head, so close that against my will, I ducked.

He gave me time to relax after I straightened.

"You might be ready to listen now," he said, "but I'm worried you might show spunk later. Maybe a taste of this whip will learn you against that."

He feinted a hand move.

I grunted, fully expecting the terror of that whip against me.

He feinted again. I could not stop myself from another grunt.

Red laughed. "This is better than watching a cat with a mouse!"

Red's partner agreed. He dropped his arm slightly, as if readying himself to coil the whip, then with his own grunt, threw himself into the next whipping motion, a lash that ripped me across my wounded thigh with such force that I fell to my hands and knees.

I couldn't even draw wind to gasp. I tried to push myself up.

The second man kicked me in my ribs. "Softened up yet? Ready to move along?"

He stepped back before I could lift myself from the ground, giving me plenty of room as I fought back to my feet.

I knew then I had no hope. An inexperienced man in alley

brawls would have stood over me as I rose. Big or not, these two were showing that they depended less on size and more on not making mistakes.

The whip lashed at me again. Same leg. Same results of seared skin.

I heard a moan and dimly wondered at the strangeness of the cry until I realized it was mine.

"He'll listen now, Red."

"Get walking, boy." The second man motioned with the shotgun for me to step along.

I did. At considerable cost because of the messages delivered by my leg, the burning welts across my thigh, and my boot-softened ribs.

Ten steps later—counting was the only way in my pain to force one foot in front of the other—salvation arrived in the voice of a woman who'd left me on a moonless night nearly fifteen years earlier.

CHAPTER 32

HER VOICE CAME from the interior of the carriage as it stopped alongside the three of us.

"Gentlemen," she said. "I wish to interrupt."

We three turned to the sound of her voice. The carriage had an oil lamp set in an iron ring on its side, and while the interior of the carriage was as dark as the night around us, the lamp showed clearly a rifle barrel resting on the sill of the carriage window.

"Red, she's got me covered." The man with the bullwhip edged sideways to give Red a better view. It put Red at the corner of a triangle. The rifle from the carriage at the second point. Me at the other.

Red shifted his shotgun to the new threat as his partner cleared the path to allow him a clean shot at the carriage. That was his mistake, taking the extra second to wait. Had he fired without warning as she first spoke, the carriage would have been shredded, and he would have had time to swivel the shotgun back again in my direction.

But he'd taken his eyes and his shotgun off me, and his partner was now only armed with a bullwhip. I drew my Colt with a slap of leather and a click of hammer that told him better than words that he'd made the mistake.

"No, you don't," I said, total focus on the shotgun and any possible movement. "So much as flinch, you're dead."

"Dead twice," another voice called. Clara's driver, from behind the reins of the carriage. "I'm riding shotgun up here, too."

"Hands on your head," I said. "Slow."

Red obeyed.

"Watch the man with the bullwhip," I said to the driver as I hobbled several steps to stand behind Red. "He's blue lightning with that six-shooter."

The driver chuckled. "Not when he's dropping the holster at his feet and kicking it away."

Red's partner took the hint.

I placed the barrel of my Colt against the back of Red's skull and with my free hand reached around to pull loose his shotgun. I stepped clear and instructed him to drop his own holster.

"I'd like to see them on their stomachs," I said to the driver as I cocked Red's shotgun. "Hands clasped on their necks."

They hesitated.

"I'm not a top hand with a bullwhip, gentlemen," I told them. "But I have had some practice and am not averse to more."

Slowly, each dropped to his knees, then onto his stomach. Only then did I risk another glance at the carriage.

Clara's rifle remained where it was. She'd been silent since first speaking, and I wondered if I had imagined it was her voice.

Her driver spoke before I could ask. "I'll scare up some law if you want."

"No," I said after a few moments consideration. "I'd just as soon shoot them and call it self-defense. That is, if you're disposed to standing in court as an impartial witness."

"I could do that," the driver said. "Best ask them to turn over, though. Self-defense is tough to support if they've been backshot."

I allowed myself another glance. This one upward to the driver. All I saw was the outline of a man sitting on the buckboard, reins loose in his hands.

I looked down at the prone men. "You heard him," I said. "Roll over. Unless you'd care to tell me who sent you."

"Don't know his name," Red told me.

"Roll over."

"He didn't tell us," Red insisted. Fear tinged his voice. "He just gave us money. Told us to work you over good. Rope you even better. Take you to a mine shack outside of town. Guard you till he shows up."

"Roll over."

"Don't be stupid," Red's partner said. "We're hired guns. We don't care none about who paid us. We'd tell you if we could."

"Hired guns. How much you ask?"

"He offered us $500 each. Half up front. Half on delivery."

"Was he wearing snakeskin boots?" I asked.

"Don't know," Red told me. "We had a message to meet him in a livery after sundown. He stayed in a horse stall. Made it so we couldn't see his face, let alone his boots."

I was conscious of the dark, silent interior of the carriage and who might be inside.

Yet I was equally conscious that these two were what I'd flushed loose. I couldn't walk away from them.

"Show me the money," I told them. Only if the driver

started moving the carriage would I worry about losing the woman inside. "Take your time. I'll be watching for pocket guns and fancy moves."

Minutes later, I had a roll of bank notes as thick as my fist. It would cover triple what the lawyer Brian Scott had promised me earlier in the day he'd charge to look into Leakey's mine dealings with Bob Nichols.

These hired guns, however, weren't as easily disposed of as a lawyer's bill. I could not shoot them. I could not let them go.

The horses stamped restlessly in front of the carriage, reminding me of how I wanted inside that silent dark interior.

"Driver," I said, "have you heard of an undertaker named Morgen?"

"Yup."

"From what I saw, he lives right next door to his funeral home." I peeled off some bank notes. "I'd be obliged if you could pay him what it takes for the inconvenience of calling at this hour for a couple of extra large coffins."

Later, inside the carriage, with the light of the outside lamp spilling inward upon her, it broke my heart all over again to look into the face and eyes of Clara Johnson, now Clara Lanigan.

I didn't trust my voice, so I swallowed hard and waited for what she might say after all these years. My hands felt like large rocks, and no matter where I placed them, they felt awkward in my lap.

She stared back, her face soft in the darkness cast by the hood of her bonnet.

Heartbeat followed heartbeat and still nothing was said.

The carriage was moving now, and we both swayed with the jolting of the road, each in our own corner of thought and memories.

I'd met her first when I was fifteen. That was '54, the year my brother Jed drifted us into Denver, where Clara was just another dance-hall girl at the Golden Slipper.

Jed and I were orphans—Jed as wild as I was shy—the only survivors of a Crow Indian attack that had killed our parents on a lonely wagon trail beyond the shadows of the Bighorn Mountains. We'd spent a fall and winter with the mountain men who'd found us, then time with friendly Shoshoni in the grassland basins north of the Greybull River.

I followed Jed in our driftings after the Shoshoni simply because he led. In Denver, he'd firmly announced he wanted to travel alone during the summer and with equal firmness announced that I was to stay there to wait for his return. I'd agreed, simply because he'd declared it that way.

I wasn't the only one who Jed could mesmerize by the force of his will. Jed found me work and lodgings at the Golden Slipper, an arrangement that resulted from the infatuation of the dance-hall matron who saw me as a good way to insure Jed would indeed return to her.

That summer at the Golden Slipper I chopped wood, swept floors, toted water—and from May until September spoke less than a dozen words to the girls who made their living at twenty-five cents per dance, the cost for a cowboy to spin them for five minutes around the floor to the sounds of tinny music. This was common enough. Many dance-hall women were straighter then a deaconess, and their job was to dance with the men, talk to them, flirt a bit, and induce them to buy drinks—but nothing more. So little did I know about women and men that I assumed all the other dance halls were similar. On the day I discovered that red lights at the other halls meant the spins there cost more and involved less clothing, I was so shocked that a light wind would have sent me tumbling down the street.

When Jed returned for the winter, he hired on as protection at the front door. Already, he was good with his guns and unafraid with his fists. I chopped wood—much more wood as it got cold—and toted water and swept floors.

Jed left again the next summer. At his directive, I remained. Shy to the point of pain, happy to be ignored, I quietly chopped wood, toted water, and swept floors.

Clara, the dance girl closest in age to me, but infinitely wiser in the ways of the world, took pity on me in my ignorance and shyness. She made it her habit to try to engage me in conversation, a difficult task on her part when I was unable even to lift my eyes from the floor to look into her face. Because of that habit, I knew her feet well and could describe every pair of shoes she'd worn that summer, but I would not have been able to describe the color of her eyes—green as I saw on the day she lifted my chin to gently kiss my forehead.

That kiss was a reward. One drunk cowboy had been particularly insistent that his five-minute spin become something more. He'd followed her to the back of the building where she'd gone for fresh air. Her cries alerted me, and I'd found her struggling to push away from his arms. I'd waded in without thinking about his friends or his revolver. That was when I learned that chopping wood, toting water, and sweeping floors do add considerable muscle to a gangly frame. He went down without a sound. She fled for the safety of the interior of the dance hall. The next morning while I sat at breakfast, she stopped beside me and, to the applause of the other girls, bestowed upon me my reward, that first chaste kiss.

It took another summer before I was brave enough to speak to her on a regular basis.

No one in Denver was prettier as she blossomed into womanhood. Her face was not quite chubby and had an alluring pout that drew men like moths to flame. Her hair was blond and fine and promised as much softness as the rest of her ripe body. It was a package that hid a razor-sharp mind. By then, she had convinced several businessmen to help her purchase the Golden Slipper. Her first official act as owner was to promote me to hired gun in Jed's absence, for he spent his winters at the dance hall teaching me gunplay, knife throwing, and fistfighting, all the education he'd been acquiring during his summers away from Denver.

At the end of the summer of '57—I was eighteen then—she inexplicably chose me as the only suitor in her life and all the following winter was the most glorious time of love I have ever experienced.

I should have stayed at the Golden Slipper in the spring and summer of '58. Instead, I listened to Jed when he suggested I follow him to hunt wanted men for bounty.

It was a decision that killed Jed and left me in jail in Pueblo, facing death at the end of a rope until—like this night some fifteen years later—sweet Clara and sweet salvation had arrived together to save my life.

CHAPTER 33

"HELLO," SHE SAID, voice soft as her touch in my memories. "It is you, isn't it? I mean, the scar, it is from Pueblo all that time ago. . . ."

I briefly squeezed my eyes shut against those memories. It seemed all my years of hunger and aloneness and pain of unanswered love for her had compressed into this tiny moment.

"It . . ." I swallowed past a lump in my throat. "It is, Clara. Only I go by the name of Samuel Keaton. Seems I left my other name behind, along with a lot of other things."

The carriage hit a bump. Neither of us lost the eyes of the other.

"I missed you," she said. "Fifteen years I've wondered about you, prayed you'd return, and other nights prayed that you'd died and would never return to haunt me. I've asked myself again and again why I let my pride send you away that night in Pueblo. Just when I'd managed to put you out of my life, you were there, in the back of my restaurant, wearing the same gentle and lonely fear that first made me care when you were a skinny kid who hauled water without saying a word. I thought I was a girl all over again, the way I shook and trembled."

She laughed. " 'Course, to see you safe after fretting all these years, I nearly took out a gun myself and shot you right where you sat. How dare you not come back to me!"

"You saw me in the restaurant," I repeated, because that was easier than thinking through everything that was flooding me.

"Even if I hadn't at first, how could I have missed you later? Not many drag out their meal over four hours."

"You followed me."

"I didn't trust myself to stop at your table. Worried I might make a fool of myself. I didn't know if I wanted to follow you, either. But I knew if I didn't speak to you, I'd spend another eternity regretting the lost chance."

"You saved my life again. Sure that's a habit you want to acquire?"

"I may want to," she said. "But it won't happen. We have until the carriage stops."

"Then what?"

"You go where you were headed before you stopped at the English House. I go back to my husband."

She must have taken my silence as disbelief.

"Yes, I'm married. My oldest boy is the same age as you were when I first saw you at the Golden Slipper. While speaking to you like this is not wrong, if people see us together, they may take it that way. I will not shame my husband in that manner."

She paused. "We will not talk again."

"Don't break it to me so gentle," I said.

It caught her off guard, the dryness in my words. She blinked, shook her head, blinked again, and clapped her hands together in delight. "You've found a sense of humor!"

I cocked my head, a silent question.

"As a boy, some days you'd take the world so serious. I'd catch a look across your face as if you'd been run down by a buffalo and hadn't seen it coming or going. It always made me think of how your ma and pa had passed on and what you'd been through, and I'd want to hold you tight and tell you everything would be just fine."

"You loved me because you pitied me?" I wasn't sure I liked this, seeing myself through her eyes.

"Hardly. What touched my heart was your braveness. I felt sorry for you, but you never felt sorry for yourself. You'd never quit what you started. When you lit into that cowboy for me, I saw for the first time that you had fire. I eventually realized you were strong, much stronger even than Jed, but didn't know it yourself. Then you filled out and had that crooked grin that made all our hearts flutter and . . ."

"You must be talking about a different person than what I remember," I said. "You were the one I always dreamed of but never once expected to look twice in my direction. Like an angel you were. You'd fluff that blond hair of yours . . ."

I stopped, for she was pulling loose her bonnet. She tossed her head a few times to fluff it like she'd always done, except now, even with the dim light of the outside lamp, I could see it was no longer blond.

She laughed more delight. "You were so innocent, you never once figured I dyed this, did you?"

"No, ma'am. You're still the vision I remember, though."

She was. The years had taken from her face its chubbiness, leaving a classic beauty that would not diminish as she grew older. Her hair, still thick, was brunette and fanned a promised softness across her shoulders.

It was all I could do not to reach across and touch that hair, if only to let me believe this was not a dream.

There was the creaking of the carriage suspension, the slap of horses' hooves on dirt, and the irregular jouncing of our leather benches. All of this reminded me that I was awake, that I truly was with Clara as we rode aimlessly through the streets of Denver.

Perhaps she felt the same as I did, for she lifted her hands from her lap. She set one down on the bench between us, leaning forward on it and bracing against it as she reached with her other hand to touch my cheek.

"Last time I saw this, it was still an open gash," she said. "I shouldn't have been surprised to see this scar."

I brought up my hand to hold hers, but she drew away, placing the distance between us again.

"Why didn't you come back to me?" she asked.

My turn for disbelief. "You'd sent me away," I said when I found my voice. "I clearly remember your last words. They were the words I heard every night as I tried to find sleep. 'Ride off the face of the earth,' you said. 'My hatred and scorn will follow you until you die.' "

"I was angry."

"Evidently."

"You should have known I wanted you to come back begging for me."

I sighed. "I was the one who couldn't even tell you dyed your hair. Someone tells me to ride off the face of the earth, I figure it's more than a hint. 'Specially after what I'd done."

Clara sighed. "Strange thing is, next morning when I'd cooled down, I saw it in a different light. She'd walked into your hotel room. She'd thrown herself at you. And from what you'd said, you pushed her away before giving her a chance to prove her intentions. I had no cause to send you away."

Clara shook her head in sadness. "But by the time I saw it in a different light, you were gone and I had no way to call you back."

I said nothing. My memories of the weeks in Pueblo were painful enough.

"Worst thing is," she said, "I sent you away the one time

you needed me so bad. I could see it in your eyes, the way you told me everything from behind the cell bars. You needed me to forgive you, and I sent you away."

"They were not easy years. How Jed died stayed with me for a long time."

"Is it easier now?" Her question was whispered.

I shrugged. "There was more to how he died than me being with his girl."

I told Clara what I'd learned in the months before my marshal position in Laramie, how the girl in my hotel room had set both Jed and me up for our deaths, why I was still alive, and about the man she'd been working with and how I'd finally faced him down earlier in the summer.

There was long silence after that. I had no idea of how much time had passed since leaving her restaurant. It wasn't until a jarring bump that a wince of pain reminded me that I'd hardly given any thought to the new damage to my leg.

She noticed. "Those boys didn't have a tea party in mind. May I presume they're part of the reason why you're here now?"

"You may."

I explained to her what had brought me to Denver. It was easier than talking about the chances with each other we had lost.

I told her about the double murder. Missing money. The murder attempt on me. The death of Clayton Barnes. About Dehlia. David Girard. She laughed at my descriptions of Mayor Crawford and of Brother Lewis in the jail cell with a horse. She clucked sympathy at my confusions, nodded agreement at my assessment of those two fine men, Doc Harper and Jake Wilson. And when I finally finished, she posed her next question without pause.

"What in the world do you intend to do with the coffins?"

"Leave them," I said. "You heard what I told those men."

"You weren't serious."

"Sure I was. The most harm it'll bring them is a little thirst."

"They'll wet their pants," she protested, not without a trace of giggle. "Two days in a coffin?"

"That's all I need," I said. "Two days. It'll give me time to wait in the mining shack and clear this straight through."

I winced at another bounce. "Wet pants ain't nothing compared to how my leg burns. Least they could have done was lashed the good one."

"And if two days isn't enough?" Clara asked.

"Set those two loose so they don't die," I said. "Then send your driver to the mine. At that point, if I'm not dead, I could probably use help."

CHAPTER 34

I FOUND THE MINING SHACK in the gray of a cold drizzling mist that hid the mountains during my entire ride from Denver. The shack stood alongside a small stream at the head of a steep-walled valley, where the water riffled a shallow path down a bed of gravel. Low cloud cover muffled all sound except for the gurgle of the stream's water, and when I'd first seen the shack as it loomed into view from the cold fog, this silence had heightened my impression of a ghostly, shrouded silhouette.

That mining had taken place here for years was obvious. Aside from the shack, there were piles of rocks and a Tom at the side of the stream. This rock would have been dug by pick and shovel from the stream bed, thrown back onto the Tom, and once washed, thrown back onto the bank. The Tom—a long trough that worked like a miner's pan—washed bits of gold free of sand and gravel. It was open at both ends for water flow and was long enough that three or four men could work side by side at the same time. Long since abandoned and without water flow, the center of the Tom showed chunks of gravel that glistened with rain.

It had been a long ride from Denver to reach this site. I'd followed a deeply rutted wagon trail, its double gash of passing wheels long softened by several seasons' growth of long grass. The trail took me upstream as the valley narrowed, until in the last few miles the broad plain of the valley bottom had become little more than the width of the banks carved by the stream, the road steeper with the twistings of the stream's curves.

My vantage point was above the final twist in the road, where it turned suddenly to reveal the shack in its forlorn decay. From where I was lying in a shallow depression in the ground behind a low bush, I'd already paced the distance down to the wagon trail. Five running steps. And from there, another ten steps to the sagging wood door of the shack.

It was a very small world, with the fog so low that visibility was down to the sparse trees immediately around me, the far edge of the creek bank, and the shack those fifteen steps away.

Despite the ease of ambush given by the gray drizzling fog, by my cover, and by the steep slopes and the twisting road, I'd hoped for better.

David Girard in his snakeskin boots—I expected no one else—would need no more time than it took to creak open the door to see that the shack was empty.

I had done the same, to find an old bunk and iron stove. The bunk was a rotting frame of wood slats held disjointed by rusty nails. Straw poked through holes in the rain-stained mattress where mice or squirrels had eaten through the gray canvas. The stove's chimney pipe had been partially dismantled, as if halfway through someone had decided it was not worth the effort of stripping further. Cobwebs, scattered mice droppings, and the vague staleness of fermented mold all convinced me it had easily been years since any miner had used the shack as a shelter during breaks from the exhausting labor of shoveling stream-bed gravel onto the nearby Tom.

In short, Girard would not need to step inside to realize no one waited him. Since I didn't want to shoot him—dead or badly wounded, he would be unable to answer my questions—I had to be ready on the road behind him when he turned away from the doorway. I needed to be waiting with my rifle steady, giving me enough of a drop on him that he wouldn't risk going for his gun to force a shoot-out.

That gave me precious little time to cover those five running steps after he passed by.

I didn't like my chances. Not with my leg as it was. The lashing of that bullwhip had not helped my healing bullet wound. Neither had a lack of sleep and a long ride here from Denver on a hired horse. I'd allowed myself only three hours of rest after stepping from Clara's carriage at dawn. If that weren't enough, my slicker was little protection against the drizzle, not when rainwater pooled beneath me where I lay waiting. The wet and cold had already numbed me so badly I wondered if I could push myself onto my feet without stumbling.

My consolation was that I *could* count on Girard to pass below me and walk all the way up to the shack, if only because I'd taken three horses in with me. One I'd ridden, the two others I'd taken behind me for window dressing. If Girard had any eye for tracks and was looking for evidence that nothing unusual waited him, the three sets of tracks would lull him into believing three men had gone to the shack. Me and the two he hired to take me.

If, as I expected, he first hailed the empty shack from the road below me, I believed the nearby horses would encourage him to continue to the shack. I'd tied the horses to a post near the shack, and that would be exactly what he'd expect to see when he rounded the corner.

It helped, too, as I endured the discomfort, that I fully

expected Girard to arrive here, and before nightfall. After all, I had Red's word and his partner's on both—with confidence that they were plenty motivated to tell the truth from where each had been helpless in a coffin with hands and feet bound.

Getting them into that motivating situation—while worth it—had taken effort. Clara's driver had first held a gun over them to let me bind their hands and feet and gag their mouths. He'd helped me roll them into a dark alley, where I stood guard for an hour until he returned with the coffins on a wagon. In the early quiet hours of the morning, we had lifted them into their wooden prisons, shut the coffins, loaded each onto the wagon, and ridden with Clara through the empty streets to the plains outside of Denver. There, beneath the light of moon and stars, we'd moved the coffins several hundred yards apart. I opened the lid to Red's coffin and informed him that unless what he told me matched his partner's words, he would be buried alive. I'd said the same a few minutes later to Red's partner. It came as no surprise to me that, ungagged, neither had disagreed with the other's version on the instructions to finding this mining shack.

They'd had a vested interest, too, in telling me as much as possible about Girard's arrival time, for Clara's driver had taken me and the coffins back to Denver, where we stored them in a back room at Clara's restaurant. The coffin lids had been shut long before then, so that neither had any idea of his location, and each believed that unless I returned, he would not be released.

Yes, I'd done as much as I could to ready myself for this ambush.

That should have eased my mind as I waited, but it did not. I still had no idea why Girard—if indeed it were him—wanted me captured. I had no idea how he was connected—if indeed it were him—to deaths in Laramie. And I had little idea of what I would do once I had him at gunpoint—if indeed I would be lucky enough and fast enough to get him there.

I settled in for a cold, aching wait.

My bladder betrayed me.

Not my leg, as I had feared with the cold stiffening me more and more with the passing minutes. But my bladder.

I gritted my teeth until well past the point of urgent pain, and I debated the best method of answering the one dilemma I could control as little as the weather. Relieving myself in the shallow trench, while safe in terms of ambush position, was unthinkable. I was already miserable and shivering. I refused to allow myself to soak myself further.

Yet where was the nearest and most effective cover? Should I face the road? Or away?

Finally, I decided to move up the hill a half-dozen steps. At most, I'd be in the open a minute—although with the need I felt, I wouldn't have been surprised if my estimate was several minutes short—and I told myself that the odds against David Girard appearing during that one minute were ridiculously small.

Naturally, that's how David Girard found me—shivering and shaking, weight on my good leg, standing behind a tree as I tended to nature's business.

If I hadn't expected my bladder to betray me, I expected even less that a dog would contribute.

David Girard in his rain slicker rounded the bend on foot, leading his horse by the reins with one hand, an extended revolver in the other. An ugly hound beside him caught my scent and barked a low warning.

Girard's reactions were no less superb than the cultured appearance he'd presented at the bank. His hand was up instantly in my direction, revolver steady as his words.

"Get your hands up where I can see them," he commanded.

There were fifteen, maybe twenty, steps at most between us on an angle so straight that even in the mist between us his gun barrel was a deadly eye of black that didn't blink or waver. All that kept me from obeying him was stubborn dignity—once I got my hands up, there was no telling when he'd let me drop them again to adjust my clothing.

So I continued what I had started, telling myself that if he wanted me dead, he would have had Red and his partner gun me down earlier in Denver.

His gun exploded and the bullet shredded bark above my head. That did test my willpower and desire for dignity.

"Girard, I can't shoot even if I wanted," I said with some disgust, most of it directed at myself for the stupidity of this predicament. "My holster's covered by this slicker, and my rifle is leaning against another tree."

His answer was another explosion, echo muted by the fog and drizzle. Another instant slash of white on the bark of the tree. Crows somewhere nearby began to caw alarm.

"Raise your hands," he said, no anger in his voice.

To me, the second miss was more proof he didn't want me dead. I began to button my pants.

The third bullet was lower down, a zing that brushed my cheek with a puff of air.

I raised my hands.

"Tie the other leg."

I'd already tied my right ankle to a post of the bunk bed and knew how much it hurt to lean forward to reach for the left ankle. But I didn't have a choice.

Girard stood in the doorway of the shack—hound behind trying to nose Girard's knees aside to watch me, too—and gave himself enough room to fire several bullets should I make an ill-considered rush toward him.

Girard watched with no expression as I used the second piece of rope he had tossed at me. When I finished, he smiled. He could afford to. My Colt and Winchester were back on the hillside where he'd forced me to walk down with my fingers interlocked on my head.

"Why am I not surprised you're here alone?" he said. His continuing smile held much less charm than the one I'd seen at the bank. "From the beginning, you've been on my trail like a starved dog after partridge."

"What say we trade answers," I said. I was sitting upright again on the edge of the bunk. My hands were still free, but with my ankles secured to bedposts, I was so helpless that my hands would help me little. "You tell me why you've gone to all this trouble."

"Trouble? What I had in mind was more like pleasure." His face showed it. Skin tightened around his cheekbones. The concentration of a boy pulling wings from a fly. "See here, Marshal, I want everything you know. And I needed a place this remote. Folks won't hear you scream."

He fired a shot into the dirt between my legs. "I killed a man once—took twenty bullets to do it. Had to throw water on him three times, though, to bring him around for the next bullet."

He stepped away from the doorway, leaving me a view of the trees and fog and drizzle. Before I could contemplate much his intentions, he reappeared, holding a battered canteen which I presumed he had taken from his horse.

"But I believe a man should be inventive," he continued as if he had not departed. "And I've never burned anyone to death."

Staying out of my reach, he sloshed the contents of the canteen against the walls of the shack. The acrid smell of kerosene filled my nostrils. He threw the empty canteen at my head and laughed as it bounced off my blocking hands.

Girard departed again and returned to empty another canteen of the oily liquid against the inside of the shack walls.

When finished, he leaned back against the doorframe and studied my face.

"So talk to me. Tell me what you know."

Despite my predicament, I snorted. Nothing about this or the murders made sense.

"How much do you know?" His voice held less cheer. Maybe it frustrated him that I wasn't cowering or begging.

"How much does anyone know?" I said, thinking with fondness of Doc.

Girard shook his head. The glee came back into his face as he dug a match from his vest pocket. He held it high, admired it, made sure I could admire it, flicked it against his thumb, admired the flame, made sure I could admire the flame, then tossed the match.

It fell in the dirt, just short of a splash of kerosene.

"I'll repeat myself," he said. "How much do you know?"

"About you?" I said. Probably more quickly than I wanted. The kerosene smell was strong, and even with the drizzle on the outside, the interior of this shack would go like whittled kindling. "Obviously I know very little. Why else would I have come out here hoping to waylay you?"

He gazed upward as he thought about that, then grudgingly nodded. More thought. A foxy look crossed his face. "My wife tell you anything?"

"Never met her," I said. "I had no reason to visit the mansion. And don't you think you'd have heard from the servants if I'd called on her?"

He grinned a triumph I did not understand.

He dug another match loose.

"I am going to kill you," he said—in conversational tones that chilled me. This was not a sane man. "And as you might guess, in a way that'll make you wish I'd shot you dead at the Bar X Bar. Barnes, at least, never knew what hit him."

He lit the match. "Shame of it is, I almost owe you thanks. Whatever you did to those boys saved me having to kill them, too. And that might have been complicated."

Girard stared at the flame of the match.

"Indulge me," I said. "What's this about? Is it Dehlia? You and her robbing banks? What?"

He blew out the flame. Hatred crossed his features. "In my dreams, she'd be here tied with you," he said. "Screaming in the same flames that will turn you into a puddle of sizzling fat."

"You killed Nichols and Calhoun?" I asked.

"Marshal, don't waste your breath. I already learned what I needed. Now I get to stand outside and listen to you die."

His skin tightened across his cheekbones as that leer of pleasure took him again. "When I was a boy," he said, "I had this neighbor, who tanned me good after he caught me stealing eggs from his henhouse. I waited some, then one day, I stole his favorite hound. Put him in a crate and done just what I'm doing here. Soaked the wood with kerosene. Touched a match to it. How that dog did howl. Surprised me, too, that dog could draw breath as long as it did."

He was going to kill me. I could see it in the slate of his eyes. He was going to kill me and take satisfaction from it.

An overwhelming sense of peace filled me. As if Someone had breathed it into my lungs. Doc had told me the most blessed thing about faith for him was letting go of his worries. Me? I'd just discovered I wasn't afraid to die. How could a man ask for more than this during his time on earth?

Girard took a third match from his pocket. "See, I got to watch you first two times I lit a match. It's going through your head, is he going to light this fire? I enjoyed that."

He flicked the match with the edge of his thumbnail, and it popped into flame. "I'll enjoy more watching this shack burn, hearing you scream."

He threw the match at the nearest patch of kerosene-soaked wood. " 'Course," he said, "maybe you'll pull loose and make a run for it. I'd like that, too, shooting you down."

The match bounced off the wood and its flame died in the dirt.

"What a shame," Girard taunted me. "I'll have to try again."

He did.

And the next match caught.

CHAPTER 35

At first smokeless and silent, the flames formed a dancing necklace of blue and yellow as they raced along the surface of the kerosene-soaked wood.

I clawed at the cords around my ankles.

Under Girard's supervision, I'd been forced to pull the knots tight, but much of my effort had been show. The knots *would* give to my fumbling fingers—indeed I could feel a grudging twist and slip already—but I doubted I had the minutes it would take.

Leaning forward as I was, I felt no heat for the first frantic seconds. Then it was like the sun warming my back, and I glanced up to see that the flames had begun to eat into the wood with a deadly hiss. Already, gray smoke stung my eyes.

As I watched, the flames crawled high and fast, deadly writhing snakes. Knowing that any frenzied struggle would only tighten the knots, I fought against the urge to pull, strain, yank at the cords that bound my ankles to the bunk.

I fumbled at the knots.

My fear became the drenching sweat of panic and effort as the flames began to roar, and my mind screamed panic at the disorienting and unfamiliar sensations of heat and sound and at the prospect of death beyond the most horrible imaginings.

One cord broke loose. I gasped relief, an action that sucked the thickening smoke into my lungs, and I sputtered for air.

The smoke was dimming my vision, even as the flames began to leap for the roof. With no hole in the shack to pull the smoke free, clouds of sparks and ash and smoke broiled and edged closer and closer to the ground.

I could not resist the panic more, and I yanked at the other cord.

Nothing.

My next glance at the flames showed only the smoke, now a swirling blanket that mixed ash with the tears burning in my eyes.

I finally realized I had to drop. Find air.

I fell onto the dirt of the shack and paid the price with a twisting of my bound leg that seemed to shear my leg with agony. A flaming chunk of wood crashed beside my head, threw sparks into my face, and spurred me to a frantic kicking. I screamed against the pain of my caught leg, and that pain ended as abruptly as it had hit. I'd broken the bunk's frame and pulled loose. My leg was free.

All I could think was to bolt. To push to my feet and crash through the flames of the nearest wall into the drizzle of cold mountain air I had been cursing such a short time before. Yet Girard waited me, ready to shoot me as a fleeing dog, ready to laugh that cold delight at the sight of my body jerking to the dance of his bullets.

As I lifted my head, it put my eyes back into the settling, choking smoke, and I was forced to drop to draw another breath. I remained with my face in the dirt.

The heat pressed on me.

My shirt seemed to be melting into my back, the rivets of my jeans searing like branding irons. I knew then I'd rather die by bullet, go down in raging futility than allow myself to meekly accept this hell.

Another chunk of torched wood slammed downward, this one bouncing off my shoulder. I rolled in desperation at the burst of flame on my shirt and crunched into something solid.

The stove.

Time had shortened for me, and I measured it gasp by shallow gasp. The heat and noise and pain and fear had crazed me; my first thought was that I'd found a shield. I'd grab the stove, wrap my arms around it, smash through the wall, and charge Girard so fiercely that I'd be on him before he could fire around the heavy iron.

At that moment, in the blind unreasonable waves of terror that swayed me, I believed I could do it, too—lift and carry a cast-iron potbellied stove.

I buried my face, sucked in air, then rose to a squatting position that put my head into the smoke again. I closed my eyes against the grit and ash and reached downward in a squatting position, gripping the bottom edge of the stove between its short, curving legs.

With a roar, I pushed up with my legs, ignored the punishment of ripping thigh muscles and the iron edges that cut into my fingers and heaved with every ounce of effort I possessed.

Incredibly, the stove toppled.

Even as it was falling, though, I knew I was about to die. The stove was so heavy that the effort had spent me, and as sanity returned, I realized that not even two desperate men could right the stove, let alone pick it up and run with it.

I ducked down from the smoke to sob for more air and lost my balance, falling forward onto my knees.

As I landed, the ground gave way with a splintering that I

felt rather than heard. And the ground beneath me disappeared. My head crashed into something hard, sending me into a darkness that overwhelmed me with the cool relief of total silence.

———

Water woke me. Cold dripping water that seeped into my clothes and made me aware that my knees were pressed against my chest, that a great weight bowed my shoulders.

I blinked. Saw nothing. Just inky blackness that led me to doubt whether I'd even opened my eyes.

Water ran down my face. I licked, tasting gritty ash. I tried to wipe it clear but could not move my right hand. Neither my left.

But I was alive.

I knew that because of the aches and pains and chill of soaked clothing.

I struggled to move and felt the weight on my shoulders shift. Then it slid, scraping hard down my back, leaving a warmth of pain and a thud of wood against wood as it landed somewhere behind me.

Nothing more but blackness, the steady drip of water, and the numbness of a body that would not move. My eyes became heavy again, and the numbness left me as I fell back into the void of unknowing.

When I woke again, it was with a bright shaft of light piercing my eyelids.

Sunlight.

I groaned, shook my head, and groaned again as I mustered the strength to open my eyes and turn away from the direct sun of a clear dawn.

A confusion of charred beams of wood crisscrossed most of the blue of the sky above me. My wrists were pinned between my chest and my knees. And I was stuck in a crouching position in a narrow, deep pit.

It was common enough that miners would have a hiding hole like this somewhere near their efforts. Because they went to town only once or twice a season, they needed a place to stow the gold or silver they extracted. Obviously, the miners who built this shack had decided to cover their hole first with thin planks that held dirt, then with the stove that had straddled the hole. I'd crashed through knees first, wedging myself almost at the bottom of the pit, barely safe from the fire that raged above me.

Only now I wondered if I had gone from the fire to the frying pan. Unless I was able to push loose, this would be a much worse death.

First, I wriggled and pulled at my hands. Slowly, and eased by the wetness of my clothing, I was able to move them from where they were pinned against my chest. I was rewarded for this by the agony of returning blood circulation, a stabbing of pins and needles that made me want to stomp my feet. If only I could.

After a rest, I grabbed the loose pieces of wood that had tumbled into the pit with me and threw them clear. It gave me some wriggle room, and I reached to test one of the beams in the pile wedged above me.

The beam creaked protest.

I tried another. And another and another until finally I found a beam that did not move as I pulled down. I pulled harder and at the same time pushed upward as best I could with my numb legs. The skin of my back took most of the punishment as I rubbed it raw in my efforts to get into a standing position.

Progress was slow. A half hour later, I was there. The top of the hole was barely above head, and my shoulders were in a gap among fallen beams. I could rest my chin on one of those beams and did.

It felt good beyond measure to be straight and uncramped, so good that I greeted with cheerful chuckles the new rush of agony that came with returning blood circulation.

All that remained was clearing the beams above that had me trapped.

By sunset, I was still there in the pit. Able to dance and hop. But unable to find enough room to haul myself upward, for the gap was too narrow, the beams too heavy, and from my limited position I was unable to get the leverage required to untangle the beams from the top downward.

I was thirsty by then from all my efforts. Twice I'd wrung my shirt, desperate for what water I could squeeze into my mouth. To make it worse, I could hear beyond the gurgle of the nearby stream.

But I was alive.

I settled down into the pit, making a seat of a pile of wood, leaned back, and tried to make myself comfortable.

I was not without hope. Clara knew where I'd gone. She'd wait the two days, then, I believed, send her driver to see why I had not returned. Those thoughts made it easier to endure the prospect of another night here.

With darkness came the stardust of a clear mountain sky and the occasional howls of coyotes and muted hooting of owls.

I tried to sleep. Although the day had become warm enough to finally dry my clothes, the night air cooled rapidly and reached past my clothing to draw from me all my warmth. When it became too cold, I would rise and dance and shiver.

I gave up on sleep and waited for daylight.

As the sky darkened, one star caught my attention. The Evening Star. My mind naturally turned to Rebecca. And in thinking of her, to what Clara had said about Rebecca.

———

After stowing the coffins, Clara and I had gone back to the privacy of her carriage. Her driver had simply ridden aimlessly, giving us the precious sadness of spending time together while knowing it would be our last, for Clara had made it clear that we would not meet again after our good-bye.

We had talked ourselves out in catching up on all that had happened in the years apart, until Clara had fallen asleep with her head on my shoulder. While she slept, I pondered new guilt. Guilt that Rebecca could be so far from my mind. Guilt that I had chosen not to tell Clara about the one woman who had been able to replace her. Guilt that I was betraying both.

Dawn had approached that morning—was it only yesterday—and Clara stirred at the growing light. Sat. Pushed her tousled hair from her eyes. Blinked at me and smiled.

In that moment, it felt like granite was falling away from my heart. I did love this woman. And could say it. To her. And to me. All the years I'd pushed her from my mind, forced myself not to care. With that one gentle smile, I was helpless against the surge of joy and pain and sorrow that came with realizing I loved her so deeply.

I wasn't sure I liked it. Losing rein over my feelings.

"You look afraid," she said. "I'm sorry for you. For us."

"Me too." I could not take my eyes off her face. "Must this be good-bye, never to see you again?"

Her smile was knowing and sad. "All night I've been asking myself the same thing. I have a husband and child, yet if you asked me to leave Denver with you, it would be difficult to refuse."

Was that an invitation? I grappled with the immensity of such an act. The price she would pay for me. How in the presence of Clara—despite what I felt now for another woman— it was easy for me to forget promises made.

I groaned. What was this that a man could be so torn and confused?

"Clara, can a body love two persons?"

We shared a long silence, until she finally said in a quiet voice that I could barely hear above the creaking of the carriage, "You always did ask me difficult questions. I love my husband. And you . . ."

"You always did appear to know the answers."

"Not now." She took a deep breath. "Life is complicated, confusing. Here with you proves it. And long ago I stopped looking for simple answers."

More silence. "Can a body love two persons?" she said. "You tell me. Can you create something as true as love and ever expect it to die?"

I shook my head.

"There's your answer." She rubbed her face. "My husband knows you were and are my first love. He knew that when I married him. He's endured the many times I mourned you. Your memory has always been a ghost between us. That's why John sent me from the restaurant to be with you tonight."

I must have gaped.

Tears began to roll down her cheeks. "That's how much he loves me. He gave me the choice. He's praying I return, and that when I do, your ghost will be gone."

She ignored her tears, tracks shiny in the gray of first light. "Can a body love two persons? I do. I told you if you asked me to leave Denver with you, it would be difficult to refuse. Yet I would. I learned to love John. He stood by me when I needed him. I cannot and will not abandon him. That's part of love, too, loyalty. It is killing me to know that as we share this carriage, he waits, afraid I may not return."

Clara took a deep breath. "Can a body love two persons? Yes. Sometimes it cannot help but happen that way. Should a body act upon both of those loves? No."

She wiped her eyes. "Who is she?"

I told her. And felt cleansed.

"I hate her," Clara said. And smiled to show otherwise. "Don't run from her like you did from me."

I tried to protest.

She leaned forward and touched my lips with her forefinger to silence me. "I sent you away. It is my eternal regret. It could have, should have, been you with me. Yet the action was taken, and because others love me and need me, I cannot undo it." She whispered it again. "I sent you away." Her eyes searched mine. "Still, you could have returned."

Tears fell fresh again, and she began to sob. "You could have returned. Tried to fight my refusal. I waited. I waited until I could no longer wait."

She shook away my efforts to comfort her. Light was strong enough to cast shadows into the carriage before she had composed herself.

"Don't keep running from Rebecca."

"I haven't run from her," I said. "She is among the Sioux because she needs to know if she should live as a Sioux or as a white. She—"

"Stop," Clara said. She set her jaw. "You can also tell me you didn't return to me because I sent you away. But you could have returned. You knew where Denver was. So ask yourself why you've allowed Rebecca to be apart from you. With me, and with her, you've given yourself the ideal excuse not to commit. Ask yourself what it is you're afraid of. Letting go and the risk of pain it brings?"

I had no answer.

She softened. Touched my cheek lightly with the back of her fingers. "I do love you. Always will. The boy too stubborn to beg or quit. The man too stubborn to realize he's lonely."

The carriage jolted. A reminder of our limited time together. Clara closed her eyes. Held her head straight, magnificent in her sorrow and the new tears.

"Please leave," she said, eyes closed. "Tap the carriage so that the driver stops and leave without saying good-bye. I cannot bear this any longer."

She refused to open her eyes as the carriage jerked to a stop.

The coward that I was, I had stepped from the carriage into gray dawn. And left Clara again. Without protest. Again.

CHAPTER 36

"GONE FROM DENVER?" I said, surprised.

"Departed." Despite my outcry, the woman in David Girard's bank office spoke in dull tones from where she sat behind his desk. She was staring down at the mess of papers, elbows on the desk, face supported by her hands. She hadn't lifted her head to speak. Otherwise, she would have noticed the two bank tellers behind me, afraid to pull at my sleeves but equally afraid to walk away.

"Gone," I repeated.

I'd endured that pit the entire morning before Clara's driver appeared. I'd ridden back to Denver at a jolting trot, rushed to this bank, bolted past the startled tellers at a running limp—my torn and smeared clothes stinking of sweat and fire—crashed open the door of David Girard's office, gun in hand, to confront him, and now this lady behind his desk was telling me he was gone?

One of the bank tellers did muster the

courage to place a hand on my shoulder. "Sir—"

I slapped his hand away.

"When?" I asked her without looking back.

I don't think it was my sharp question that got her attention.

Rather, she sniffed. Not disdain. Not tears. But as if she was testing the air. I didn't blame her. I had never been more rank, even after weeks on the trail.

She lifted her head.

Her face registered no surprise to see me, as if it were an everyday occurrence in the bank to see someone in filthy, ripped clothing, three days of beard growth, and a gun in his hand as he blocked the doorway.

"Departed. Yesterday."

I realized her face did not register surprise to see me because she was numb with shock, reflected by the monotone of her words and the lack of focus in her eyes.

She had graying hair. A lean face, strong thin nose, and flesh just beginning to sag, now drawn with weariness. Her dress was simple, but offset by the gleam of pearls on the necklace that matched her earrings. The hands that held her head were adorned with the greens and reds of expensive jewelry. Altogether, she was not unattractive.

"Mrs. Lesley Girard." I holstered my revolver.

"Mmmm." An acknowledgment that was more like a distracted hum.

I spared a questioning glance for the two tellers behind me.

One shrugged.

I flipped open my vest to show the marshal's badge and motioned for them to back off. They did, probably happy to have someone with a mantle of authority take over, no matter how false the mantle or how disheveled his appearance.

I shut the door behind me.

"You smell," she said, continued lack of concern in her voice.

"I *would* like a long hot bath," I allowed. "It was more important, however, to speak to David Girard."

"Yes. That would be nice."

She was childlike in her shock. I wondered how she might be under different conditions, and I decided that someone from a wealthy family and accustomed to running a bank might be someone much less pliable in normal circumstances than she appeared to be now. It was a terrible time to take advantage of her. However, I'd give myself the luxury of worrying about that later.

"Will he return soon?" I pressed her.

"He left me." Absolute hopelessness.

"How do you know he won't return?" I asked.

"He took the money." She spread one hand across her cheek so it could take the entire weight of her head and lifted the other hand to point at the papers. "He cleared all these accounts and took the money."

"Any idea where—"

"He had everything," she said. She was speaking to herself. "The mansion. Easy work here at the bank. Me. All there was in the accounts to take was five thousand. He left everything I could give him for that meager five thousand dollars. I wasn't that much older, you know. Only a few years." She was rambling now, in a sing-song voice. "Of course, I always knew he might go. That's why he never got more than a thousand or two at a time. He—"

I reached forward and slammed my fist down on the desk.

She blinked once. Twice. Finally met my eyes.

"He tried to kill me yesterday," I said.

Her mouth opened and closed.

"He's killed others, too. And may have killed two men earlier this month in Laramie."

Slowly, her eyes began to focus on me.

"Why are you here." She said it firmly, a statement, as if she were coming out of a daze.

"I'm the marshal from Laramie."

Lesley Girard pushed the chair back from the desk. When she stood, I discovered she was tall. Thin, to match the lean in her face. She took a deep breath. Composed herself.

"This is an affair of the bank," she said. "Private."

"I'm not looking for him because of this bank."

She began to shrug.

"He tried to burn me to death. If we discuss him here, that will remain private, too. Otherwise . . ."

She considered that. "All right, then."

She sat again. I pulled out a chair myself. Set my hat in my lap.

"Any idea where he might go?" I asked.

"No." Had she said it quickly and immediately, I would have guessed the denial to be a lie. But her slow statement had a ring of truth to it.

"Where was he from?" I asked. Maybe that would give me an idea of his habits.

"He never talked much about it," she said. "Whenever I pressed him, he got all cold on me."

That stumped me briefly. I remembered Dehlia.

"Didn't his daughter claim she was from the South? Did you learn anything from her?"

"Dehlia?" Her sniff now was definitely disdain. "I spoke to her as little as possible."

"Is she still here in Denver?"

"No," Leslie said. "She left two or three days ago. I thought it was finally over, whatever they had."

Her new ironclad composure cracked along with her voice. "Now I'm wondering if he left to be with her."

I remembered the expression of hatred on David Girard's face when I'd asked him about Dehlia.

"Mrs. Girard, I can assure you that would not be true."

She took a breath. "I shall choose to believe you."

I gave her some time to collect herself once more, then asked, "Does David have any connection to Laramie?"

"None."

"No business there?" I could not keep disbelief from my voice.

"None. If you won't accept my answers, don't bother with the questions."

She'd recovered quickly.

"What did he do here at the bank, Mrs. Girard?"

"Loans. Mainly to cattle operations."

"Forgive me for asking," I said. "Any of those ranches in Wyoming?"

"Possibly. He often went to the Cheyenne cattle market."

"Any chance of knowing which ranches?"

"I can have a list drawn for you," she said. She paused. Squinted puzzlement. "My apologies for my previous abruptness. There was one ranch *near* Laramie. Bar something or the other."

"Bar X Bar."

She nodded.

No surprise. I had no idea how that fit in, but it was no surprise.

"This may be troublesome," I said, "but I'd appreciate a look at the loan papers." That might give me an indication of what was behind this.

She frowned. "Banking is a private business. It's built on—"

"Trust. I know. But in the last while I've been shot at and missed, shot at and hit, bullwhipped, burned, and buried alive. It hasn't put me in good humor, and while I have no grounds to force you to show me the papers, it would improve my mood considerably if you did."

That brought her first smile. She moved out from behind the desk, walked past me, opened the bank door, called one of the tellers, and moments later whispered instructions.

She stepped back inside.

"You must think I'm a fool," she said. "An old lady smitten by a younger man. I was. But money, no matter how much you have, doesn't hold you at night. And you can't force yourself to love someone, no matter how much you wish you could. Much as I looked, I found no one to interest me. I feared I would grow old alone. Until David Girard. He had a way about him that made it impossible not to be smitten. So I permitted myself the luxury of marrying him and never regretted what it cost. I loved him, and my money kept him nearby."

She had my sympathy. Because of Rebecca, and more recently, my time with Clara, I understood lonely. Money meant little in the face of it.

"I wish you the best," I said.

She smiled apologetically. "I always knew he might go someday. That's why I never left enough in these accounts to make it worth his while. . . ."

She let her voice trail away.

I couldn't think of anything to say, so we shared silence for a few minutes until the relief of a light knock on the door. She opened it enough that I could see the teller's anxious face from where I sat, but she did not invite him inside the office.

"No record of the loans," I heard him say.

"Impossible." Her voice was sharp.

"I checked the files. The bank vault for copies. Everywhere. No record."

"The ledgers?"

"Three pages missing, Mrs. Girard."

"Impossible." But she didn't say it like it was.

"I can look again."

"No," she said, "I'll sort this later."

Lesley Girard dismissed him and turned back to me. "Strange. You don't suppose . . ."

Eagle concentration filled her face. I admired her toughness.

"Suppose?"

"I always knew he couldn't be trusted," she said. "That was part of his attraction for me. Everything else in my life was tame. You don't suppose he drew up a loan to someone who didn't exist. . . ."

"Unlikely," I said. "I've been to the Bar X Bar myself."

"Why would he help out some rancher so far north?"

"Help?"

"Unless we can find records of the loan, there's no proof. Without proof, we can't expect repayment. Not unless the rancher volunteers his records."

"Was it a substantial loan?"

"Without a doubt. David didn't deal with loans under ten thousand."

"And his ceiling?" I asked.

"Fifty thousand."

"Fifty thousand dollars." That would be enough to justify leaving his gilded cage.

"Find the money if you can," Lesley Girard was saying. "But if you can, leave him be."

"Ma'am?"

"Don't hurt him."

"He tried to murder me."

"I know," she said. "But I love him."

CHAPTER 37

My return to Laramie was not a hero's welcome. Not when the only person to greet me was Brother Lewis in his jail cell, still as ungrateful as ever for my efforts to spare him from future sins.

Jake Wilson was delivering a load of feed to a nearby ranch. Doc Harper was on a sick call in the opposite direction. And I had no hankering to discuss my Denver trip with Mayor Crawford, mainly because I barely knew more than what I had left Laramie with in the first place.

My first stop after dispensing with greetings to Brother Lewis had been the Red Rose Saloon. Dehlia's brothers sat playing poker but were unwilling to share with me the whereabouts of Dehlia.

I'd then walked well clear of Benjamin Guthrie's store, because all the sleep I'd absorbed on the train ride back from Denver was not near the amount I needed to put me in a mood that would make discussion with him any sort of tolerable.

With everyone out of town, all that remained for me to do was pay a visit out to the Rocking N.

Which is why I found myself a few hours later staring into the barrel of an old Sharps rifle.

———

"Have mercy," I said from atop my horse.

Helen Nichols lowered the rifle. The bush behind her still shook from her recent exit. It was a big bush—she'd been completely hidden before stepping onto the trail.

"Recent habit?" I asked.

"Yup," she said. "Being out here alone as I am. The boys told me they'd seen someone headed this way."

I shook my head. I still hadn't dismounted. "You had the rifle cocked. One shaky trigger finger from down there, it would have taken out the bottom of my chin."

"I know what I'm doing," she said.

I wasn't prepared to disagree with her.

I began to swing off my saddle. Stopped with my weight still on my good leg. What was bothering me?

"Marshal?"

I gave my head a shake and completed the dismount.

"Just distracted," I said. "Got any bread and ham handy?"

Her broad face creased into a smile. "As much as you can pack into your belly."

I led my horse and followed her around the bend in the trail to the soddy. What I really wanted to do was sit by myself and puzzle why I was so bothered. Something important had passed me by. I knew that with a gut-deep certainty. But what had it been?

Her three boys ran up, white grins in dirty faces.

I found a couple of coins and flipped them in their direction. "Think you boys are old enough to water a horse and brush him down?"

"Yes, sir." They'd each said it, but all together, and it sounded like one.

They took the horse's reins, serious determination showing in the rigidness of their small bodies.

"By the way, boys, when you get the saddle off, take a good look in the saddlebag. I believe you'll find some licorice sticks. Can't eat them myself. Doc Harper says I'm too old."

They whooped delight that continued until they'd reached a far shed.

Helen was already in the soddy.

I eased myself in the shade on the same stool I'd used on my earlier visit.

She returned with water and strips of clean white meat on thick bread. "Chicken this time, Marshal," she said. "Cooked yesterday, and with the cooler weather, it keeps plenty good."

She was right. I swallowed it down with cold water.

I grinned.

"Anyone else here but me," she said, "I'd swear you was in a courting mood."

"I do have good news," I said. "Been looking forward to delivering it."

She had not yet sat. She placed her massive fists on her massive hips and looked down on me.

"Pray tell."

"You're a wealthy woman."

"Marshal, you have no call to jest."

I gulped more water. "No jest. A lawyer named Brian Scott, back in Denver, looked into the mining papers you believed were worthless. Turns out you own a regular producing vein of silver. Mr. Scott there figures it won't bottom out for a couple of years."

I reached inside my vest pocket and handed her the envelope that Brian Scott had hand delivered to me in my Denver hotel. By then, of course, I'd had a hot bath, shaved, rested some, and was in shape to understand most of what the lawyer had explained about his tradeoff with Leakey. All documents immediately transferred to Helen Nichols. No further inquiries into his crime.

Helen Nichols did not open the envelope that assured her that she never need approach another bank for a loan.

"Marshal," she finally said with the first trace of helplessness I'd seen upon her, "I cain't read."

I gritted my teeth at my stupidity. To assume she'd been schooled . . .

"Me neither," I lied. "I was hoping you'd be able to tell me what it said."

I snapped my fingers. "Ask Doc next time you're in town." I added a grin. "And I'd get to town soon. What I did hear was the first lawyer looked for a way to steal it from you, and the second lawyer got it all straightened for you. From the way the fella in Denver was talking, you might just be able to buy the next bank you see."

She studied my face, and when she decided I was not playing a cruel joke, she clutched the envelope to her massive bosom.

"My boys," she whispered. "I can move them from here and all the bad talk about their pa."

Her eyes began to redden, and she began to sniffle.

"If it ain't asking too much, I could use another bite or two." I held up my empty plate. A person don't mind helping out, and this hadn't taken much anyway, but she was ready to bust into tears or give me a big hug. Both prospects promised sentiment, and in general, I find it pays to duck that kind of difficulty.

She returned with another chunk of bread and sliced chicken that I had to force down, and because I was eating more slowly, she filled the silence.

"Didn't mean to give your heart a jump with that rifle,"

Helen said. "Just that I did hear about you getting shot, and how Clay Barnes died, and what with all the dying in these parts, I figured it don't hurt to be safe."

I nodded and swallowed hard. At least she wasn't sniffling.

"Old Emma, too," she said. "You heard?"

I nearly choked. "Emma Springer? Dead? How?"

She nodded. "In her sleep. At least that's what I heard. Peaceful like."

"She was strong like a mule," I said.

Helen shrugged.

That bothered me. Greatly. Two deaths—Emma Springer and Clayton Barnes—out at the Bar X Bar. Two deaths in Laramie—both somehow tied to David Girard in Denver. And David Girard in Denver tied to the Bar X Bar through the cattle loan.

I opened my jaw to take another bite.

Jaw . . .

It sprung loose, the distraction that had been worrying at me like a bur under my saddle ever since Helen had stepped out suddenly with that rifle. If she'd shot upward, her bullet would have taken out my jaw.

In a flash, I saw clearly her husband's body in the bank vault. Shirt and vest and dusty jeans. Hat off and crushed beneath his head. Gray-and-black beard matted with blood, blood that had pooled from a hole torn in his throat, the exit wound at the back of his skull hidden by his hat and hair.

And hadn't I told Doc that the bullet that killed Bob Nichols was going upward, a fact that proved Calhoun hadn't killed him?

Now, if my guess was right, it was the path of a bullet fired in the same manner as Helen might have fired at me. From a man on the ground shooting a man sitting on a horse.

Helen tried to say something.

I put up my hand for silence. I wanted to think this through.

Yet it was ridiculous to think that Nichols had been on a horse in the bank vault.

I closed my eyes again, pictured what I'd seen in the bank vault.

Then I smiled.

"Helen, when your husband left the ranch—"

"You mean that last time?"

"Yes," I said gentle, and reminded myself that this was not a puzzle to her, but the death of someone she would grieve for years. "Did he take a coat? I mean, it is fall and nights get cold."

She thought some. "Why . . . why yes, I believe he did."

Of course he did. I had my own coat rolled back of my horse's saddle for when the sun set.

"That may be enough to clear his name," I told Helen. "If not legal-like, at least cleared in folks' minds. Your boys might not have to hear much bad about their pa."

"How's that?" She was hesitant, but hope shone from her eyes.

"Helen, he didn't have his coat with him at the bank. Nor was it found on his horse. I think I can make a case that he was . . ."

I couldn't say it to her.

"Murdered," she said. "You don't have to go easy on me."

"I think I can make a case it happened somewhere else. That his body was then taken to the vault."

I wasn't going to detail my theory about the bullet that took his life coming from a man on the ground while he sat on his horse. Not with her grave eyes fixed on me.

"But the landlady," Helen protested. "She says she saw Bob visit Lorne Calhoun. Everyone says Bob forced Calhoun back with him to the bank."

I disagreed with her. "By the time I got around to asking the landlady, she'd already heard about the two men who were found in the vault. Easy mistake at that point for her to assume it was Bob. Dark hallway, low voices, I'll bet if the landlady thinks it through, she'd never be able to swear on a Bible that it was Bob."

Especially, I thought, if Bob had already been shot somewhere else, then brought into Laramie late at night by the person who then knocked on Calhoun's door. If Bob had been shot just after leaving the Rocking N, that would explain his three-day absence before appearing dead in the bank vault.

Except for one thing.

Blood.

The blood around both bodies in the bank vault had been sticky. Fresh. Not four days old.

"Marshal?"

I realized I'd been quiet too long.

"Helen, it's . . ."

I'd been about to say that it's impossible to explain the fresh blood. Doc's voice echoed in my mind and cut me short. *"When I cleaned the entry wound, I was low to the ground, and I found something in the blood between the two bodies. Bits of feather stuck in the blood. Like feathers from a pillow."*

"Helen, first time I visited, you'd just finished butchering chickens. I saw the claws and feathers on the ground near your chopping block. Tell me, how hard would it be to lop off a chicken's neck and hold it by the legs so that its blood drains into a bucket?"

I knew the answer already, but I wanted to hear it from her.

Her square face shifted in puzzlement. "Not hard t'all, Marshal. Why ask? What's this got to do with—"

"Last question," I interrupted. I couldn't force myself to involve her in my guessing game. Not about her husband. I had a good idea of how he'd been murdered. All I had to figure out was who, and I had my ideas on that, too. I asked the question that on my first visit I had forgotten. Back then, the question had little importance when I'd believed four days had passed between Bob's departure and his murder. "Helen, which direction was Bob headed when he left that last morning?"

I swept my hand vaguely in all directions. "He could have gone north along the river or south. He could have cut across the river or taken the trail back toward Laramie. Did you happen to notice?"

"Certainly." She blinked back the sadness of her memories. "I always see him off. It's just how we were."

"Which direction?" Now I was impatient.

"He took the trail," she said. And pointed in the direction of the Bar X Bar.

CHAPTER 38

I RODE. AND THOUGHT.

There was what I'd just considered. Two deaths had taken place at the Bar X Bar. Two other deaths—Lorne Calhoun and Bob Nichols—were related to the Bar X Bar through David Girard and Denver. Bob Nichols' last ride had been in the direction of the Bar X Bar.

The easy conclusion was that someone at the Bar X Bar was behind all of this.

But was it David Girard? How could he be in Denver *and* Laramie?

Eleanor Ford. She was also a common tie to Lorne Calhoun and Bob Nichols. Jake Wilson had told me Bob Nichols on his return from Denver mumbled a comment about stopping by the Bar X Bar to see Eleanor Ford. Lorne Calhoun had his letter of instruction from her.

Eleanor Ford owned the Bar X Bar. And Eleanor Ford had access to the bank vault at the First National in Laramie.

Was it her, the murderer, the person who

had shot Nichols as he sat trusting on his horse looking downward at the person about to take his life?

I told myself it could not be. Eleanor Ford was not big enough to handle the inert weight of dragging the dead Bob Nichols into the First National bank vault. Eleanor Ford would not have been mistaken for a man by the landlady who had seen Lorne Calhoun's late-night caller.

The frustration was killing me. I felt as if all the pieces were there, maybe even assembled, but somehow I was failing to recognize the completed puzzle.

All right, I asked myself, what did David Girard and Eleanor Ford have in common?

Banking.

She owned a bank. He'd worked in a bank.

She owned a bank. He'd married someone who owned a bank.

Anything else?

The Bar X Bar. She owned it. He'd loaned to it.

I gnawed on that for a while.

Nothing.

I was maybe a half hour away from the Bar X Bar. My horse flushed the occasional jackrabbit. More often a sage hen. The bowl of the afternoon sky was a pale blue, painted with the wisp of high, white trailing clouds. Usually I enjoyed the ride, but now, not even the serene freedom of horse travel through the great grassland basin of the Laramie Plains gave me any sense of peace as I rode.

I realized all of my thoughts had been focused on the murderer—logical, but with no results.

I decided to try it from another approach. Why not wonder about the victims? I'd include myself as murdered—after all, David Girard had left Denver so quickly he would have no idea I was still alive.

Bob Nichols, Lorne Calhoun, Clayton Barnes, Emma Springer, Samuel Keaton. Take Emma off the list; maybe she had indeed died a natural death. Take Clayton Barnes off the list; he might have died as an innocent bystander or been killed simply because of his involvement with the dead man's horse and the missing ten thousand in bank notes.

That left Bob Nichols, Lorne Calhoun, and Samuel Keaton. All three of us had seen David Girard in Denver. All three of us were from Laramie. All three of us had been to the Bar X Bar.

Impossible as it seemed, if it was Girard, what could he be trying to hide through our deaths?

Bob Nichols and Lorne Calhoun might have known. I didn't.

What then could Nichols and Calhoun have in common that I had missed and Girard hadn't? What had they seen that I hadn't?

I gnawed at that, too. Found nothing.

It jolted me when I finally realized David Girard had asked me essentially the same question. *How much do you know?* That was his question at the mining shack. *How much do you know? My wife tell you anything?*

Why would he be so concerned what I might have learned from Lesley Girard? Unless he feared that I had passed along that knowledge and before I died needed to be certain I hadn't.

My wife tell you anything?

Girard had accused me of being on his trail like a dog on partridge. From the beginning, he'd said. *Before* my arrival in Denver? But how could that be?

My wife tell you anything?

Girard had admitted to shooting me and Clayton Barnes. How'd he know the Bar X Bar country so well? Why could he ride through it and not fear that somebody might comment on him being a stranger? Both suggested, of course, that he was no stranger in these parts.

My wife tell you anything?

Calhoun and Nichols had been around Laramie enough to know who was a stranger in these parts. And . . . I hadn't been around long enough! Now things begin to click.

My wife tell you anything?

If Girard wasn't a stranger in these parts, I needed to figure out his connection to the Bar X Bar.

My wife tell you anything?

It hit me then. Not Lesley Girard.

Wife? Which wife?

That's why I had my gun out when I stepped into the barn at the Bar X Bar ranch. That's why it didn't surprise me when, at the sound of my voice, David Girard turned from the horse he was saddling.

CHAPTER 39

ON MY HORSE, in the shadows of the barn, I extended my Colt at face level and looked down my barrel at him. "David Girard," I said. "Or, since this is the Bar X Bar, would you prefer I call you Cyrus Ford?"

"No," he said. "Not possible. You're dead."

"You lie down," I said. "Right there. Right now. And clasp your hands back of your neck."

It was the best way I knew to stop a man from pulling fast.

He looked at the ground. It needed shoveling.

"I shot a man once," I said. "Unlike you, I hated doing it. Unlike you, it took only one bullet. And there was no amount of water that could splash him back to life to feel the next bullet."

He lowered himself.

I kept my gun carefully trained on him as I walked a wide circle to get behind him. There's a move called a road agent spin, where you hand the gun across, barrel mouth toward yourself, then suddenly flip it so the handle slaps your palm, leaving the gun upside down and barrel now pointing opposite, giving you the chance to fire safely, all within the space of a heartbeat. I know, because I've practiced it lots. I wasn't going to ask him for his gun and take the chance of finding out whether he'd practiced it, too.

"Nope," I said as he turned his head and body to keep his eyes on me, "just keep looking toward the door."

When I got around him, I stepped up close to his back and plucked the gun loose from his holster and threw it aside. Much safer.

I pressed my revolver against the small of his back. Firm, to pin him to the ground. It was another method to discourage a hero attempt. With my other hand, I patted the sides of his legs and boots. He had a derringer in his left boot.

"Work that boot loose with your right foot," I said as I stepped away. "Then kick the pocket revolver away."

He struggled.

I didn't watch his feet—but his hands. That was the only place I could expect trouble. There was none.

"Sit up," I said when he was finished. "Keep your hands clasped behind your neck."

Straw and clumped balls of horse droppings clung to the front of his shirt. He stared at me with cold rage, his saddled horse standing patiently beside him.

"Let's talk," I said. "A friendly talk."

Silence.

"David Girard?" I asked. Silence. "Cyrus Ford?"

"I'll see you dead," he spat.

"You tried that once," I said. "Back in Denver where you called yourself David Girard. 'Course, this was after you shot me in the leg here at the Bar X Bar where you call yourself Cyrus Ford."

"Prove it."

"The names? Or the murder attempts?"

"The murder attempts. It's your word against mine."

I nodded. "Maybe."

Girard snorted. "Maybe? You name the time. Eleanor Ford will testify I was with her. In Denver? Name the time again. Lesley Girard will swear I was beside her."

I studied him.

He laughed. "Nobody's been hanged for being married to two women. And don't expect either to send me before a judge anyway."

His face, even with that hateful laugh, was a model of perfection. And he carried himself like a god. In the face of betrayal, Lesley Girard had still asked me to get her money, but leave him alone. I didn't doubt Eleanor Ford felt the same.

"I'll tell you the way I read it," I said, "You had the perfect life. Whenever you needed to leave the Bar X Bar to be in Denver, you told Eleanor Ford you had ranching business in Cheyenne, because, of course, Cheyenne was the stopover, and your train ticket would indeed show Cheyenne. Once in Cheyenne, you would purchase another ticket to Denver. Same thing, but reversed, with Lesley Girard whenever you needed to leave Denver."

He gave no reaction, but I knew I was right.

"Then one day," I said, "out of the blue, Bob Nichols walks into the Denver First and sees you as David Girard. You see him. Maybe he's too surprised to say anything because he knows you as his neighbor, Cyrus Ford."

I drew a breath. "Bad luck for you. Who would guess someone like that would see you in Denver? You know that as soon as Bob Nichols gets to Laramie, he'll say or ask something that puts your double marriage and the good life that comes with it to an end. So he's got to go."

"Do-gooder wanted to talk to me in private first," Girard said. "To give me a chance to right my wrongs. Wasn't hard to right that wrong with a bullet."

"Of course," I said, "it'd be the last thing he expected. He rides up to you on his horse, and you shoot him from where you're waiting on foot."

"You think this will accomplish anything . . . Marshal?" He said *marshal* with a sneer. "There's no proof."

"Humor me," I said. "About this same time, you're feeling more heat in Denver because another Laramie man by the name of Lorne Calhoun is doing his best to set up an appointment with you, Mr. David Girard. You've managed to avoid it a couple times, but eventually he'll be there. In your office. And you'll be facing the same problem all over again. Someone who knows you as Cyrus Ford and finds it quite a surprise to meet you as someone else in Denver. Someone who can ruin your good life the minute he gets back to Laramie. You might even suspect Calhoun is nosing around at your wife's request. But with Calhoun, you'll nip it before it becomes a problem."

"An ounce of prevention, Marshal . . ."

"And two birds with one stone. Bob Nichols is already dead. Why not get rid of Calhoun and lay the blame on Nichols? Drag Nichols into the bank vault. No problem. After all, he's too dead to fight back. And it's your wife's bank. One of your wives' bank. You know how to get into the vault." I took a breath. "Stop me if this gets boring."

"People like you are always boring," Girard said. "It comes from a misguided belief that good must prevail over evil."

"You force Calhoun inside the bank vault. Nice accident that the landlady later identifies you as Nichols. You shoot Calhoun. Put a slug mark in the opposite wall so it looked like Calhoun shot Nichols. To make it look more authentic, you pour chicken blood over Nichols. Then while you're there, you find a way to steal ten thousand or so from your wife's bank. Which means later you'll have to kill Clayton Barnes, because when the marshal starts to ask him questions, good ol' Clay might spill something about how his boss told him to expect to find a horse about where he did when he did. Good ol' Clay might tell that marshal how you instructed him to bring the horse to the nearest livery after turning in the money he saw. Good ol' Clay. Not very sharp, I've heard, but hardworking and honest. Just a kid with peach fuzz, probably worshiped the ground his boss walked on. Do anything for his boss. Include taking a bullet in the chest."

Girard shrugged, not an easy thing to do with hands clasped behind his neck. "Dog-eat-dog world, Marshal."

"I do have some questions."

"Marshal," he mocked. "You don't know everything?"

"Crawford had to know you could get into the bank vault. But I can't see him in on this."

"I went to Cheyenne with Crawford once. He loved it when I took him to visit some fine ladies in one of their less respectable establishments. He didn't like it when I showed him the photographs of him with those fine ladies. What the fool didn't know was that nothing happened. He was too drunk. Them ladies could barely get him down to his undergarments, he was so heavy. Fact is, they dropped him once, and he never even woke."

"Sure," I said. "And a bank is built on trust. If folks in Laramie ever saw those photographs, where's the trust Crawford can't live without?"

"There's more." Girard smiled, and I saw the traces again of a boy pulling at the wings of flies. He must have enjoyed the pressure he put on Crawford. "I was bleeding Crawford through blackmail. That's why Calhoun found something wrong in the books. That's why Crawford couldn't lend money to Nichols. There wasn't much around. Especially after I forced Crawford to get all that Union Pacific payroll cash on hand for me to steal."

"I appreciate that," I said. "Emma Springer?"

"She asked me a question too many. Turned out she'd

seen me follow you from here when you went looking for Clayton Barnes. All that took was a pillow across her face while she was sleeping."

I'd mourn her later. Maybe with Doc. I hadn't known her too well, but what I did know told me the world had been diminished with her passing.

"And Dehlia?"

His face began to twist in purple hatred.

"Blackmail?" I asked. "The blackmailer gets blackmailed in return? That's why you finally took all you could in Denver and ran?"

He spit.

There is a certain satisfaction when hunches pay off. That had been the only explanation I could think of for both her presence in Laramie—guarded by her brothers—and her late-night visit to me. She knew what was happening, of course; she'd been making money from it. Only when people started to die, she had second thoughts.

"Dehlia promised me all the answers in one week," I said. "That's all you had anyway. One week. With me dead or not."

"You do think you know everything, don't you?" Even his sneer was handsome. "Dehlia left Denver the day before I did. She had no way of knowing that I'd cashed in my chips there. She had no more hold over me."

"How about here?"

"She made a visit expecting more money. She didn't expect me to pull a gun and throw her in a dry well. So she's dead if I don't return. But a good bargaining point if her brothers show up at an inconvenient time."

"I'd say this is inconvenient."

He shook his head. "All you have is speculation. Or your word against mine."

I shook my head. " 'Fraid not. You're forgetting two things."

He snorted disdain.

"One," I said. "The chicken blood."

"Try convincing a judge of that."

"Shouldn't be difficult," I said. I tried to remember completely how Doc had explained it to me. "See, there's this gadget called a microscope. Like a telescope, but instead it magnifies things real close to you. In a clear drop of water, you can see creatures wriggling like bugs."

"So . . ." It was a wary statement.

"So what it can do is give a good look at blood." I was bluffing now, but what was going through my mind seemed logical. And it was my bet he'd buy it. "Under that microscope, the difference between chicken's blood and human blood is night and day."

Girard spit again.

I didn't exactly know where I was going with this. I just wanted him off balance. And I wanted that sneer of total confidence off his face.

"Two," I said. "There's the letter you missed when you searched Calhoun's room."

I was bluffing on the blood. I figured I might as well continue. If I had to, I'd write the note myself and fake Calhoun's handwriting and signature. "He explained lots in that letter. Enough that ties in with what I can prove now."

I paused. "When we get back to Laramie, I suggest you make a clean breast of things. Judge will go easier on you that way."

He stared at me, as if giving it serious thought. Then he smiled.

A heartbeat later, I understood why.

"Drop the gun, Marshal."

His smile widened. The voice behind me came from Eleanor Ford. And it didn't sound like *she* was bluffing.

I dropped my gun.

CHAPTER 40

"MOVE BESIDE CYRUS," she said.

I lowered myself onto the dirty straw litter, clasped my hands behind my neck, and waited.

She stood where I'd been standing, a derringer fitted into her right hand. Twice in one day, a woman with the drop on me. Only this one wouldn't smile and serve up lunch like Helen had barely an hour earlier.

"My darling," Girard said. "Thank you."

He started to struggle to his feet.

"Stay," she said.

"What?"

"You heard me." She waved the derringer for emphasis. Anything past ten feet, it was a useless pistol. She was close enough. The up-and-down double barrel of the derringer held sufficient promise of death that Girard remained beside me.

"When a marshal comes to call and asks for a woman's husband," she said, "it does raise questions. Especially if she's had a few of her own in the last while. When I saw the marshal ride up today, I followed here to the barn, stood outside, and heard everything." Her voice lost its braveness.

"Everything," she whispered. "Another wife? Why?"

"Love," he replied softly. "Love for you."

Her derringer dropped slightly.

"Remember when we met," he said. "How it was between us?"

She nodded. "It's still that way. For me."

"And me. I loved you so much I couldn't bear to tell you about the horrid woman who kept me in Denver. And when I saw you returned my love, I decided I could use her money to help both of us."

"But I have enough."

"Wrapped up in the ranch and in the bank. Not money we could take when we needed it. I used her in Denver. Don't you see? I used her because I loved you so much."

He was able to get a sad, choked hitch in his voice. "In fact, darling, I left her this week. You can ask Keaton here. That bridge has been burned. All for you."

She sighed. But did not completely lower the derringer. Kept it waist high, aimed somewhere between Girard and me.

"Darling," he said with the same reasonable tone. "All you need to do is shoot Keaton. Our problems will be solved. He's the only link to Denver."

She continued to stare at him. When I'd first visited the Bar X Bar, her petite figure had been strong and alluring. Now it sagged with weariness. The remarkable face so clear of wrinkles now looked ten years older. "I . . . I . . . don't know what to think."

"Think of love. Our love," he soothed.

If ever I wanted to hit a man's face without warning and unfairly, it was now. I felt dirty at the oiliness of his words. Yet each time he spoke seemed to soften her more. What kind of hold was this?

"We're two of the same breed," he soothed. "Remember.

Our love was so strong you helped me get rid of your husband. I got rid of my wife, but later, when it best suited the both of us. After I'd taken her money. I saw no need to worry you with things you might not understand until they were finished."

"What he's saying," I finally interrupted, "was that her cash was tied up in Denver, and he couldn't leave. What I'd understand if I were you is that he's still here with you for the same reason."

"No," she said.

"Haven't you been trying to sell the First National? And the ranch? Ask yourself if you believe he'd still be here once he got his hands on that?"

Girard rocked me with a punch.

She didn't shoot him. Nor me.

I spit blood. "Eleanor, you had your will changed. To take this man out should you die an accidental death?"

She flinched.

Girard raised his fist again. I was ready and smashed an elbow into his face.

"You changed your will," I repeated. "In your heart you know you can't believe whatever he says now."

"Eleanor," he warned, "if I go to jail, so do you. We both know how your husband died."

"He was old," she said to me, helpless. "So old. And Cyrus loved me. The money would have set us free if it hadn't been in the ranch and the bank shares."

"We *are* free," Cyrus urged. "Just shoot Keaton. Or give me the gun. I'll shoot him. We'll have forever together. I promise."

She swung the derringer so that it pointed directly at my chest. Her knuckles whitened. My head, I'd have a chance of ducking. That gun carried only two bullets. But she was pointing at my chest.

"Freedom?" I asked. My mouth was dry. It was tough to speak clearly. "What about Dehlia's brothers? You heard him say she was taken care of. He'd only risk her death if he knew he'd be riding away from those gunmen. And away from you."

"Cyrus?"

"Not so," he said. Untroubled. "I'm only holding her as hostage to show them they can't push me around."

Weak reply. We all knew it. Her derringer was back to a point between us.

A sudden thought. And I was speaking almost before I finished thinking it. "Dehlia," I blurted to Eleanor. "Ask yourself about Dehlia. How'd she know he lived two lives? Was she married to him before? Tracked him down?"

"Cyrus?"

"Not so," he said. But had nothing to add to it.

"Why," she said. "Why?"

With no indication it would happen, she moved her hand and pulled the trigger. It was only a small pop, but the impact of the bullet into his chest threw Girard onto his back, almost beneath the hooves of his saddled horse.

I froze. For I knew she'd helped murder her first husband. And she knew I knew.

"I did it for love," she said. Strangled voice. "I murdered my first husband because I loved Cyrus. But all those nights alone, it haunted me. When Cyrus was with me, I knew what I'd done was all right. But when he was away . . ."

She drew a breath to steady herself. "And now I killed my second husband for love."

When I saw what was about to happen next, I began to scream. But it wouldn't come out. Like a bad dream, I saw the derringer swing slow, as if we were swimming in time. Yet despite the horror of the slowness, I could not move fast enough. Frozen, unable to even lift a hand, let alone rise and dive.

She pressed the barrel of her derringer against her breast and pulled the trigger. Blood blossomed, a rose of tragedy on the fine material of her dress.

She'd taken Girard's promise and held him to it.

The two of them. Forever together.

Epilogue

"Doc, anyone else's arm you want to break?"

We were sitting in the Chinaman's. My casual question hit Doc so hard he sputtered on the coffee he was about to swallow and jarred his cup down to slosh more coffee over the sides.

"Thought so," I said. I'd never seen Doc squirm before. It was enjoyable. Especially since I'd only been half sure with my speculations. "It's a real shame, though, Doc. As lawman, I don't think I'd ever be able to prove it was you that done in Benjamim Guthrie. Means I can't ever take you up before a judge. Or even talk to other folks about it."

Doc glared.

I smiled.

Doc pulled his spectacles off and began to polish them.

"Doc," I said, "you need more time to compose yourself, go right ahead. Those glasses weren't any dirtier than they were last time you cleaned them." I gave another smile. "Two minutes ago."

"You are so very funny." He quit polishing and set the spectacles back on his nose. "How'd you know?"

"I finally got over to the Guthrie house to tell him I'd had no luck yet. Got there 'round suppertime. Met his wife and little boy. She had two black eyes. Not recent black, but puffy and yellow and blue and green by now. Said she fell down the stairs a few weeks back. The boy couldn't say a word, he was shaking scared so bad to see someone as big as me in the doorway. Little gaffer had a broken arm. His ma said he'd fallen down the same stairs about the same time. That you'd splinted it for him."

I gulped back some coffee. Looked Doc straight in the eyes. "Wasn't it you, Doc, said a sawbones has a moral obligation to keep secret what a patient tells him? I saw that boy's broken arm and her black eyes and got to asking myself what kind of secrets you'd know about them. I got to asking myself what I'd do if I were you, if a mama and her boy came in and told you it was her man that hurt them both. You can't go to the law, not unless she gives permission. And she's too scared."

I grinned and leaned back in my chair. "Let's make this a what-if situation, Doc. Tell me what you'd do in a case like that."

He shrugged. A theatrical shrug. "What if? Well, say it happened that some Rebs ride into town, and say folks might blame it on them, anything that might happen to Benjamin Guthrie. In a situation like that, I'd surely consider giving that man a taste of his own medicine. I'd probably soak a burlap bag in chloroform, throw it over his head, and whack his arm as good as I could. Then I'd probably charge him double to set it, that is if he came in the evening and inconvenienced me."

"I'll bet few would blame you, Doc. I had my own words with Benjamin, private-like."

Doc raised an inquiring eyebrow.

"I mentioned that if his wife or son ever fell down the stairs again, I'd gut-shoot him from an alley. He seemed to understand I was serious."

The Chinaman stopped by with more coffee. He returned again with a rag and tsk-tsked Doc as he cleaned up the spilled coffee. Doc accepted the chastisement and waited until the Chinaman disappeared into the kitchen before he leaned forward and whispered across our table.

"Samuel, your secret is safe with me, too."

"What secret?"

"Folks are ready to make you a legend. They're still talking about how you shot both snakes. I happened to notice, though, that neither shot put a hole in the tent. Was it buckshot you sprayed from your revolver?"

"Bring your medicine bag like I asked?" I wouldn't give Doc the satisfaction of hearing he was right. " 'Cause I got something you'll need with it."

I unbuckled my holster and set it on the table. "Go ahead," I told him. "Strap it on."

"I've never worn a gun before. I will not start now."

I removed a couple bullets from the belt, and just as I'd done in Mayor Crawford's office, I began to work the lead loose from the casing.

"Fine," I said, "I guess it'll have to be Jake Wilson who shares all the pleasure in my doings with Brother Lewis."

Doc squinted suspicion at me.

"Yes." I spoke firmly. "Pleasure. It's time I moved Brother Lewis out of that jail cell. But I'd hate to see him back in the revival business again."

Doc didn't even ask what I had in mind. He took the holster and stood to buckle it on.

The first lead pellets landed on the table with light clunks.

Some grains of gunpowder followed. I'd brought along small pieces of cloth, and I stuffed one into the casing to keep the powder in place.

"You're taking Brother Lewis more serious than most lawmen would," Doc commented as I began to pry at the second bullet. "Why's that?"

He sat and waited for my answer.

"I'd like to tell you it's the same reason you have," I said. "A woman got snakebit and died. But when I ask myself, I think there's more to it."

I set my knife aside. "Doc, a few months back I almost got killed. Discovered I wasn't ready for it—that I hadn't given thought to the beyond."

I explained to Doc that I'd realized there was a simple decision to be made behind a question I'd ignored all my life. Either God existed or He didn't. It had led me to realize that despite the compelling matters of living, much of a man's business was to decide matters of his death and his soul. To choose to believe God did not exist. Or to accept faith and from there try to search for what that meant. I told Doc how it bothered me to see someone as skillful, powerful, and charismatic as Brother Lewis taking advantage of the confusion too many of us had.

"Worst part is, I still can't figure out how he could reach into those snakes and come out unhurt. Nor how some of the others could do it."

"You might recall," he said with a smile, "I'd once mentioned how little we know. I won't even try to explain that one. Sure enough it did happen, and sure enough it might happen again. Just because you can't understand it, though, don't close your mind to it. Fact is, Samuel, if a man doesn't predispose himself to disbelieve in God, and he tries to figure out how the world works, soon enough he'll have no choice but to believe in God. That's when the fun starts. After you get faith, looking for more answers."

"I haven't found it particularly fun," I said. "I thought believing was supposed to give you the answers, not get you started with more questions."

"Some folks do look at it that way," Doc said. "You'll notice they surround themselves with all sorts of church rules and let those rules serve as answers. I don't mean that unkindly, and I have no doubt God welcomes those folks."

He paused. "The older I get, it seems, the more I know how ignorant I am. Especially in the face of God. And folks rarely talk serious like this, so indulge me when I try to share what I've learned through watching people live and die over all my years as a doctor."

My coffee was getting cold. I only had one bullet prepared. But I was ready to indulge him.

"Some people approach faith to hide from the infinite mystery. They just want rules to get them through life," he said. "Others approach faith to seek the mystery behind it. I believe I know which road you're on. I promise you it won't be easy."

He swirled his coffee and stared down at it. "This black tar the Chinaman serves. You don't know how bad I wish it was whiskey. Even now, first thing in the morning. Every day I fight the urge for just one shot. The bottle cost me my family before I decided to quit."

We both gave that statement respectful silence. I thought of how he'd repeatedly declined my offers of whiskey at the Red Rose, and I made a note to quit that habit around him. I thought of the inscription in his book from his wife, Sarah. The rumors of a successful practice abandoned. This was a tough man, not to have quit on life.

"Will it help, Samuel, if I tell you I've discovered faith isn't much different than my fight against the bottle? All you can do is hope to win a day at a time. Keep searching, and the truths come in little doses here and there."

He pulled the revolver from his holster and examined it

critically. "Speaking of truth, young man, I believe you owe me an explanation."

I provided it as I worked over the last few bullets. Girard and the chicken blood had given me the idea.

Doc grinned when I was finished.

I carried Doc's medicine satchel during our slow walk across town to the jail cell. As we walked, I explained to Doc what I'd learned from Dehlia. She'd been easy to find—the foreman of the Bar X Bar knew of only two dry wells nearby, and she'd been at the bottom of the first we searched.

I had been right about one thing. Dehlia had been black-mailing Girard, bleeding him slow with malicious joy. She'd armed herself with the four Rebs—not her brothers, but hired on and posing as brothers—because she knew she needed protection as she threatened to expose his double life. After all, as she had sweetly explained to Girard, if she died, those Rebs would not only track him down but give the entire story to both Eleanor Ford and Lesley Girard.

Blackmail had forced Girard to set up a phony loan to the Bar X Bar from the Denver bank and made him desperate enough as Cyrus Ford to steal the bank notes from the bank in Laramie.

It was the perfect setup for Dehlia. As long as Girard needed both his wives, she could squeeze him dry. And he couldn't leave, not when most of his wives' wealth was tied up in cattle, land, and bank assets. It was so perfect, she knew she could aggravate him by posing as his daughter in Denver, just to spite him more.

Her mistake was in failing to realize when Girard had de-cided to run from the situation. Her death, then, and the fol-lowing revelations would make no difference to either of the wives he left behind.

She'd met Girard at a prearranged place on the grasslands

to get more money. He pulled a gun and forced her to the dry well, believing if the Rebs caught up to him in the next few days, he could use her as a bargaining chip. Otherwise, as he'd happily explained to her, if he'd put enough days between himself and the Bar X Bar that she was finally dead of thirst in the well, it was also enough distance that the Rebs would never be able to track him down.

If I'd been right about the blackmail, I'd been wrong about the why. Dehlia had never been a wife to him. Dehlia's mother had, a wealthy woman down south some half dozen years older than Girard. The marriage lasted as long as the wealth—after Girard had diverted all he could, Dehlia's mother had died mysteriously one night, and a bribed doctor called it heart failure. Girard played the role of grieving widower for only a month before he fled. Dehlia, a daughter determined to get revenge, had finally caught up to him after a soldier friend passing through Denver had spotted Girard at the bank and wrote back to her with the news. She went to Denver and watched him for several weeks, which led her to follow him to Laramie and discover the double life. Blackmail, to Dehlia, had seemed the ultimate justice.

What I didn't tell Doc was that Dehlia had openly expressed interest in staying on in Laramie and deepening our acquaintance. Nor did I tell Doc how I'd had no regrets in gently declining, something Dehlia had understood from my eyes even before I spoke the words. Clara in Denver had helped me more than she knew—I would not permit myself or my heart to flee from Rebecca, no matter how easy to justify in the face of temptations or my worries about what might happen to Rebecca's love for me during our time apart.

I also held back from Doc the conversation I'd had with Mayor Crawford upon my return to Laramie from the Bar X Bar. Physicians aren't the only ones with moral obligations to hold some things secret. Crawford had already been punished greatly for his mistakes by Girard, and as Laramie did depend so much on a strong bank, I made my own judgment and let the matter lie. Maybe I didn't have the right or foresight to make such a judgment, but there hadn't been anyone else to take from me the responsibility.

Resolving so much of the previous weeks' happenings, however, didn't rid me of the problem of an irate, abusive revivalist preacher and the too-slow territorial movement of a circuit judge who still might not arrive for another month.

Which was why I was stepping into my own marshal's office with a leather bladder of chicken's blood beneath my shirt, a Bowie knife tucked in my belt, my holster around Doc's waist, and two saddled horses reined to nearby posts.

"Sun's been up two hours, Marshal," Brother Lewis called as I opened the door. "Where's my breakfast? And—"

Doc Harper stepped in behind me.

Brother Lewis softened his voice. He'd learned quickly how far he could push before we went through the trouble of bringing the horse back into his jail cell. "I sure am glad you got a sawbones in here. My throat's been aching bad for days."

"My own thoughts are that you don't shut up enough to rest it," I said as I moved to the hook that held the jail cell key. "But to make you happy, I'll let Doc Harper explain that in fancy doctor talk."

I opened the cell door for Doc to enter, then moved to my desk, sat with my back turned on them, and busied myself with paper work.

It didn't take long.

"Samuel?" Doc's voice had tension.

"Yes," I said without looking.

"Samuel!" More urgent.

I sighed. Turned around. And yelped. "Doc!"

"I'm sorry, Samuel," Doc said, shakylike. Brother Lewis

stood behind, left arm wrapped around Doc's neck, right hand pressing the gun barrel into Doc's ear. "He took it from my holster while I was reaching into my satchel."

"Let him go," I warned Brother Lewis. "You'll never get away with this."

Inside I groaned. Couldn't I come up with anything better than a line from one of Ned Buntline's dime novels?

Brother Lewis didn't notice. That was my gamble. That he would be so wrapped up in this, he wouldn't notice odd details.

"We're moving out," Brother Lewis said. His face was white with strain. "Don't force me to shoot."

Brother Lewis pushed Doc into the jail cell door, swinging the iron bars open. "He stays with me until we're well clear of town. Anyone follows, I shoot him dead."

"No," I said. "I don't believe you'd kill a man."

"Don't call my bluff," he warned. They were halfway to the outside door now. "I'm serious."

"So am I," I said. "If you shoot Doc here, you have no hostage."

I pulled the Bowie knife loose from my belt. Whether or not he was capable of killing a man in cold blood, I figured he'd shoot in self-defense.

I held the knife high, giving him a good look at it. I took my first step toward him slow, letting Brother Lewis see my intentions. Then I rushed.

Brother Lewis pushed Doc aside and fired into my body.

I twisted, screamed, fell, made sure I landed on my belly. The leather bladder burst blood against me. I rolled over and over, screaming, gurgling, and ended in a collapsed pile against my desk, pressing my shirt into my belly, letting the blood seep through my fingers.

Then I let my head fall back and my eyes close.

"You killed him!" Doc shouted.

"Shut up or I'll kill you!" Brother Lewis was in a panic,

the frenzied edge in his voice a sure indication that all of this had happened so quickly that he bought it completely.

All that remained was for Doc to get him out of the office.

"Please don't kill me!" Doc said. "I'll ride with you! I promise! I won't do nothing to put you in danger! Just let me go when you get far enough away!"

It seemed too staged to me. But I needn't have feared. Brother Lewis was holding a smoking gun, looking at the bleeding body of a Wyoming Territory marshal and realizing he'd hang for it. He was in no condition to spare any other thoughts for logic.

"Get moving," Brother Lewis said. "Walk calm when we're on the street. One false move and I shoot."

"Anything!" Doc said. "I don't want to die!"

Moments later, I heard the creaking of the office door. Then silence.

I relaxed. Doc would point out the saddled horses reined at the posts if Brother Lewis in his panic missed them. As they rode, Doc—safe because my Colt now had only one blank and empty chambers—would also point out the dangers of future public appearances as a revivalist, now that Brother Lewis would be on every Wanted poster in this territory and the neighboring ones. And I'd be rid of the problem of taking before a judge someone accused of throwing snakes.

To be safe, I lay on the floor for another five minutes.

Jake Wilson walked in just as I was ready to sit up.

"Morning, Marshal," he said. "Things work out fine?"

"Just fine, Jake." I got to my feet. Wiped my hands free of blood against my pants.

"Good. That preacher was a tiring man." Jake grinned. "You'll be wanting to clean up. So I'll hold this letter for you till you get back."

"Letter?" It couldn't be from Rebecca among the Sioux. Not unless she'd found a way to get it to the nearest fort outpost.

Jake held it to the light and his grin became a leer.

"Wish I could read through the envelope," he said. "Looks like it's traveled some to get here. Smells of perfume, too. What's this on the outside? Some Injun symbols. A drawing of the moon. Marshal, it—"

Moon? Moon Basket. Rebecca.

I grabbed it from his hands. Had it open before I was sitting again. Totally forgot Jake was standing there with a wide-open smile across his face.

Dear Samuel, it began. *I love you as fiercely as I miss you. . . .*